For Dakotah and Angelie, my beloved children.
In you my heart has found a home.

Our lives begin to end the day we become
silent about things that matter.

Martin Luther King Jr.

The Earth is a living thing. The Mountains speak.
The trees sing. Lakes can think.
Pebbles have a soul. Rocks have power.

John (Fire) Lame Deer

TABLE OF CONTENTS

Chapter 1: Coulee   1

Chapter 2: The Boarding House   13

Chapter 3: Adoption   16

Chapter 4: The Boarding House   31

Chapter 5: Badlands   35

Chapter 6: The Boarding House   50

Chapter 7: Indians   52

Chapter 8: Buffalo   60

Chapter 9: Hobo   68

Chapter 10: The Boarding House   75

Chapter 11: Gone   78

Chapter 12: The Boarding House   93

Chapter 13: Campfires   95

Chapter 14: Search   110

Chapter 15: The Boarding House   117

Chapter 16: Horses   118

Chapter 17: Found   128

Chapter 18: Graveyard   139

Chapter 19: The Boarding House   163

Chapter 20: Drunkard   166

Chapter 21: Dead   176

Chapter 22: The Boarding House   187

Chapter 23: Cabin   188

Chapter 24: The Boarding House   202

Chapter 25: Hide   204

Chapter 26: Care   226

Chapter 27: The Boarding House   243

Chapter 28: Safe   244

1
COULEE

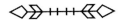

"What's wrong with this family?" I gripe into the dog's ear, brushing my lips over its soft velvet until I calm down. It takes awhile. Grabbing his scruff, I bury my face deep into dog breath heaven. The good dog knows the drill and holds steady, then attacks. Kisses for giggles, the aim of a happy dog.

But right now I need to concentrate. I'm in trouble.

Think fast.

"Dog needs out, Mom. And uh, sorry about the other," I say, hoping the sweet pull of caramel in my voice will call off her temper. I've made her mad without even trying.

I live in contrasts, a calm hand stroking the collie's coat while trouble tightens the back of my throat. I aim to sneak off, so I ease the front door open without a squeak… then yep, almost closed. Whew, made it! Chief and I careen off the porch and around the corner before I take a breath.

"Yee haw!" I twang in fake cowgirl, "Git along li'l doggie!" as we gallop off the edge of the deep, wide ravine we call a coulee that runs behind the house. Chief soars, long hair floating, tail raised. He lands on his back legs partway down the slope, and when his front legs join him he slides into a puff of dust before loping to the bottom.

I dig in the heels of my cowboy boots as I gallop down, arms circling backwards to keep from landing on my face. "Whoa there, Nellie," I yank on the reigns of pretend, stopping just short of the bottom to fall flat on my back against the steep bank. Chief's tail can be anything short of a weapon, and right now it beats itself silly beside my ear. He points his long nose at me, seeming to smile.

"Safe!" I holler, throwing my arms out like an ump at the little league field up there on the other side of the coulee. We've hit our homer, run from base, and Mom can't catch us now. Or find us. The coulee promises a hiding place if we need it, wedging between slabs of concrete that were bulldozed down here like it's a garbage dump. Re-bar juts out from the slabs to hook chunks of kid flesh. I've learned to steer clear of the rusty metal.

This time of year the coulee has run dry, the rushing water of springtime gone from this gully, leaving a bottom of mud and sand. Coulees cut all through this land, and this one runs from out of the badlands and along the backyards of the houses on our street. Each of our lawns ends at the slope into the coulee. It's where adventure starts, and the trail to the badlands begins.

Except I'm wheezing like a geezer, but so what? I'm used to it. With Mom, every victory counts, and asthma won't wreck this one. I'll hightail it home eventually, but for now I'm a drifter on the wide Montana range. I've found a wild pony, and I'm as free as a tumbleweed blowing over the sage.

In a mess of a life like mine, you'd best pretend. What seems real just can't be, and it all starts me to wondering. Nobody would make up a story like this, no matter how much attention they needed, and attention is the last thing I'm looking for. But I wonder if maybe in the telling of my story, some sense could be made out of this big heap of trouble.

I call myself Coca Joe Stratmore for no other reason than I like it. It doesn't mean anything that I know of, but I must have heard something, somewhere, to give such a name to myself. Pretending who I am is all I got that's real.

I squint into the sky to see if there are any messages hidden in the wispy clouds, telling me how much trouble I'm in with Mom. She let me run off without hollerin' out the door after me, so maybe she's just plumb worn out and needing to be mad at somebody, anybody, me. But for goodness' sake, getting mad just because she caught me reading again!

Well, it's my fault. I know what she thinks about me reading.

She thinks it's a sign of laziness. And if there's trouble to be caught, I can catch it even with the reading of a book. Mom has something against lying around. She tells me I can vacuum instead.

She says, "Don't go filling up your head with other people's ideas. It'll take you nowhere fast." I've thought this through. If I'm going nowhere, I can't get there fast.

Mom thinks reading makes me sneaky, and she hates sneakiness, coming around a corner to see me fumbling to hide a book. Mom says she's trying her best to raise me right. I guess in her book, I'm partial to wrong.

Chief does a nuzzle-sigh into my ribcage, hinting towards a move-along, his eyes begging up at mine. He's the one book I can read cover-to-cover, inside outside upside down. Our eyes lock. 'Never look a dog in the eye. Never look a dog in the eye,' repeats in my head. Another lie from Dad. Chief holds me in focus, eye to eye, but not for long. He's the closest thing to family I have, but he's not as human as I make him. 'Always look Chief in the eye. Always look Chief in the eye.' I nip at the lie and chase it off.

I let Chief know it's time to go. He leaps to all fours in one swift move, no scrambling, nothing awkward. He's a beaut.

We wander along the bed of the coulee, me looking to crack some mud. I love cracking mud when it's in that rare sun-baked state. I spot a patch and am hopeful. Down on one knee, I scold Chief to move back, to not crush my masterpiece. The mud on the top has dried away from the mud on the bottom, making a couple dozen perfect mud potato chips. Each chip has so many snappy layers lifting up its thin crispiness, it almost makes me hungry. Black mud, silky and mysterious, hides under the lifted chips, protected. I lie down. I'll be here awhile.

Chief jumps up and looks ready, for what, I don't know. I push up on my elbows jerking my head around to make sure this mud crackin' isn't being witnessed by some bully. I'm not breaking any laws, but feel excited enough to be. Small town fun, it's just that.

"Chief, lie down!" I command, but there's a thrill in my voice that confuses him. I pat the earth to invite him down. He drops to the spot, stretches his head out on his paws, and exhales, nostrils blowing up sand dust. "Hey, Gracie," I tease, and nudge him with my elbow, giving just enough lovin' to this dog who eats and breathes to be with me. It's the same for me, I eat and breathe to be with Chief, he's my everything. If anyone spots one of us without the other, you can bet it isn't our idea, someone is forcing us apart.

I'm lucky my wheezing is settled down because the kind of asthma I have is out to kill me. It's tried. But I'm still here—breathing. I'm lying with my face in the dust, and I'm allergic to dust, so I'd better be careful or I'll have to go home for extra medicine and that would end my get-away.

Asthma is dangerous and moody like mom and dad, coming out of nowhere and getting out of control fast, threatening me with death and not messing around. It's fussy and doesn't fit someone who wants to be pounding through the badlands with Chief.

Crackin' mud doesn't seem dangerous, but it can be, so I play it safe. I move the mud chips aside instead of crackin' them on top of the puddle because I'm leery of what's under the chips—gumbo—a mud worse than axle grease. This sticky mud hides and lies in wait for any sucker who doesn't know its slippery ways. It's taken me down in the badlands so fast I never saw it coming, leaving its gooey mark all along my backside, and this is on a good day.

Gumbo is a hungry mud, known for eating shoes. It can look dry and cracked-up on the top, just like this puddle does, but if I dare put a foot in, it will keep my boot and try to keep me.

I test it with my fist, pumping in and out of the mud.

This makes a sucking sound that grows suckier the more I do it. It's impossible not to laugh. If I didn't know better, I'd think someone is down there, grabbing hold of me tighter and tighter with each punch down into the mud. This doesn't stop me. The more I punch the harder it is to tug my hand free. It's a real fight!

I struggle and grunt with effort to get my hand back. Then, when I'm all punched out, I open my hand flat and can pull it right out.

Ha! I win.

It wouldn't be good for Chief to get stuck, because it's a death trap. The more an animal struggles, the tighter gumbo takes hold. Livestock die in gumbo. They'll wait days to be rescued, stuck belly-deep near the creek edge where shallow water hides these silt deposits. Ranchers and farmers use a lariat to rope the animal from afar to avoid getting stuck themselves, and they tie it to the hitch so the truck can pull the animal out. For such a silly name, gumbo is a serious threat. That's why I play in it.

I rub my hands together to clean them and go back to crackin' mud, twisting off a mud chip using gentle fingers. It's globbed onto the wet mud underneath, but with patience, it comes to me. I set it aside carefully so the chip's many layers do not crackle. Looks good. Most of the chips around the outer edges lift off, but the middle of the mud puddle is still moist. It needs a few more days of sun, warm coulee breezes, and no clodhoppers.

Now for the fun! I stand up to crack the mud with my boot tips, to coax the sound out of each and every layer. Crackin' is one of the most satisfying sounds of summer, like popping the top off a bottle of Squirt on a hot and sweaty day. I can't keep myself from chugging the end of a soda, just like I can't keep my feet from doing a wild stomp to crack every last chip.

Done with crackin' mud, I stretch out in a sand bed and lace fingers beneath my head. I am shocked by the perfect blue of the sky. "Roo—t Rew," I fake whistle, my signature call if I've seen something surprisingly beautiful. I ask in a soft and slow western drawl, "Would you look at that, Chief?" He answers with a quick bark as if he can see it too. My eyes had been stuck on the color of dirt for so long, this knockout blue does just that, and I shut my eyes. It's Chief that lets me rest, and Chief that gets me up and going again, nuzzling my shoulder like a horse until I move.

Even he knows pushing it with Mom never works out well.

Next to the path home is a culvert that dumps into the coulee. The culvert is half as round as I am tall. It whispers my name as I slip on by, calling me back into its dark tunnel. I go, it's just one of those things to do. All kids know that sissies aren't allowed in here so it's a good thing I'm not one. Even Chief, who's usually stuck to me like glue, never follows me in. While he sits on guard duty at the mouth, I imagine he'd whine like Lassie does whenever Timmy disappears. When we watch the Lassie show on television, Chief and I lie side-by-side, propped on elbows, with my cowboy boot tips in the carpet. I can't help but egg Chief on, nudging into him and whining in his ear to see if he'll whine along with Lassie. Somehow he knows better and won't fall for my pranks.

Once inside the culvert I hear the sound of voices coming down through the street grate. I crawl in halfway, just past the cartoon drawing of a bald-headed man with a big nose peering over a wall. I've seen this same cartoon in the underpass near Main Street. They both say 'Kilroy Was Here'. Mom says it's something from the World Wars that has spread across the country. I thought Kilroy just likes dark places.

I start crab-walking, creeping silent. One careless pebble would alert the kids and end my spying. I squat in a patch of darkness under the street grate, pleased to hear Double Trouble—my older brother and his sidekick Split, a neighbor kid nicknamed for his split lip, which often oozes blood, proving his love for roughhousing. My older brother doesn't have a name right now because I'm mad at him, as usual. These two are really up to something with their excited whispers.

"No, let me do it. I've had more practice," my brother says.

Split argues back, "No way! I don't need practice. Give it over."

In the scuffle that follows, the cherished 'it' drops down through the grate and lands in front of me in a shaft of light. Usually for me, bad ideas come faster than good ones. A firecracker juts out from the fold of a matchbook. I scoop it up, and after three strikes of the match I light the firecracker and toss it back up through the grate. Just as Double Trouble seems to notice the sizzle, it booms, loud and echoing in the culvert. They jump higher and scream louder than any sissies I'd ever seen.

Stooped over, I race through the culvert without catching a boot heel on the corrugated metal or bonking my head. They'll already be running fast across the empty lot above in hopes of trapping me like a sitting duck. As I fly out the opening I fight off the urge to hoop and holler from the thrill of duping my brother! I scramble into a hiding place with Chief right beside me. Knowing this coulee like the back of my hand saves my skin once again.

I watch Double Trouble attack the mouth of the culvert, fists up and ready for a fight. They look like total goofs from here, jeering into the culvert at their trapped enemy, daring them to come out and show their face. When no one does, they crawl in to drag 'em out. I can't help giggling into my hand. They come back arguing, start shoving each other and almost come to blows themselves before getting interested in some other bad idea.

My big brother is actually pretty dang smart, but he hides it well.

I make a plan to celebrate later at the family dinner table by asking my brother real casual-like, 'Do you have any more of those firecrackers?' The dad we have—who keeps himself strong and fit on our backyard chin-up bars, who wears a crew cut that means no fuss but keeps his cowboy boots polished up, who expects us kids not to be kids—will be interested in my question, never a good thing for my brother. Double Trouble has met their match.

When the coast is clear of smelly boys, Chief and I creep like the common criminals we are along the coulee edge passing behind our backyard shrubbery and lilac bushes, ducking under crab apple tree branches, and sneaking along the fence of the side yard. I hear

the loud, open-mouthed laugh of mother ringing across the backyard.
Fearing trouble and hearing laughter instead is such a relief, I stop in
my tracks and feel my stomach unwind its knot. Hanging back, I smell
cigarettes and hear Mom's neighbor-lady friends, Hazel and Priscilla,
laughing along. Hazel is extra short with the compact strength of
a circus performer. Her soft-brown hair is not soft at all, but hair-
sprayed six inches high into a bouffant to help her seem adult height.
Mom isn't tall but she makes herself visible with her showy personality
and her sparkly jewelry, some that she makes jingle on her wrist. Even
her everyday sandals have jewels. Once I overheard Hazel call Mom
a sex kitten, which I don't get. Maybe it hints at Mom's one-shoulder
dresses, tight around her behind with a hidden zipper on the side and
a slit up the back that brings on a wider wiggle to her hips. Meow.

Priscilla somehow gets away with wearing a housecoat out of her
house. She keeps her mousy-brown hair short by cutting around a
bowl on her head. These things are not very attractive, but the too-
orange lipstick on her too-large mouth is just plain wrong. She's nice
though. All three of 'em sound like wrestlers from smoking cigarettes,
lighting one after another as if in a race. As much as Mom cares about
looking pretty, she sounds like she has hair on her chest. Right now
she's using her smiling voice, so I might not be in as much trouble as
I thought. I've got a plan to keep her friendly.

I swing in the front door to scrub off the dirt, not easy, and brush
out my long braid. It's as old as I am, twelve, because my thick hair
has hardly been cut. Some kids have blonde hair that's yellow or the
color of gold. Mine is silvery blonde, like it's not quite sure it wants
a color. I change into clothes Mom ordered from the 1967 summer
catalogue from Montgomery Wards, or as us kids call it, Monkey
Wards. She likes this stuff, a midriff top of summery white eyelet and
light purple shorts with matching eyelet trim. My legs are on the long
side, two sticks with knobby knees in the middle. My fingers can roll
my kneecap around until it pops up like a doorknob. I like to knock
on it, twist it open, and pretend to answer the door in a low, spooky
voice, "Ve—lcome."

I head into the backyard sort of bouncy-cutesy, turning on a big smile. I widen my washed-out blue eyes and skip on out to their lawn chairs. Right on cue, Mom's friends dote over me, running their fingers through hair floating past my rear end, waves from the braid trapping the light. The train whistle blows a couple miles off, adding drama to the stage I'm setting to butter up my mother. Presentation is everything to Mom, and she eats it all up. The charmer recognizes her handiwork, and through her latest stylish glasses she gives me a wink. I recognize myself as winner of our earlier battle and wink back.

Chief holds court too, wooing the ladies. He's a natural attention-stealer, being the breed of the nation's most popular animal movie star. But where Lassie looks sweet and smart, Chief looks powerful and smarter than you. He's stunning and knows it, posing now with his head high to show the beautiful white mane flowing down his chest to a point just above the ground. He expects people to get their hands on him, and they do.

When I say Chief is powerful, he is. He lives up to his name as an Indian chief putting all others first and protecting his tribe. I am Chief's whole tribe, and I'm enough to keep him busy.

When I say Chief is smart, he knows things. The other day he sniffed out something under my bed that I didn't put there. It's a mystery to me, which isn't all that unusual. Nearly everyday things happen that I can't explain. Like I put something one place, and it ends up in another, or I lose it for a while, stuff like that. I try to get used to this, but it can make me mad. Sometimes things are destroyed, like my favorite Barbie's hair, cut off stupid. And one time I found a pair of her pink high heels in the sandbox, sitting pretty in a scooped-out bowl of sand. I get after the family, especially my brothers, but everybody swears they aren't messing with my things. Still, somebody seems to be playing tricks on me.

Anyway, under my bed, Chief found two washcloths that were folded in half. Each one had a pair of my underwear rolled up tight, wrinkled from being twisted, but clean. Why would anyone do that?

After Chief showed me the underwear, I rubbed the wrinkles out with my fingers, pressed them flat with my hands and put them back where they belong in the dresser drawer. I've learned to dismiss these happenings without another thought. It's like I rub a giant pink eraser over my memory and sweep the pink worm-shaped droppings back under the bed where my underwear had been.

At church when I learned what devotion is, I thought only of Chief. God gets this. He gave me Chief, guardian angel and all. I mean this seriously for the saving of my life he's done.

Our backyard coulee is a dangerous playground, and somehow Chief knows it. In summer there's bullies to keep an eye out for, to say nothing of the rattlesnakes. Water is the biggest scare year round. It's hard to fathom on a bluebird day like today, but when gully washers rush out of the badlands headed for the Missouri River, it's a trap for youngsters. Long before I learned to swim, I was washed away in one of these flash floods and it was Chief who saved me! Chief dragged me out facedown and halfway to heaven, his powerful jaws clamped to the waist of my pants, and he wouldn't let go until he climbed all the way up and out of the coulee while I was coughing and spurting water.

I just wish that somehow, someway, he could have saved that frozen girl. Or saved me from seeing it. In winter the rule is drilled into you seemingly every day of your life in threatening voices to never, ever, ever go down on that ice. I learned why. On a day windier than all the windy days and colder than all the coldest days, I hear heavy machinery struggling to keep running in the bitter cold. When you have a coulee for a backyard, it's hard to miss anything major going on down there, and when you're a girl like me, you're bound to investigate anything happening. I follow the sound to the coulee and see a yellow ditch digger reaching down towards the ice, and heavily-bundled people scurrying back and forth along the upper edge. Their frantic voices send a jolt of fear through me and I start running towards the bridge to be close, but not too close. I hear Mom shout at the top of her lungs to "Get back in this house right now!" but somehow this makes me run faster.

Then before I could unsee it, the ditch digger brings up something in its bucket. I'd never spent even a minute thinking about what falling through the ice would be like, but here, right before my eyes, I see. I'm horrified at the purple. I recognize the coat and tiny boots of a neighbor girl, but all I can think of is why is she so purple lying there in the bucket of the ditch digger, looking so small, so crumpled? Thank God Mom grabs me just then and buries my face in her thick parka. Chief pushes behind me so I'm sandwiched between them, limp, and scared inside. I have one clear thought of relief, that this dead girl isn't my best friend Frankie. It could have been. We are both rule breakers.

I'm carried home beside the dark, scary water that's under the ice in the coulee. The squeak of freezing snow under Mom's boots sounds like a child screeching. I cover my ears with thick mittens before noticing this sound is in my throat in rhythm with each step, like a blind kitten, crying, lost from its mother.

I worried for a long time after this whether purple could still be my very favorite color.

Her cold, purple body seemed to move into my room, frozen to the color I call mine. I have loved purple since I was tiny, always choosing it first ... lavender walls, purple clothes, and a fancy bedspread with purple lilacs bringing the hope of springtime to dark winter days. A lavender kitty of soft rabbit fur rests on my pillow, the hospital prize when my tonsils were yanked out. I love that kitty with all my might, right down to its purple whiskers, but now I wish it was pink-pink-pink.

In our small northern town of Hell Creek, Montana, winter never quits. Long past May Day, snow can smother the cheery apple blossoms any time it wants. And fun doesn't just come knocking on your door, you gotta go find it. I was scared to go out. My mind got slippery, seeming to slide down that steep slope into the coulee with my dead friend. I kept imagining I heard the ditch digger and would run to the window, frightened that it was coming after me too. I started confusing the rusty yellow bucket as the monster that killed the girl, instead of her being pinned under the thin ice and dragged by the shallow current toward my house.

Life seemed to drag on after the drowning accident, heavy and awkward. The tough tomboy in me left. I wanted to stay in my room, or I begged to watch more television. Fear grew in me. My thoughts turned to worries, yipping and howling like the coyotes at night. My heart lost track of things it loved, burying them beside the dead girl.

Mom and Dad never seemed that pleased with who I was before the drowning, but they didn't much care for this stand-in, either. They went back to their happy-face rule. "Nobody wants to see your sad face," they'd say, "so put on a smile before you leave this house." I did. It's the ticket out. Smile! Smile a big smile. Without it I must be ugly, or worse, like Dad says.

Chief sniffed me out daily, dogging me until I finally returned to be his child. I went back to living more outside than in, as soon as the weather turned. It's safer out there, more predictable, even with all the danger that rides in on this land.

Lately I've been standing outside peeking in the kitchen window of our house wondering, who are these people that adopted me? I watch Mom rinse the dishes before placing them in her sparkling new portable dishwasher, and see Dad get a glass of water from the tap, reaching around her with a powerful arm. I notice her stiffen and lift an eyebrow off its normally stern line. How did I end up with them? I just gotta wonder.

2
THE BOARDING HOUSE

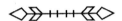

The Boarding House is not visible to the naked eye and yet here you are. The simple form of the clapboard two-story is graced by a revolving door of brass that is weather-pitted and tarnished. Day and night residents of The Boarding House spin in and out of the glass triangular pie shapes of the revolving door. In the blink of an eye.

Her eye.

This place exists only in the mind of Coca Joe, but even She does not know it's there.

If you were to enter the mind of someone with multiple personalities, what would you see? If these identities could speak to you, what would they say? The answers are as varied and stunning as a snowflake.

Step closer. This is Coca Joe's snowflake.

Behold, The Boarding House.

Inside The Boarding House, the residents exist unseen to those in the outside world. They are tucked safely away, waiting. There are many rooms in The Boarding House, just as there are many residents who live here. The sitting room is the largest, fronted with single-hung windows, and holding overstuffed chairs and a chaise lounge with worn silk upholstery and sagging cushions.

Gangster pushes up the hidden trap door from the underground apartment and the rug that covers it slides to rest. Like always, he flicks dust off the padded shoulders of his fine pinstripe suit and sets his Fedora low over his eyes before reaching down for her. It's a sight to see, this routine, no matter how many times The Boarding House residents see it. Poised fingers in a long, pale-pink satin glove rise out of the hole in the floor. Gangster sets his hand under hers and when she's ready, when she's sent the diamond rings worn over the gloves sparkling around the room, she takes his hand. They pause, always, which can make some residents hold their breath unawares.

"Watch your step, Sweetheart," he says, sounding just like a gangster from a movie out of Chicago. He says the same lines every time and could seem like a flat paper doll if he didn't mean every word spoken. She's his everything and he is hers. Without him she'd be dead.

Platinum hair sways opposite her shoulders in response to the va-voom of her hips as she climbs the stairs out of the hole. She's good, and needs to be. It's her strength. As good as this show is, the residents' favorite part, the one worth waiting for, is the girlish giggle as she shakes soft curls back from her face. She's loaded with sex appeal. She's The Babe.

Gangster swings a Tommy Gun from behind his back to rest under his arm, then sweeps it around the room. It's no prop. Once he deems the room safe, he hooks The Babe with his free elbow and walks her a few steps so he can shut the trap door. The Babe lets a knee go soft and her hip releases. She's tired from work but still stunning, and she never moves, not once, away from Gangster. No resident of The Boarding House has ever seen them apart. He leads her to the oriental silk chaise lounge, never rushing, so The Babe can move as only she knows how.

"My Princess, your throne," he says in adoration.

She sighs as she places herself on the lounge, a long pearl necklace swinging from breast to breast.

"Sit with me," she welcomes, rolling her knees to the side to give him room. His finger rests near the trigger of the gun, ready if needed.

3
ADOPTION

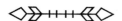

I don't fit with this family. I'm different somehow. As early as I can remember I've known I was adopted, and I've been taught only one thing about it. Mom says, "It took more love to give you away than to keep you." This is all I know about the lady that had a baby and that baby is me.

But this sounds like a grown-up load of bull, especially when I think of Chief. Now if Chief was caught in quicksand and he couldn't get out and I couldn't get him out, I'd jump in with him. We'd get swallowed up together. He's my biggest love, and I'd never walk away or ever give him away. Chief is family and I love him for keeps. I don't say this to my folks, adoption being the touchy subject it is. Adopted kids learn this pretty fast.

Sometimes my parents' reactions to the topic surprise me. Recently Mom acted shocked when I asked her about my beginnings, saying that she had completely forgotten that I was adopted. I stared open-mouthed for so long she finally said what I already knew, that it took more love to give me away than to keep me. This has made me very suspicious of love. Not with Chief or my badlands, they are safe love. But what if someone falls in love with me, with more love than ever before? Wouldn't he have to give me up rather than keep me? I think so. I'll be steering clear of anyone like that.

Thing is, until I am old enough to have a baby right outta my own belly, I am equally related to everybody. I am also equally related to nobody at the same time, and that's the sad part.

I've learned to milk this sad tale. The words orphan and adopted seem to be magic and can really get me stuff. Not from my parents, but from other moms and dads and their kids. Like one time I was swinging with Frankie, my best friend since I was five years old, on the huge swings in their back yard. Frankie spotted her mom heading out to pull sheets off the clothesline and said she wants the best swing now. Her mom, who is a beautiful strawberry blonde with a quick smile, said, "Sweetie, let her have the best swing." Then I overheard her whisper, "She's adopted, remember? Let's be extra nice."

Telling kids' parents about my sad beginnings is like striking gold. They give me the last cookie because I'm adopted. If bacon is served I get the best slices because, according to me, I'm a sad, sorry orphan. The list of treats is endless: purple suckers, last turns, and special sad smiles aimed right at my heart. My little pity party is like having a birthday every day. I never aimed at being special, but I like it!

Oh, I know it's wrong, but it isn't like word would ever get back to my parents. It would shame them if it did.

Adoption is hush-hush and there's power in that.

I'd like to hound them about who I came from, since it's something that circles 'round and 'round my mind, but it wouldn't matter, their answers are always the same. Dad tells me it's something to ask Mom about, and Mom says she didn't listen to a single word she was told about my parents because I was hers, and that was that. I think this is pretty weird. Couldn't she have listened to even one word? Like, the word asthma. That would have been helpful since I've got it so bad.

Before we knew I was allergic to stuff and that is why I wheeze, Mom took a younger me on the train to the closest big city to Hell Creek, Montana so that my asthma could be treated by a specialist.

Memories of that trip are fresh.

It's just Mom and me on the train in a sleeper car, a small playhouse with a floating bed. I'm practicing saying our destination, chugging it with the train's rhythm: Minneapolis, Minnesota ... Minneapolis, Minnesota, a real live city. I get to be the first grandchild to meet Grandma Naomi, who lives there. She is Dad's Mom who, for some mysterious, secret reason hasn't gotten to be a grandma to me until now.

Way too soon after boarding Mom says, "You're driving me nuts with your 'what if this, what if that.' I don't know!" She's talking loud. "I don't know how you will keep from falling out of the berth but you will not, and you *will* be sleeping up there. Your damn pestering needs to stop this instant!" Her angry hand digs into her purse, then holds a dime so close to my face I pull my head back. I don't reach for it because she hasn't told me to take it yet. She grabs my palm and digs the coin into it. Ouch. What did I do wrong? "Go get candy from the snack bar and when you come back you will stop driving me nuts. Are we clear Miss Muffet?" She opens the door but doesn't shove me.

I'm in trouble too soon.

I've been taught not go out the door to the gangway because it's very dangerous, but being curious isn't a crime. It takes a lot of practice to scare myself to death, so I pull the heavy railcar door and squeeze out. I seem trapped in an in-between land, a thrilling beginning. I'm slipping on the moving floor that connects the train cars, my slick patent leather shoes like ice skates on the metal. The crashing and squeaking out here is loud. I dare myself to look down through the little crack at the dizzying ground flying by, thinking this must be where danger lives.

I keep my balance for a quick moment, but the loud train whistle startles me and blows me right over. My shoes slip and I crash onto the metal floorboards that are churning against each other. There is nothing I can hold onto or reach.

Crying out is like yelling into a strong Montana wind; the sound goes nowhere. I can't even hear myself. I try to get to my knees, but the moving floor is teaching me a lesson, to mind my mama. I'm stuck. I went looking for trouble and found it.

A faraway voice with a drawl says, "Miss? Miss?"

I hear it through the loud ruckus and get confused. Squeezing my eyes shut tighter I worry *Where am I? Where am I?* and I fight to be brave enough to open my eyes.

Before me appears a dark black face and gleaming white gloves reaching down to me. I snap my eyes shut because I have a foolish imagination. I steal another peek. Yep, still there. Where in the whole wide world would there be a face like this? Heaven? Yes. Heaven. I'm relieved to have figured out where he came from. I smile in great surprise to have made it up there. My mom will never believe it!

"Miss? Take my hand," the voice shouts over the noise.

"Yes, Jesus, I'm comin'," I say to the bright white coat and soft chocolate eyes.

I reach up to him and shout, "Jesus! The Sunday school pictures sure painted you wrong!"

Cradled in his arms, my head resting near a shiny brass button, I tell him I'm ready to be in heaven and that he can go on up now. I snuggle in for the ride saying, "Oh Jesus, I didn't know you wore such a fine-looking hat." Mom would have been so proud of my nice manners.

He chuckles so hard I'm jostled. "Oh! Do you think the snack bar is heaven?"

He carries me into the train car and sets me on a stool in front the polished glass bar that comes up to my nose.

Once I've adjusted to the idea that I didn't die and go to heaven, I place Mom's dime on the glass top and he laughs again, saying he figured I was on my way here when he found me. Then he chuckles some more and shakes his head, "Heaven," and smiles wide at me. I look inside his mouth for the light that makes his teeth glow so white.

"May I help you, Miss?"

Eyeing the candy, I taste each one from memory before I choose: caramel Sugar Daddy scrapes my tongue raw; white, chewy Big Hunk lasts forever but grabs my teeth and won't give 'em back; salty Salted Nut Roll...

But then I remember the version of mom I'll be going back to and start to reconsider things.

"Miss, can I get something out for you?" he says, the deep voice stirring me.

Good manners nudge an answer out of me. "I can't pick... yet."

Deep dimples carve into his shiny black face.

A couple of older girls giggle their way to the snack bar, ignore me sitting there, and address this man as Porter, telling him what they want. They know little kids like me take too long.

I start again, returning to my candy dreams. Cracker Jacks are too much money, but oh, a toy too! Chocolate is my favorite, but I gobble it so fast it's like I never had any candy to start with. I hear a deep laugh and catch my tongue going around and around my lips, tasting as I go. It's the porter getting a kick out of me.

Finally, I make the choice I must: black licorice—something I hate but Mom loves, because sometimes candy isn't really for me.

"I got this for you Mommy!" I burst into our miniature room. But she's made her switcheroo, with a cocktail clinking ice and a cigarette glowing, staring out the window. "Put it in my suitcase, Pun'kin," she says, taking a long drag off her cigarette and still not looking at me or my gift, "and don't bother me now."

I straighten my shoulders. I won't let her see them droop if she looks.

I study her to note our differences because when she acts like this I don't like being her girl. Her nose is narrow at the top and slightly pudgy at the nostrils, instead of my wider, bigger nose, and her face is a thin oval instead of my round face with cheekbones that lift when I smile. I am always on the lookout for people that closely resemble me. I fear that I will miss them—that they will pass me by if I'm not paying attention—and then I will have missed my one and only chance of finding my real mom or dad, since it's all up to me now to find them. I have to believe my mom and dad must be searching for me too. How could they not be? What if they are? That could be my ticket out, boy.

This idea drives me to keep looking, drives me to imagine a happy reunion right on an ordinary sidewalk somewhere. Our eyes will spark with recognition! Our hearts will leap in our chests. We will hug for a long time, afraid to let go. I will be lifted off the ground and swung around in circles with my feet flying high by a mother who found her lost daughter, and a daughter who found her mother. We will laugh and cry and be so filled with the wonder of finding each other, knowing it is because we never stopped looking. I will never stop. It's like being a bucket of water with a pinhole in it, little leaks of me dripping out, trying to find the rest of me.

Since no one will ever tell me the history of my adoption, a kid like me is bound to make something up. I always listen to people tell their tall tales, sometimes there isn't anything better, so I figured out my own adoption tale at a young age. Then, after telling this story over and over, it became the truth I believe about myself.

It goes like this: My real dad is a big, burly miner, nice but dumb. My mom is a pretty sixteen-year-old, sweet, but dumb. My mom wasn't allowed to marry my nice dad because she was too young. The two of them couldn't figure out what to do with me, (here's how I know they were dumb), so they took me to an orphanage and left me on the steps.

My mom empties her glass and puts it down on the small, wooden sideboard with a too-loud thud. I peek at her out of the corner of my eyes, investigating. She's not paying any attention to me.

The mom I have is like stormy weather, you never know when it'll hit. I wonder if she would be less wound-up-tight and ready to go off if she had married a man who didn't move her to this place she says is a God-forsaken town trying like hell to blow itself off the earth. Sometimes when she is mad about living in Hell Creek she yells, "It was bad enough being raised in alligator country by alligator people!" This is all I know about her mom and dad. I don't have any trouble picturing these grandparents: human bodies with alligator heads, huge teethy mouths speaking in southern drawls, the grandpa wearing overalls and a ragged baseball cap shading his alligator eyes.

Apparently there are "damn good reasons" these relatives aren't in our lives, but Mom will never say what they are.

Dad is the same way about his father and stepmother. "There's no welcome mat where they are concerned," is how he puts it. I pressed him to tell me at least where they live and he said, "So far east and cold nobody can get to it." So if Mom's folks are alligator people, I picture Dad's as Abominable Snow Monsters with overly large, wiggly eyes and growly things to say.

Though the storm called mom doesn't seem about to strike, I decide to get out of reach anyway. As I climb up into the overhead berth of the train, I wonder how Grandma Naomi is going to fit into things. I lie flat on the mattress and hang my head upside down so my long hair dances with the rocking of the train. It's a good position for considering things. My dad's mom is not part of the alligator people or the Abominable Snow Monsters. All I know about her is the special gift she sent me. My brothers got stuff too, but mine is the best and I'm wearing it now. It's a gold-link and tiny pearl bracelet with three charms: a tiny mustard seed in a see-thru plastic box, a gold and mother-of-pearl oval of Jesus the size of a baby ant with his arms welcoming me to come to him, and a Moses-type tablet that is thumbnail-size engraved with, "If ye have faith as a grain of mustard seed, nothing shall be impossible unto you."

On Grandma Naomi's note she wrote that she has prayed all my life to be able to meet me, her granddaughter, and that she has always had faith that God would make this possible. For a tomboy cowgirl, you'd think I wouldn't like this bracelet, but I do. I cherish it like Mom does her jewelry, not because it's glittery, but because I already invited Jesus into my heart and now he's hanging on my wrist. When I try to picture Grandma Naomi, I see a fairy godmother flitting about.

I could sure use one of those.

Not able to stop myself, I ask Mom for the umpteenth time when I will meet Grandma Naomi. She only shushes me.

I sigh and try to settle into the rhythm of the train. Trains are a big part of my life, with the tracks being close to home. I can almost feel them rattling the house, and their whistles are just part of any normal day. Now I feel this train pull the top of my head toward this new grandma I don't know. I like the feeling in my brain. It seems to be making room for her up there.

At the Minneapolis depot the train takes forever to stop. When we finally find Grandma Naomi she says, "Oh, yo—u!" like her breath is plum taken away by me. She holds my cheeks in gentle hands and her eyes are lit like she's never seen a little girl before. I'd try anything, do anything, to get Grandma Naomi to say "Oh, you" that way again, and to look at me like I was really something to see, like the best present ever, like I'm cupid and she is love.

We go right to Dr. Mattenstadt's office in a high rise. At first I'm excited and feel very special to be seeing an important Specialist, but once the nurse spends all day in half hour slots sticking shots into me, I don't feel so special. She scrubs my upper arm with stinky rubbing alcohol, like I'm dirty and hard to get clean. I count the twelve metal syringes each time as she rolls my arm out toward the wall and makes a prick just under the skin, squeezing in a bubble of liquid.

The nurse lied to me about it all first. "This won't hurt, because I put it just under your skin," she'd said, not looking at me, putting one needle down and getting the next. The nurse makes row after row of nasty shots so that by the end of the day my mom has to drag me back to the little room for my last few rounds, hissing in my ear how embarrassed she is on account of my "having a fit." After we leave, I count the rows, twelve, and I count the shots, 144.

My bed at Grandma Naomi's is on the summer porch, thick with quilts. I think I am in trouble and not allowed to stay inside the house. Only Chief sleeps outside at our house. I'm afraid out here, with all the big city noises. I kneel for bedtime prayers and lay my arms out, palms up, chin on the mattress, and view the lines of blistered shots, angry red ants trapped in a bubble of skin, marching toward my elbows. I let the shots feel the summer breeze coming through the screens and rest my face on the pink and green gingham squares. "Now I lay me down to sleep. I pray the Lord my soul to keep. If I should die before I wake,

I pray the Lord my soul to take. Amen. And tell Chief I love him and miss him and wish he was here with *all* my heart. Amen."

"Amen," Mom says from behind me. "Stand up and let me see those cute pajamas I bought you. Oh, Punkin', those look so pretty on you." Mom cares an awful lot about pretty things. Kind of like happy faces. "Now up in bed." The cool satin pajamas cause goose bumps down my back as I slip under the quilts. Being in a good mood, Mom tucks the covers around my body. I wince when she pushes against my tender arms. Her happy face is gone in an instant. "Listen, you won't get any sympathy from me. You're going to have to get tough and stay tough at the doctor's tomorrow. I won't put up with another of your fits like I witnessed today. You hear me?"

I hear the liquor on her breath. Mom acts like I got asthma on purpose just to bug her.

"Will you send Grandma Naomi in, please?" I'm extra polite, hoping to invite a better mood.

"Yes," Mom says grudgingly, "but don't you go getting her upset now when she's unstable."

She disappears without another word and soon Grandma Naomi comes through the door in her slim polyester pants with a tucked in blouse. She's not ready for bed yet, like I am. I see the twinkle in grandma's eyes even in this dim outside light. She sits beside me, so trim she hardly leaves a dent. "Oh, yo—u!" she says and giggles, like I'm the sweetest piece of pie during the most hungry time of her life. I let her eat me up. Why does she have such joy for me when I haven't done anything for her yet? "Oh, you dear, dear girl." I watch her closely, drinking her in, ready for disappointment to crease her face and slip out onto her tongue like it does with Mom, ready for her to act unstable in some way. "May the Lord bless you and keep you," she whispers with a sweet smile. "Snug-as-a-bug-in-a-rug." She kisses her fingertips and lightly touches where she had seen my upper arms were covered in shots, as if somehow knowing they itch and throb under the covers.

I see her salt and pepper hair and grandmother face that isn't too old and wrinkled. I see her hipbones stick out and the slight rounding hunch of her back, but still, I think an angel can be in anyone it wants. I don't want her to go, and this makes me miss Chief so bad, tears slip into my ears.

"Tomorrow we'll just see how much that fancy doctor knows," she says, soft but firm. Like she'll pop him one in the eye if he doesn't do right by me. I wonder about him, a short bald man with wire-rimmed glasses, a German accent, and nurses that hurt kids all day.

"Okay, Grandma Naomi." I like this old lady. "You know what? You're already my favorite person ever." I hook her to Jesus, knowing she must be a friend of his, and put her right beside Chief, imagining Chief wagging his tail.

She tells me I'm beautiful inside and out, and points over my heart saying in her shy way, especially there. I know what she means, and it helps dull the pain.

I fall asleep with the little smile she put on my face but wake under this huge pile of quilts from a nightmare. Voices say, 'You breathe because we let you,' over and over. The voices are familiar. I'm being choked and something heavy pushes down on my chest. My wheezing grows worse but the voices keep saying, "We let you breathe. We let you live." Whatever is around my neck starts to feel like hands, and I cough and cough but can't get the hands off my neck or the weight on my chest to stop. I eke out a plea, "No. No. No!"

I wake to the sound of birds chirping next to my head. My face is pushed into the window screen, my neck wrenched like the low hanging tree branch next to me. As I dig my way out from under the quilts I feel the fear of the dream and gasp for air.

Grandma Naomi arrives soon after and rubs soft fingers up and down my back. I decide she is a fairy godmother after all.

All too soon, I have to say goodbye to spend another afternoon at the doctor's office, so he can tell us I'm allergic to most of what the nurse shot into me, forbid me to run or play rough or ever get out of breath and get my wheezing started, and give me five prescriptions and instructions to see our local doctor for allergy shots once a week. We're to come back for more tests in a year, which I dread, but at least I can see Grandma Naomi again.

As much as I hate asthma, it did bring me my most favorite person in the world. She's the only family I have that I actually wish I was related to by blood.

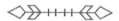

I'm afraid something is wrong with me. As many times as Mom has said to me, "You're up to no good," I've wondered if I am no good. Trouble does seem to find me. Sometimes my heart hurts from feeling cold, like ice. I try to warm it up by thinking, 'I have another mother, a real mother, and a real father, and they really, really love me.' Maybe something is stuck inside me, something bad from my real parents that makes me unlovable. Maybe I'm just not the kind of girl people hope for.

Mom says that adoption isn't easy. It was worst with my older brother. She and Dad had surprise inspections any time, day or night, where someone would knock on the door to check the house and make sure this couple is good enough to adopt children. Mom said it was horrible to be spied on by someone who acted real nice but was just looking for mistakes. I know what that's like.

I'm sure the inspector lady did her very best. It must be near impossible to tell what happens once the front door locks.

I didn't come from an agency, so there were no inspections, and it was the same with my baby brother. He came to us like this.

One day, without any warning, suitcases are loaded into the trunk of the car with my brother and me in the backseat, and when Mom gets in the passenger seat, Dad drives off. We aren't told anything, so my mind worries that they're getting rid of me for good. I'm convinced. I'd heard them quiet-talking a lot lately, and when I'd come in the room they'd stop. These thoughts shouldn't come to a kid at any age, but for adopted kids like me they do, like they took me in and now they'll turn me out.

"We're going on a trip!" I say from the backseat, chasing fears away by being bubbly. My brother's back curves in a half circle as he hunches away from me like I have fleas.

"Not exactly, Little Missy," Mom says, turning towards the backseat to smile big. Great big happy smile! I wonder what has her so happy. Her eyes are hard to see behind thick cat-eye glasses.

Dad clears his throat. "Your mom and I have a special trip to make."

"And we're bringing back a big surprise!" she adds, sounding like she might pop.

"Are we going too?" I ask.

"You can't." Dad has a way of slamming the door on any more questions.

We pull up outside a strange house that Dad says is Mrs. Peterson's. My brother groans long and loud. Mrs. Peterson is a nice lady, but she's only come over to sit with us at our house. We've never gone to hers.

"We're sleeping at some old lady's?" Big brother asks.

Dad means business. "It's only for a few days." He sits with the car keys in his lap and looks like he's squinting into a bright sun but there isn't one today. This look means don't give me even an ounce of grief. They drop us off here without telling us where they're going.

Mrs. Peterson gives us the tour. She's old and has this skin I can't figure out. It hangs down so far off the backs of her arms, I mean really far, that when I'm near her I can't think of anything else. I stare in the worst way and can't stop myself, even though I know it's bad manners. I watch it like it's alive, flapping back and forth, wiggly-jiggly. When she waves me downstairs for lunch, I'm sure it will slap her in the face. I'm thrilled by it.

I would die to touch it, but can't think of how. She isn't the hugging type. We don't touch. Mrs. Peterson is kind and tucks me in at night, but I know I can't ask her about it. It wouldn't be enough, anyway. I want to play with it like putty, pull it out as far as it'll go and see if it'll snap back like a rubber band.

This won't do. There is no way. It drives me crazy. When she wears a light cardigan in the chilly morning, it looks like there's a little gerbil up her sleeve, wiggling for a way out. Between this and being a little girl who misses Chief, I'm miserable.

When at last my parents' car pulls up, we watch out of the window as Mom and Dad fuss with getting something out of the backseat. We see their heads huddled together, bent over. When they finally turn, a pale blue blanket is gathered up high in Mom's arms under her big smile.

This is how it happens for adopted siblings: one minute they aren't there and then POOF, another kid comes home. This isn't a surprise. It's a mistake.

They come in and Mrs. Peterson fusses over the little blue bundle. It's soon clear that my older brother and I have turned invisible. We look back and forth at each other confused by this new competition. "We got him in Cheyenne, Wyoming," Mom says in a voice that would spread butter. I wonder if that's a store where you buy babies. Mrs. Peterson coos like a mourning dove.

Mom smiles down at the new baby with a smile that reaches all the way to her eyes. I wonder if she smiled at me like that when I was new, before she found out I was up to no good.

Mom and Dad want me to hold my new little brother. I want to be held by them. I do what I'm told.

I'm sure nothing could be as cute as Chief when he was our fuzzy little collie pup. But this baby boy with a funny, scrunched-up face is made of teeny-tiny things: hands, toes, ears and a sweet, red 'O' of a mouth. I hear myself coo as silly as Mrs. Peterson. He yawns and blinks open his eyes at me, and my heart jumps up inside. Babies have special powers. I hold him without complaining, this new brother who, just a second ago, was a stranger they got from a baby store.

Mom wants to show off her new baby every chance she gets, so almost as soon as we get him home the folks arrange a welcome party with their Couples Bridge Club members and other important friends.

That night Mom is in one of her better moods as she gets ready, asking if I want to come in her room to help her pick out her jewelry. Oo-wee she loves jewelry, going back and forth with earrings and necklaces, then rings, and more rings, and different rings, and less rings that somehow lead to just the right bracelet. I do not have a knack for this. From time to time she asks me to pick, so I've learned to keep track of her face as it studies itself in the mirror, hoping to remember which one it liked. Where did all these rules of fashion come from and how is a cowgirl supposed to know them?

Whenever there is a color to pick, she always goes for yellow. So you can probably bet that our house is yellow, soft and cheery. And daisies—she loves daisies—which start out as plain-normal-nice, then explode all over the house. The exploding fits. But it's the daisies I wonder about, seeming contrary to the mother I have. She's the darkest rose, like a reddish-black, a powerful smell, with thorns that say "stop when I say stop".

. Unfortunately for my parents, the welcoming party has turned into one of those nights I need saving from asthma. It can come any time and I can't predict just when it will attack. All of Mom and Dad's important friends are here with their wives: the bankers, the judge, the veterinarian, car dealers, business owners like my Dad, the lawyer, the pilot who co-owns a small airplane with Dad and flies for the utilities company, and our family doctor. They all golf, they all play bridge, they all drink during cards and after cards. The baby has been put to bed for the night, and the adults get louder and louder as the night goes on, but my wheezing starts to match their noise.

Soon, the doctor who is as drunk as the rest of them is treating me at his office in the middle of the night with his booze breath ready to kill me if the asthma doesn't. He pokes a thick, long needle into the vein in my arm near the place I squeeze together to look like a butt crack when I'm bored, but I'm not bored now. My eyes are popped wide in fear. He's not able to stay in the chair while he pushes the huge syringe of pus-colored medicine into me and the needle cranks around in my arm. My scared eyes beg Mom to do something.

"For God's sake, what's the matter with you?" Mom yells, and I'm not sure who she's yelling at, me or the doctor.

He yells back, wiggling the needle and hurting me more. "You begged me to bring her into the office like she's somehow my problem!"

I keep quiet, too scared, too wheezy. Sometimes I start here for treatment and still end up in the hospital.

I shake and shiver from the icy cold this medicine delivers into my body, but my life is saved, my airways opening. I will shake all night and be tired the next day in school, but not wheezy.

"Breathing is improving," the doctor reports. Mom takes out a cigarette, shaking, and lights up. She blows smoke my way without thinking. He only stares at her.

I wish Grandma Naomi could be here to rub my back the way she did when I had a nightmare. In my mind, I hear her say, "Oh, yo—u," which I know means I love you so—o much.

4
THE BOARDING HOUSE

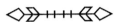

The Boarding House is not for just anybody. The residents who live there will be the only ones who ever live there. No path leads to the revolving door. No one can inquire, no one notices.

The fast clip of hard-soled shoes and the rustle of a crinoline slip announce Katrina before she turns from the hallway and into the sitting room like she means business. A basket she carries is brought to her lap as she sits straight-backed on the couch exclaiming, "Big night, too much to do! Oh, the messes, the mending, the constant need for comforting. I must catch up. It's only me, only me."

She takes freshly washed and wrung out underwear from the basket, lays them in washcloths that she folds in half and rolls up tight. "It's only me, only me." Her hands fly through the mending, sewing a lavender button on a cotton blouse.

Katrina's eyes are large for her heart-shaped face, and she pops them even bigger when speaking. She's a rosy-cheeked girl, with naturally dark lips, the upper lip heart-shaped. Her hair is medium long, black, and curled along the bottom. She keeps it pulled back from her face and tied with a pink velvet ribbon with pretty loops running along the edges. Katrina is hardworking and precocious, with the job of an adult even though she is not. She is treated like a grown up, and that is what matters in The Boarding House.

Katrina wears a pretty, dark-pink dress of raw silk, with a full skirt and billowing sleeves. A petite black velvet bow is affixed at the throat. A dress so beautiful proves her stature as a leader in The Boarding House. Katrina's constant work requires a crisp pinafore to protect such a dress. Its cap sleeves with wide rickrack add a jolly touch to this overly responsible resident. Gold hoop earrings set her apart, adding to her value, and are admired by the children she cares for who try to touch them but are discouraged from doing so by Katrina's no-nonsense manner.

The seriousness of her job leaves creases between her lovely arched eyebrows, and her constant movement puts off anyone intent on admiring her beauty. Katrina looks like a doll but acts more like a matron.

Nearby, Gangster sits by The Babe, who lounges long and sleek, like a cat. Outwardly, The Babe and Katrina couldn't be more opposite, but as far as work goes, they both give their all. They respect each other and both know full well what lies behind their masks.

"Gangster, is The Babe up for a chat?" Katrina inquires, widening her eyes to take in the powerful figure he cuts. Every resident in The Boarding House knows to go through Gangster first if they want to talk to The Babe.

"I can ask." His hat brim shades The Babe's face as they whisper and he reports, "She's up for a chat. Keep it snappy."

Katrina's eyes return to her work. "Thought I heard the trap door last night."

"Nothing new," The Babe answers in her breathy voice.

"And earlier too. Did you get cookies?" Katrina licks her lips.

The Babe turns her face away, already tired of Katrina's routine. "You know my work schedule. You watched me go out the revolving door. I brought a cookie back for someone special."

Katrina knows the cookie isn't for her. "I wish my work brought cookies and ice cream cones," she sighs.

"No. You don't." The Babe's icy delivery stops Katrina.

Katrina tries to make up for her mistake. "I know, I know. I'm always stuck in The Boarding House, never leaving," she talks faster and faster, "always fixing, mending, taking care of others, busy-busy-busy. Going out once in a while sounds good."

"There's nothing good out there." The Babe tries to get back to her sweeter voice, "Just jobs to be done," then covers her mouth with the back of a gloved hand to hide a yawn.

Gangster stands up quick and Katrina recoils slightly, but the barrel of his Tommy Gun is pointed to the floor, never at her. "That's enough, Pipsqueak. The Babe's done with you." He sits, turning to the love of his life. "Right, Sweetheart?"

Katrina sighs deeply without making a sound, secretly wishing she had a Gangster to take care of her.

A faint voice from the hallway says, "I'm all alone."

Katrina puts down her basket and does one of her many jobs, caretaking. She goes to take the hand of Lonely to sit her close beside her on the couch.

Lonely curls in a ball and whimpers, "I'm sad."

"Yes." Katrina strokes Lonely's thin hair. "You have a sad, lonely job but you are still precious. And you are here with us, so you are not alone now. Stay with us for a quick minute and then you can go back to your room."

"I'm too lonely." She leaves the couch in bare feet that match her threadbare nightgown.

"I will make you a new nightgown, Lonely. What is your favorite color?" Katrina asks in her direct way.

"I'm too lonely for colors."

"Then I'll make it yellow to bring some sunshine into your life."

"Yellow likes itself too much." Lonely scrunches her face as if she's hearing a loud sound. "It's always shouting."

"I will pick another color then, maybe a warm cream. You would look lovely in cream."

Gangster says, "Hey Lonely, come 'ere. The Babe has something for you."

"Here's your cookie, Lonely," The Babe says. "You do such a good job being you."

Lonely takes the cookie. "Oh. Only one. It's lonely just like me."

Katrina says, "With you it makes two, you and the cookie, see? So you aren't lonely."

Lonely takes the cookie to her room, holding it in open palms like it's a sheer wonder.

5
BADLANDS

An early morning sun bounces off the lavender walls of my bedroom, a new day after a bad night of the folks fighting over me. They probably didn't think I could hear them between two doors, a hallway, and a bathroom between the walls. I wish.

Dad accused Mom of being too rough with me, saying that she could damage a kidney giving me a bruise like that. Mom hissed about his visits to my room but Dad cut her off, bringing up a past argument about her liking to lock me out in the winter cold and only letting me in so I didn't freeze to death.

When I heard that, my body did shiver, but they can fight over me all they want, I don't know what they're yelling about. Never have. Never will. I don't feel a thing. Nothing. I don't know about how the bruise got on my stomach, but with a wild badlands girl like me, it could've come from anywhere. I don't know about Dad coming in my room either. He never bothers himself to come in during the day, why would he care to come in at night?

I have a trick when they fight like this. I sit under one of the high bedroom windows and rock my back against the wall, rocking, rocking, imagining that I slip out the window and drop onto the back of a white horse waiting for me below with Jesus on its back and we ride like never before, like this horse is a bolt of lightning, charged and glowing through the night sky. Once I hit the back of the horse I'm gone. I fall asleep rocking by the wall, but Jesus must do some powerful saving, because I wake in my bed, like I did this morning.

I lie still, holding my breath to listen, to see if I'm cooked this morning or not. I can tell Dad's gone to work. My baby brother, who is five and isn't a baby even though I still call him this, doesn't sound like he's up yet. My brother two years older than me, who I still wrestle and real-fight with, isn't making any noise either. Chief? He knows to wait. I like the sound of today.

This might be our lucky day to spot the herd of wild Mustangs galloping through the badlands. Chief and I have been looking for them for years, and we know they are here, they're just deep in there, knowing they'd better hide, I guess. Ever since our sweet ol' mare Whitey died, I've been hoping to catch a replacement, which is a long shot, but my folks aren't budging on getting me another horse. She died when I was nine, and I remember every piece of that day. Whitey didn't glow as white as the horses on the movie screen ridden by cowboys racing through canyons that look like our badlands, poppin' pistols under their armpits behind them. But I remember running toward the gigantic white balloon that was Whitey's puffed body, with my dad chasing me and telling me to get back in the car. It was too late. Whitey was buzzing with flies, and her ears didn't twitch to shoo them and her tail lay still. My high spirits died down for weeks, squeezing under the bloated horse, squashed flat. Nobody told me how to lose a love. But looking for the wild horses out in the badlands helps me feel better and gives more power to my prayers that God will bring me another horse someday.

How soon I make it outside always depends on Mom and what she wants from me. Mom is the boss of this house. Mom is the boss of me. She's the type that wants to tell me what to do, and I know better than to ask for what I want, which is to get up, get dressed, and bolt out of here quick to get up into the badlands. With her, I need to earn it. So I get to it.

I make quick work of it, too. As I make a peanut butter and jelly sandwich to take with me, I go through the list of all the chores I've already accomplished. But Mom adds one more, a smelly one: feed the cats. I look for our Siamese brother-sister team, Stormy George and Suzy. They're misnamed. Stormy is fat, lazy, and easy to find, lounging in some sunny spot, but Suzy is an all-out scrapper. She's the stormy one, ornery, skin and bones, always looking for a fight.

Suzy, as usual, is perched at the top of the telephone pole on our back corner lot. Near as we can figure she thinks she's in charge of the birds. They dive-bomb her as she's scratching the eyes out of the sky, sometimes rising on her back legs. Then she uses her innersprings and leaps, spreading all fours, using the skin under her armpits and the puff of her guiding tail to fly. Batting at the birds, she lands on the grass. She sits casually and licks her bottom just to prove that being a flying cat is no big deal.

Mom had come to the door to watch Suzy. "Did you ever clean up that juice spill in the basement?" Uh-oh, Mom's veering off course, looking to add more chores.

"I'll go see how it came up." Doing what she asks right away is best when Mom starts her day like this.

First, I call the cat to feed her. "Suzy! Here kitty, kitty, kitty." Suzy looks at me from mid-lick on her tummy, cat eyes little slits that say, 'Are you talking to me?' Mom sees this and smirks.

"Hey, Mom, will you please go get her?" I am always very careful to say 'please' and 'thank you'. It doesn't always help, but today she strolls out and scoops Suzy up, proud that she's the only one who can approach this fur ball. I hold the door open for them, plastering myself to the wall out of harm's way. No matter how unpredictable Mom is, I'd place bets on Suzy clawing my eyes out any day.

My brothers are up now and in the basement in their pajamas, watching television as I race around doing Mom's bidding. I'm not gonna start anything with them, I've got places to go, so I act like I don't see them and their sleepy faces and mussed hair, I just clean up the spill and report to Mom. Finally she says my favorite words, "Go on now," and they must be her favorite words too, getting me out of her hair. I nearly bowl her over running past her to get outside, and I yell a quick sorry as I slam the back door behind me and run across the yard, with Chief on my heels and passing me in a flash. We leap the edge of the coulee making our escape, but out of habit, one ear listens for Mom in case she thinks of something else to yell out the door to keep me a prisoner. Nope, nothing.

"Yi—ppee!" Chief and I race along the bottom of the coulee, today a grabby mix of mud and sand. Tough going. Heaven opens to us just under the bridge near our house where the badlands start.

Badlands.

What's so bad about this land? I know what bad is, and it isn't out here. I've heard people use words like drab and stoic when they see the badlands. There's plenty of plant life and color out here, but it doesn't hit you over the head. You have to notice it.

As proof that trees grow here, the tip of my cowboy boot hooks on a juniper root not too far up the coulee from home. "Chi—ef!" I scream as I fall flat on my face taking in a mouthful of sand. Trees like these come to the badlands with a strong will to live. The root is thirty feet from the tree, and the tree is hanging so far off the side of a hill it's begging to die and take me with it. "Ow!" I gasp as I get up, spitting sand.

Chief stretches into a deep bow, yawns for a lifetime and lies down on his haunches.

"I—ck!" I yell, grossed out at the feel of a sandwich squished on my belly. My face-plant smashed the lunch I carry inside my shirt where it tucks into my jeans. Now there's peanut butter-grape jelly goo on my stomach and probably into my belly button. I crane my neck around to see if any other kids are watching since all types of trouble can be hiding out in makeshift forts or sitting up on the hills throwing rocks. I'll need a secret hiding place to lift my shirt and clean up this mess because any kid spotting me now would spread gossip around school nicknaming me Squishy for life. And since Frankie moved away the summer after third grade, I'd have no feisty friend to stick up for me.

I know just where to go.

Chief and I take our normal route, running through the drainage to Big Elephant, which I named for its top that feels like I'm sitting right on the animal's back. My badlands are made of giant ridges, grassy bluffs, large formations, and acres of hill-size mounds stretching as far as the eye can see. Everything is layered in pale colors. Shapes form in this land of shale, sand, silt, and clay made by rushing water and howling winds. These shapes must have called out their names to me over time: Big Elephant, Sleeping Lion, Indian Brave, Sand Circle and many other beautiful dirt friends of mine.

Climbing up the side of Big Elephant is like running up tall draperies of firm sand, made by the magic of runoff. It takes fast, light feet and lots of practice, because there are no hand or footholds. It's steep but not too steep, and it's high, maybe twenty feet, so I can't pause to think about whether I'll make it. It's charge or nothing, since firm sand is slippery under indecisive cowboy boots. Keeping my balance is rewarded with a comfortable seat across Big Elephant's wide sandstone back.

Near the smooth top, I find Big Elephant's lucky charm and finger the sea fossil imbedded in his hide. I make a wish like always. This land is littered with prehistoric fossils and dinosaur bones that I've been lectured to never take for granted. I love them and leave them. I'm a western explorer not a scientist. I can't grasp what billions of years ago might actually mean. In my mind, my parents seem as old as these gumbo hills, and that's as far back as I want to go.

From his comfortable back, I look down his left side into a circle of very fine sand. I have Chief trained, so I wait for him to run all the way around Big Elephant and elephant's other tall lumpy dirt friends that hook together and wrap around this hidden area of sand I call Sand Circle. Chief knows where the only opening is, and knows to check for snakes sunning their cold, scaly skin. I've had just about all I can handle of this gross, sticky goo on my belly, but it'd be nothing compared to snakebite, so I'd better be patient. I stay perched on Big Elephant's back until Chief barks the "all clear" then I aim myself toward Sand Circle and slide down on my rear end, rocking to dig in my boot heels to slow the downhill speed.

Unsnapping the bottom of my shirt, I peel the sandwich off me, glad that I'm no wussy because I'll need to eat this squarshed mess. This is how to say squashed in our town because we have our own way of talking and seem to be proud of it. Anyway, I'd never waste a perfect summer day tromping back to the house for another lunch. Grown-ups have one thing right, there's never enough time in the day.

I assess the mess. It's bad, widespread. I know better than to waste a canteen on cleanup, so Chief is in for a real treat. His licking tickles so bad I have to push him away for spells of relief. I'm squealing higher than my voice goes. My stomach jumps at each scrape of the long dog tongue. I laugh so hard I'm afraid I'll pee my pants because peanut butter sticks to the roof of his extra-long muzzle, making his tongue seem like a separate animal. Chief is unrecognizable. My stomach is aching from laughter, and my cheeks are begging for rest. Now I know what splitting a gut means. It's not about cleaning fish.

I've never carried on goofy like this in the mysterious Sand Circle. Normally, a serious feeling drapes over me like a monk's cloak.

In this Sand Circle, surrounded by tall earthen walls, my young girl eyes have seen without seeing an ancient tribe of Indians burning a holy fire, heard drums thump-thumping my heart while a mood lifts my feet, tempting me into dance. I come into this circle often, but can never stay. It's a place to move on from, like paying respect to my elders before running off to play.

I don't think it's strange, this Indian stuff. You'd have to be dead not to feel them on this land. I see them other places in the badlands too: a line of warriors standing along the ridge tops, horses galloping through the draw with Indians on their backs. I know they aren't really there so I'm not worried that I'm seeing things. Once I talked to a Sunday school teacher about it when we were reading about visions in the Bible and she said it's a gift from God to be able to see these ancient Indians. Her answer surprised me but I know she's right. I like it. I have a gift.

I wish Chief could clue me in on what he finds when he's sniffing out these badlands, like if his nose discovers an old arrowhead buried in the roots of a tuft of grass growing out of the sand. He's not human, so he can't tell me. I like pretending to know something about the lives of Indians. I imagine Red Bird, the son of Black Cloud Lightening, shot an arrow to kill his first deer, and a celebration to mark him becoming a hunter will be held in the Sand Circle. I pretend Chief and I are invited, and we dance around on the hard, smooth sand. It passes our time in a good way.

I dream I have real Indian blood in me. Being adopted, with origins unknown, it's possible. But if so, my Dad wouldn't keep me. He talks bad about Indians and holds a grudge that's not helped by living in Hell Creek. It doesn't sit on the reservation border but is still called a border town. He says he has his reasons, but he won't tell me what they are. Dad calls Indians nasty, dirty, and smelly, and even said that the Indian men want to steal their women. I doubt it. When I was a toddler Dad would threaten that if I was bad he was going to give me to the Indians. This worked, I behaved, but he sure did scare me out of my wits with the way he said it.

Dad calls a junky car an Indian wagon and any dark-haired drunk on the street a drunk Indian. I rarely even see Indians in our town. Dad recently blamed a robbery at his heavy-hauling truck repair shop on Indians. It turned out to be one of his hired hands, but that didn't change what he thinks of Indians.

I'm expected to share his opinions. I pretend to think like him to save my hide, but I don't. And I know Dad isn't a mind reader.

If I could tell him what I think, and I know it's not allowed, but if I could, I'd tell him he's confusing people with bad dogs. Bad dogs can happen because of bad people.

I know this from Chief. Everything circles back to him and his gold-rimmed brown eyes often so fixed on me. Right now he twists his side into the floor of the Sand Circle bringing up the damp, cool sand below. I push into him, lying against the rise and fall of his mighty rib cage. He snorts, probably because of the sand, but I imagine he's pleased at getting the peanut butter lunch. I weave fingers into his coat of many colors until I'm firmly attached to his pink-colored skin.

He's my lifeline and I hold on tight.

But Chief can't help me with everything. Dark moods aren't his specialty, and sometimes I run to the badlands for reasons other than play, like pouring sad feelings into a cave. I sing "Please release me, let me go," into the small hole at the very top of a high mounded hill. The cave echo gives me a fancy singer voice in the underground emptiness. This one line, sung only here, lays a patch on that hurt in me. I curl my body around the cave opening as if I'm sick and I guess I am— heartsick—don't know why. "Please release me, let me go." I sing into the deep, until I'm all poured out.

Chief stays at the bottom, listening, cocking his head one way, then the other, waiting. I start to get over myself, then milk it one last time, hoping it's my best. Dried pebbles of gumbo roll down in a stream beneath my cowboy boots as I scooch from the top of the mound down to the gully. They roll into Chief right along with me.

On better days I give star performances at the prairie dog town, singing the song "Don't Fence Me In." I can do the Western Shuffle and belt it out, "Just turn me loose, let me wander, over yonder, underneath the western sky." Prairie dogs are a funny audience, popping up and down, but none of them join in with their strange high-pitched call. I picture myself singing and dancing on The Lawrence Welk Show, him clapping, his baton tucked under his armpit as he says in his soft lilt, "Very nice, little lady." It's not hard to imagine Mr. Welk discovering me, since I'm singing just over the border of his home state of North Dakota and only four hours from his German-speaking hometown.

Mr. Welk wouldn't have me dancing on his show. He's got some real pros, and learning to dance doesn't come easy in our little town. Seems like all little girls, and I mean all—short, plump, or skinny-whinny—took tap dancing and ballet from a lady who packed the local Elks ballroom during the one year she must have gotten stuck in our dead-end town. She promised our parents a big show of The Wizard of Oz and I can still do the shuffle-shuffle-ball-change/shuffle-toe-heel-step while singing, "Follow the yellow brick road. Follow the yellow brick road," in a munchkin voice.

Normally, our small eastern Montana town doesn't take kindly to drama. Folks here are good humored, and most love to laugh but they have long memories. They're watching us kids closely to see if we're growing up to be fools. In this harsh, northern land there isn't much room for goofing off if you want to survive. Nobody here has any homesteading ancestors that were able to keep their land without their noses to the grindstone, and deep pockets of luck.

But drama is one thing; the threat of a Russian invasion is another. Air raid sirens go off regularly, and when the Russians attack, I'm supposed to be in our neighbor's basement bomb shelter with everybody else. I figure I'll be deep in the badlands and won't hear the loud warning. I'll come home later to find Russian soldiers yelling foreign words on our quiet streets. But I'll turn back, knowing I'm lucky that day to have carried the knapsack I keep full of camping supplies, and I'll run into the badlands with Chief before ever being crammed into the bomb shelter.

The last time the air raid whistle blew and all us designated neighbors crammed onto benches with jars and jars of green beans at our backs I ended up having an asthma attack. Listening to a kid's wheeze grow louder and louder, with air becoming harder and harder to pull in makes a crowd that is stuck in a very small space real nervous. It started to seem like other people had asthma. The men yanked their neckties loose, opened their top buttons and stretched their necks out like flying Canadian geese. The women tried not to touch their throats and failed. It was embarrassing for my parents because people took turns giving them the stink eye. Finally Mom got up and told our family we were leaving. I mumbled a sorry, because I was, and Dad said, "I guess we're just going to have to go out and get shot by the Russians," as he was closing the thick door. His tone sounded like he probably winked. That's Dad. He's good with grownups and they seem fond of him. I was the one he was mad at anyway.

Townsfolk claim that our small town of Hell Creek is right smack dab in the middle of nowhere, but for a town claiming to be nowhere, we've got an awful lot of trouble. It seems some people jump out of bed in the morning to hear bad news and spread it fast. Hazel is over here early for coffee and nothing makes me eavesdrop more than whispering grown-ups. I may have Indian talent after all, since they never hear me. Hazel is saying that her older sons told her there is a group of high school boys bragging about partying and making girls take their clothes off and doing 'you know what.' Mom gasps louder than ever and asks Hazel where they could be doing this awful stuff. I overhear Hazel whisper, "Some cabin in the badlands."

Mom blurts, "There aren't any cabins in the badlands, unless you want to count the lean-to at the shooting range."

Hazel shushes her and they both look around for big ears. She assures Mom there is some cabin hidden in a forest up there.

Uh-oh. Chief and I have already found this cabin in the junipers and we've been to it several times, stumbling on it while climbing higher into the badlands than we'd ever been. I couldn't have been more surprised when I first saw it, my mouth hung open—calling all flies, calling all flies! The cabin is tucked in there but good.

I always pile simple rock markers along our cross-country route when we explore unknown territory, since getting lost is stupid, and we never walk the main road into the badlands, because roads mean people and I am never looking for people. One day Chief and I did follow a weedy, narrow lane from the cabin to see where it goes and found that it stems off the dirt road coming from town, the one and only. If teenage boys are going to the cabin this is how I'll bet they get there.

The last time we cut up to the cabin, Chief and I had a scare, but it wasn't teen boys, it was a mountain lion! It walked toward the cabin—took my breath away and not from asthma—man-sized and powerful with a thick long tail. I froze admiring the way it moved. Mountain lions are shy animals that flee from sight, so I knew I was lucky to even lay eyes on this one. Chief barked me out of my trance and I had time to close the door but I watched out the windows as it snooped around the cabin for long enough that I was afraid to leave. The cabin is most likely in its territory. I hadn't seen it before, but that doesn't mean it hasn't been watching us. After I built up enough nerve to leave the cabin, I figured it would rather run from Chief and me instead of attack. I gave it a warning by making plenty of human noises from inside the cabin, and was grateful the huge cat was not around when we left.

I was almost late getting home, waiting out the mountain lion, which would have earned me the punishment of standing with bare legs spread while Mom whips a bamboo switch back and forth between them causing welts that rub raw in my blue jeans. These sores remind me for days the lesson I am supposed to learn. Dad's tool is the belt, and if I am long late and cause him to worry, I'd probably have to brace for the buckle on my behind. He's used it on my younger brother and I hated Dad for that.

After hearing what Hazel said about the teenage boys hurting girls in the cabin, I decide Chief and I are going back this very day to see if the cabin playhouse is still ours. I catch Mom off guard while Hazel is still here gossiping, and she seems flustered enough to let me go without making me jump through her chores routine.

We travel by way of Big Elephant and the Sand Circle, winding upwards through hilly mounds that wear horizontal stripes in pale colors of orange, light gray, brown, tan, and almost black. We weave around big blobs of firm sand supporting knobs taller than me, and around smooth, egg-shaped rocks, large yucca plants, and prickly pear cactus that must be avoided. It's rough travel that would seem never-ending if you don't like badlands, or if the strange shapes and changing dirt underfoot aren't considered fun.

There is lots of up-and-down trekking to get to the cabin. A steep climb leads to a wide sandstone saddle that is magical except for the sprinkling of red scoria: sharp volcanic stones that make you bleed if you fall on them. They like to roll underfoot, and I've shared my red blood with this red rock more than once. Why I say this saddle is magical is that on either end are tall formations that stand like proud guards to the kingdom. These guards stand out from a backdrop of steep sagebrush-covered hills. When I am on a roll I can scale pretty high on these formations, even though they are not built for climbing.

Usually I act way sillier running around up here, loping and teasing Chief, glad to be away from home, but today I feel like I better watch out. The other side of the saddle funnels into a deep bed of dirt and sand surrounded by hills on all sides. This sandy bed hints at becoming dangerous gumbo during a heavy rain, with so many slopes feeding it water. I will know to try to stay high and skirt around it if I am ever caught in a downpour, since the sandstone pass will be slippery enough when wet to feed me right to it.

Off to our right is a rare sight for the badlands, a juniper forest. Hiking up through the forest on dried pine needles makes a crunchy, musical beat that adds to the wonder I feel about there being a cabin playhouse up here. Finally I spot the river rock chimney climbing up the side of the cabin.

Whoever is the owner of this cabin knew this land well, and picked a perfect spot. Past the cabin, a huge bluff with gently rolling forested hills goes on for a few miles. The main road from town into the badlands climbs up on this bluff and circles around its edges. Past the bluff, I know, are more badlands, with formations and wide sandstone paths that travel way away into the north to the tops of mounded hills. These giant mounds go on farther than the eye can see. I have never been back there. I want to go since it's probably where the wild Mustangs are, but that stretch of badland country is way too far, unless I am aiming to be lost for good.

Trees hide the cabin the best they can. Off a ways and down a bit of a slope, a shallow ravine carves around behind the cabin and to the right. Chief is off in the forest, sniffing, and I'm hiding behind trees to be extra careful because of what Hazel said. I stop to listen for cars and voices. If I was an Indian on this land long ago I might be noticing mountain lion tracks, but as myself in 1967 I don't see them. I sneak around the cabin in a circle, giving the outside a good check. All I find is a crumpled up beer can next to the far corner of the porch. It could be new, I suppose, but I found an old beer can the first time I came here, too. It looked just like this one, dusty and like it could've been here for months. Not that I can tell for sure. Where this one was I could've missed it before, since I usually come up the porch from the other side. We don't seem to have company, and that's all I care about at the moment. I'm thirsty, so I take a break in my investigation to get a drink.

I head down into the ravine where there's an old water pump. I pump the red handle and the water spurts and bounces off the dry ground, dotting my dusty boots. I pump until it looks fresh and take a good long drink, coming up wet faced, like I survived a drowning.

I go back up to the log cabin that wears a reddish stain. As I creep closer to the door, I'm again listening hard. Those boys could have snuck off the road and trekked here on foot. It's possible they're being quiet. I hear the sound of nothing. I coax Chief in front as I open the thick, heavy cabin door that seems to want to keep us out. "Hello—o?" I say to what better be no one!

"Chief," I pat my leg for him to come back and stand next to me. He's half of my courage.

Inside the cabin, there's no one, but there's an antique wood cook stove, a river rock fireplace, cupboards, and a small kitchen counter. The peacefulness of this abandoned place is something I can feel. After all this fear, I stand in the middle and take it in. I don't know who lived here, but I love the secret. I don't notice any changes. Maybe Hazel's older sons are wrong, maybe the boys don't come here. It wouldn't be the first thing I've overheard adults say that isn't true.

Now that I know the cabin is still ours, I do what I normally do when I'm here, acting like it's mine, poking around, opening everything. The milk-glass green and cream enameled stove was once the prize of this place, but now one of the cast iron burner plates is missing. A wooden box sits near the stove with bits of bark and slivers of kindling left over from some long-ago someone making a fire in the stove or fireplace.

I continue my normal routine, fingering the raised letters of the nice cook stove, and softly mumble what I've come to know without having to read it, "Superior. Bridge Beach & Company. St. Louis." Chief circles over to my knee, and I pat him. It's these simple things I love about him.

We go outside and sit on the porch to feel the nice summer breeze. I rest my back against the logs of the outer wall, my legs straight out in front of me and my cowboy boots flopping out to either side. Chief stretches out on his side and lets out a dog sigh. He must feel the peace, same as me. As I rub his soft belly, I notice there's a thick tuft of fur stuck under a sliver of the log I'm leaning against. I reach over and pull it out. It looks just like Chief fur, so I turn around to inspect the wall more closely. There are other bits of fur stuck along the cabin logs near the porch floor. I pull some off and compare it to his sable coat. It looks like Chief's, but all this fur would be from deliberately rubbing against the wall, and I've never seen Chief do that. Maybe there's a stray dog around, and with no hand to pet it, it rubs itself against these old logs instead. That'd be sad. I pet Chief some more, rubbing both my hands along his tummy as if to make up for the other dog's lack.

My eyes travel to the names carved into the cabin's logs, most people promising to love each other For-Ever, and I wonder how that's worked out for them. My favorite is weatherworn to a faint gray, so it must be from a very long time ago. It says simply 'MARILYN', carved in capitals like a mountain skyline.

Smells ride the breezes, honeysuckle and sweet grass baking in a warm sun. When we've had our fill, I run carefully down the small ravine and Chief gallops past me, hair swimming with the breezes, his head held high and happy. I watch him and whistle through my teeth at his beauty. We head back through the forest to make our way home.

All seems well here, and I couldn't be more relieved. After all, a girl like me needs *someplace* safe to run off to.

6
THE BOARDING HOUSE

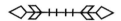

Two residents keep watch over The Boarding House, standing guard at all times: Watcher with Owl. They need each other and work in tandem, much like Gangster and The Babe. Owl sits on the right shoulder of Watcher, twisting her head as only the brilliant owl can. They never miss a thing. Watcher sits on a strong, low-hanging branch just above the revolving door. Watcher and Owl communicate telepathically with each other, and with everyone inside The Boarding House as well, alerting the proper resident to instantaneously leave through the revolving door to do their job.

Watcher is a handsome lad, dressed like a shepherd boy from biblical times, with shaggy hair and sandals on his feet. He's not visible to anyone on the outside but the residents know him and like that their guard is friendly-looking, since Owl seems menacing.

Owl is a Great Grey, barely over three pounds, so not too heavy upon the shoulder of Watcher, but she's loaded with feathers, giving her the appearance of being huge. Owl is twenty-eight inches long counting the feathers, with a large, round head so she seems to dwarf Watcher. Her intense yellow eyes are circled by ten dark rings, a ruff of facial discs she moves in order to focus in on a sound. She hears extremely well in the dark, which is when most jobs need to be done. Nobody ever gets past Watcher with Owl. Like all jobs done by The

Boarding House residents, no mistake can ever be made, therefore Watcher has Owl to see all, hear all, and be ready for all. With a bird's eye view, they never rest, since being guard is a never-ending job.

As residents go out and come back inside through the revolving door, Watcher with Owl works in tandem with the lead resident, Knower. The historian and record keeper, Knower has recorded everything that has ever happened, and is aware of what is about to happen. He knows who needs to go out the revolving door, what their job is, who the job is for, and makes sure they get back in the revolving door and back to their room in The Boarding House.

Slight, hunched, and nervous, Knower doesn't portray the leader that he is. He pushes thick black glasses up his nose too often and has a habit of clearing his throat. Normally he is seen carrying record books with him for reference, and sometimes his load is heavy. He flips through them and often drops some to the floor, but he is never ridiculed. Knower is trustworthy and loyal as he guides the residents with his tremendous memory and reliable instincts.

Knower has many jobs, but his most important lifesaving job is keeping The Boarding House a secret.

Especially from Her.

7
INDIANS

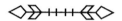

When my best friend Frankie moved away she left a barrelful of smelly feelings behind, the missing kind. I spent time outside kicking things, and inside fighting with my older brother. It helped.

But now my parents have made arrangements for me to visit Frankie. I'm not sure why, but it must be they need a break from me and all the trouble I cause.

Me on a train by myself can't be a good idea, given my record for trouble. But here I am in a seat with no one to bother me, no little brother to take to the potty again, or to chase down the j-jumpy aisle to fetch his toy under some grouchy man's seat, again. This trip is all mine, and it's heaven!

Except, it isn't. I always tug, tug, tug to get free of my family, like a kite that seems to be saying "I may look like I'm just playing, but I'm serious about getting away from you." That's me. And then once the kite is flying free, like me racing down the track away from my family, it might dive-bomb into a tangle of telephone wires and become bent and stuck. As the train chugs away from the platform holding my family, I wave like I mean it, then I do mean it, and then my insides say 'NO! Don't let me go!' at the same time saying, 'Yes! I'm gone… I'm going away from you!' I feel horrible, really.

It's a terrible mistake and a wonderful prize, all wrapped together into the few short minutes before they disappear and this metal beast speeds along the track to take me away from them.

I squish against the window to watch them for as long as I can. My cheek squeaks on the pane as the train rocks. The reflection of my eyes looks scared, but I see past them to the stain of water spots on the outside window, then farmland, and then my beloved badlands behind yelling at me—don't go!

A fog forms from my breath and I barely stop myself before kissing it, kissing the family goodbye. I hear Mom's voice, "Don't ever put your lips on public transportation, it's filthy," so I carry her with me after all, harder to leave behind than I think. This thought makes me kiss the window on purpose for even longer than I'd normally dare.

I hear trouble! It's coming from inside me—loud and wheezy. Shoot, I hadn't noticed, which is just like asthma to sneak up on me. Deep inside, my chest feels like sparks from a campfire pricking and burning. Air fights to get in, like I'm breathing through the tiny red straw that comes along with a sweet cherry in a Shirley Temple kiddie cocktail. Under my armpits and around my back it hurts like my ribs have shrunk. I plop down into the extra wide seat with the headrest hovering over me. I haven't felt this small in a long time.

There's an old Indian woman sitting across from me, but I'm too busy trying to save my life to pay her much mind. It won't do for this asthma to finally kill me when I'm on my way to see Frankie.

Stopping an asthma attack is all up to me. It's not like there's a hospital on board this train. I know the drill, so with unsteady fingers I take a soft pill from my medical bracelet and put the super sweet thing under my tongue. Big fears kick in as I wait for the effect of the medicine. My thoughts are "I'm gonna die, I'm gonna die, I can't breathe" over and over. I hate that part, it's scary and never helpful. I start to shake, but now it's from the pill, not from being scared. A few minutes later my heart races at the speed of the locomotive pounding down the track eating up farmland, while I eat up oxygen. As my breathing steadies, my body wants to get up and walk this off, but a moving train isn't good for wobbly legs and weakened lungs. I must ride this out while my body gets a hold of itself.

I feel eyes on me and look down at the feet across from me wearing soft leather moccasins with beaded designs and a long skirt of flowered cotton cloth. Brown hands with knobby knuckles sit in her tiny lap and a thin, gray braid lays down her front. I don't need to see her face to know she has dark eyes, but when I do, they remind me of the soft chocolate eyes I saw on the train so long ago. These eyes, though, are set deep into the wrinkled face of an Indian woman. As old as she seems, her eyes might have seen as far back as 1876 and Custer's Last Stand. It hurts my heart to think about that.

We watch each other, her eyes gentle but never moving, mine jumping like the wiggly kid I am. Her calm way seems to want to calm this asthma attack. It's weird, the powerful effect of her kind eyes seeming to encourage me to catch my breath and keep it. I suck in some shuddery breaths, like a baby who has cried hard and is trying to calm down. It almost feels like I'm that baby, except I end up violently gasping for breath, leaning over to grab my knees to suck in the air with all my might. When I sit back after this fight I think I feel her eyes on me again, and there she sits, watching me, only this time it seems her old eyes are beaming me some love. I smile a strained smile and she smiles back making her eyes disappear behind her cheeks. This makes me giggle for some reason and she widens her eyes in surprise and smiles big again so that her eyes disappear again. I giggle at our game, which has taken my mind off my wheezing and seems to be truly settling my asthma.

She waves a hand, curled but pointing toward the window. I stare at the hand, wondering if it works, if it can hold onto anything anymore.

She speaks her native tongue saying, "Cetan," sounding like cheh-tahn, and points toward the window, then points at me. "Cetan," she says again, flapping her hands like bird wings then pointing out the window and back to me again.

Getting up to peer out the window, nose smooshed, I spot a hawk hunting the prairie. "Cetan?" I ask, making arms into wide wings and faking a dive. "Cetan?"

She nods yes, points right at me. "Cetan." Her eyes are older than my Grandma Naomi's but they twinkle at me the same, as if she recognizes me from somewhere. She points a gnarled hand outside again, and then rubs a small circle over her heart saying, "Maka sichu," pauses, nodding, "Maka sichu." The words come from the back of her throat—mahkah seechu—as she points toward my heart.

I know these words. How could I? How could I not? Maka sichu is the Indian name for my playground, the badlands.

"Bad. Lands. Maka sichu." I say. I point to myself, rub over my heart, then point outside up to the bird long gone.

"Cetan Maka Sichu." She repeats.

I am talking to someone with another language! I never did that before. I repeat again, "Me badlands, me hawk." I try to say her words again, grabbing them from my throat, nodding yes with a close-mouthed smile. I realize I speak more like Indians do in the movies, not how she talks. Just goes to show you. She watches me closely as I practice her words.

"Yes," I say to her eyes that really see me.

I'm not alone after all. Someone else, besides Chief, sees who I am. I am a badlands hawk.

The rest of the long train ride is peaceful. We don't need to try anymore, our friendship being already solid underfoot. I like having her across from me, and hope she won't get off the train in Billings. She doesn't. She sleeps a feather sleep, so light, while I wander the train. I stand between the railcars remembering my young girl rescue, and wishing again for a sighting of my black-skinned Jesus. I could use one.

In third grade I lost Frankie to Chico Hot Springs that I overheard my folks say is a popular tourist stop with large, hot swimming pools of natural mineral water, lodging, and a restaurant with a country western bar. It's down the road from Yellowstone Park and just before Pray, Montana. Frankie's family bought Chico "to give it a go," they told my Mom.

I wonder how Frankie likes it. I'm not even there yet, but as the train winds along the Yellowstone River, I can see this part of Montana is nothing like the badlands I know so well. Closer to home, this river looked a lot like the wide muddy water of the Missouri. There the river changes into a dark-green fury, running fast off the tall mountains and the waterfalls in Yellowstone Park. Here it looks cold and angry, not at all like the river I inner tube down every summer. Across the river is a big herd of elk, some wearing racks so huge they brag of being hunter-proof, making me wonder how they ever hold their heads up. Their young bound up the steep bank at the noise of the train, and as if answering my question, the herd follows them up the bank, without a care.

Cottonwood trees line the river edge, blowing seeds like flying fairies in creamy skirts floating down to earth. I think of the tooth fairies out there hauling heavy coins to leave under my pillow, and wonder if they fly off with my teeth, just to drop them out in these woods somewhere. Mountains pop into the sky wearing pointy snow hats, even in June. I forget where I am with my nose to the window, and struggle to think. My daydreaming is often real enough to confuse me.

Out of the corner of my eye I see the peaceful old lady pull a soft-looking deerskin bag near her hip as she sits up taller. Even sitting up straight she's not much bigger than me, but she has that bit of sag in the middle that comes with age, like my Grandma Naomi. Just then the conductor comes through to announce our arrival in a singsong voice, "Livingston, Montana, Livingston, Montana." He sways past my seat and smiles down at me, touching the seat back for support. The train's loud squeal sounds like the way I feel, not as brave as I had hoped on my arrival to a new town, unsure of stopping. Out the window, the depot is the fanciest I've ever seen in Montana! Four wide sidewalks cut through bright green grass, heading to a half-circle arch of great beauty. The red and yellow brick depot wears lion head carvings. I whistle through my teeth at ornate lampposts lit with four white globes, so glamorous, and a great contrast to all the cowboy hats and boots sprinkled through the waiting crowd.

The train stops. The old Indian woman slides to the edge of the seat and slowly gets to her feet. Once standing, she gives me the smile that made me giggle and I give her a giggle again with a big smile back. I follow her down the aisle though, not minding staying close a little longer. Once on the platform, I look both ways and finally spot the big smiles of Frankie and her freckled mother with short, curly, strawberry-blonde hair and pretty white teeth. My body slumps in relief, like I'd carried the burden of waiting to be found for a lot longer than I had.

I'm wearing my usual cowgirl outfit while Frankie and her mom both wear pedal pushers, sleeveless button-up cotton shirts, and navy Keds. They look like the Bobbsey twins, except one of them has an hourglass figure you can't miss.

Just over Frankie's shoulder, I spot the old Indian woman as she disappears into the bear hugs of an Indian man and woman. This couple is my dreamy version of gorgeous, which shocks me. I had no idea I would think Indians are dreamy. She is short, but very pretty. And his thick, dark hair lying far down his back fits his extremely handsome Indian face, along with the rest of him. It makes me wonder if he is a movie star.

These thoughts are so embarrassing I am relieved to only see him now in one of my visions: wearing beaded and feathered ceremony clothing, dancing in the Sand Circle, a strong, tall man whose shadow by firelight ripples around the badlands walls, while an elder woman closes her eyes in enchantment. With my vision eyes, I look down from the back of Big Elephant to see Chief sitting up tall, wearing an open-mouthed smile, bright eyes reflecting the fire. I experience this vision so clearly that I smell the sand dust rising from the Indian's bouncing feet.

I close my eyes tight for a second to bring myself back onto the train platform. When I open them, I am back, but still staring at the Indians. The old woman catches me wonder-watching, and pokes her gnarled fist into the man's side. She points and calls to me, "Ceta—n," in her warbling voice. The man repeats this in a deep voice, "Cetan," and nods his head in greeting. I perform a deep curtsy, dropping my head in respect that I'm not faking, and I stay here longer than anyone expects. Chuckles go around, especially Frankie and her mom.

Embarrassed by my antics I stutter, "Tha-thanks for...your, your help," to She Who Rescued Me from the fear of an asthma attack.

"Cetan?" he asks, and I'm thrilled he's not done with me yet. "Is that what we call you?"

I step toward their tight group holding my suitcase in front of me, maybe for protection between them and the lie I'm about to tell, "I'm Coca Joe. Coca Joe Stratmore." A loud breath is sucked in, and my guess is that it is Frankie that did it, but it seemed to come from this group of Indians.

"Coca Joe. Coca Joe Stratmore," he repeats, widening his sparkling, brown eyes. He studies me. I gave him my secret name and he seems to be searching for the truth in my lie. I still can't move and neither do they. "Thank you for befriending, my unci, my grandmother," he says at last.

"Oon-chee," I whisper his word and smile at his grandmother. Then I stare at him—stuck. I can't help myself; his dark beauty and strength seem glazed-over with peace, both him and his language. I don't know. I take in a breath and feel my shoulders drop into a quieted me. They seem a bit stuck on me too. More likely they are not sure if I want something more. It seems I do but I don't know what, so I shrug my shoulders and give him a shy smile. He nods at me and they move away down a connecting sidewalk.

A slug to the upper arm wallops me back onto the train platform and Frankie teases, "What is...who is...what was THAT?" I stare at my feet.

I glance one last time at the group of American Indians and whisper, "Goodbye." Shifting the suitcase, I feel my neck blush and drop my face. I step toward Frankie's beautiful mother who has been standing back taking this all in.

Frankie stretches her words as far as curiosity will go. "Coca who? BRA-strap-more?" laughing so hard she holds her gut. "Geez, Jane Louisa, you're a scream!" I look back to see if offense is taken, but the Indians are talking amongst themselves. They stop to watch me for a few seconds seeming slow to go, then start walking toward the depot and it's really strange how much I want to follow them. I have no idea why, but I want more of that.

Frankie interrupts our staring at each other, the Indians and me, saying "Seriously! What's that about?"

"I'd be interested to hear, too," says her mom.

It's hard to pry loose from what just happened. I can't explain it because I have no idea, so I just shrug and smile.

8
BUFFALO

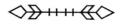

Mrs. Halstead drives their truck through steep rock walls on either side of the two-lane, like a gate, that gradually opens to a valley with huge mountains close to the road. Whoa, I say, and Mrs. Halstead says, yep, that's why it's called Paradise Valley. Pine trees drape the slopes below craggy mountaintops. Foothills climb into the trees like green cats clawing up a curtain. A river hugs the road and we bend with it, turn, turn, turn. In a corral along a straightaway, a blonde cowgirl turns her horse sharp, and it breaks away fast enough to lift her ponytail like a hooked fish.

Off the highway to the left, we take a dirt road leading across a bridge over the Yellowstone River. Frankie points out showy-snowy Emigrant Peak, saying Chico is just around this bend. Sure enough! A black horse whinnies in a corral of horses beside a gambrel barn, white with green trim. The barn's river-rock foundation is taller than the cowboy wearing chaps coming out of the huge barn doors. I stare at his shiny rodeo belt buckle until barn swallows catch my eye, flying from their mud nests on the barn.

The Chico Lodge is really neat, and I feel proud to be sitting in a pickup with its owner. It's a wide, white two-story, with several dormer windows popping out of the roof, and a covered porch going its width and around the side. Mrs. Halstead tells me that in Chico's long history it has had many famous visitors, like President Teddy Roosevelt, and western painter Charlie Russell, who'd trade his art for room and board.

We pull up at their house, a white two-story with a big front porch. The dust from the tires rolls like sausage and blows into the screened windows of the house. Frankie opens the heavy cab door and jumps out before her mom has stopped, a trick perfected over time, no doubt.

As soon as I grab my suitcase, Frankie yanks me upstairs to her room with Mrs. Halstead yelling after us to get some chow when we're hungry. Frankie's fancy lace and shiny satin linens and full canopy bed has spoiled written all over it. I am spoiled too, but only because my mom thinks it's important we have nice things to show off, and besides, I only have a half-canopy. I gape at the room that seems made for movies. She says, "Yeah, I cried pretty hard about leaving our hometown, and my best friend, er, you, so..."

"Wow, you must've cried a river," I say, and we both giggle and dive onto the prissy bed.

Next we get into swimsuits, turning our backs to each other, and Frankie gives me an over-sized T-shirt to throw over mine. She wears a crocheted white cover-up that pops her nice tan through little holes. I myself sport a bad-ass farmer tan. It's not a good look, but it's impossible to hide. I think we give it a tough name to cover our embarrassment.

Chico Hot Springs is famous for its natural warm pools so I'm excited to swim, but instead of heading to the pools, Frankie takes the wooden boardwalk to the Chico Saloon saying, "Don't tell," as she holds open the door for the cigarette smoke to waft into my face. The jukebox is playing Loretta Lynn singing "You Ain't Woman Enough (To Take My Man)."

No, I think to myself, I'm sure I'm not, but Frankie? She's acting like she thinks she is, putting one hand over her middle and holding her other hand up like it's in the hand of a dance partner. She sashays toward the bar, mimics a 'cowboy swing' tuck turn, and dances her way up onto a barstool, completely comfortable with drawing attention to herself. It takes me a minute to realize I'm still at the door, my feet planted like I'm not sure I want any part of this. I don't, especially after Frankie showing off like that, but I cover the cross-sawn log floor quickly to not make a fuss.

I climb on a tall barstool, embarrassed. Not knowing how to act, I look out the picture windows that hold Emigrant Peak in focus. Then I study the mass of names gouged every which way into the bar top.

Frankie ignores me and says like a pro, "The usual, Haskell, and rack 'em up, pretty please." I haven't a clue what she means because I'm not allowed in bars.

The bartender is a young buck. His bottom-hugging Wrangler jeans and tight cowboy shirt show off a rodeo build, small waist, and wide shoulders that make me feel shy. I look into my lap.

"The same for you, beautiful?" he asks me. What do I say to that? My eyes plead with Frankie to get me off the hot seat. I'm not ready for this kind of teasing.

"Yes, please, Haskell," she answers, then excuses me. "She's not from around here."

He gives me a smile as he lines up the funniest bit of food I've ever eaten. On bar napkins in front of each of us he makes a triangle shape of five shelled peanuts, four slices of orange, three maraschino cherries, two green olives, and one dime. "Rack 'em up!" he says and clicks two times out his mouth like he's trying to get a horse to start moving. Frankie smiles the flirtiest smile and even bats her eyes. I'm dumbstruck. My mouth hangs open.

"Don't mind her, she's practicing for when she's grown up," a woman down the bar says and winks at me. She must have seen Frankie's routine before.

I'm glad for something normal to do—eating—even if it's not normal food. Frankie eats a couple rows down on her triangle then hops off the stool with her coin and heads to the nearby pool table. She drops the dime in the slot, racks up the balls, picks two pool cues and says to me, "Winner takes all."

I hop down and go over, holding out my dime.

"No, dodo-head," she laughs, "not yet. That's for our second game!"

Where'd she get the idea there'll be a first? Geesh.

I'm not sure what's going on, but for some reason I'm nervous for Frankie. She acts like she's up to something, but I don't want to know what. I look back at Haskel to see that he isn't paying us any mind. That's a relief.

After scraping the green felt of the pool table, we finally go swimming. In the three years since Frankie and I played together, something has changed. Under her cover-up is her flirty bikini swimsuit, not teeny but still embarrassing to me, and she wears it with a wiggle out to the pools. It's not a good wiggle, too fast, and missing the fleshy parts required for a wiggle worth watching.

I'm mad because I forgot to think about Frankie being different from years before, and madder still wondering if I'm the different one, spending all my time with Chief in the badlands. I throw my towel on a lounge chair and dive in. Hearing the water's surface crack is the sound of relief getting away from her. I'm sitting on the bottom when my long braid is tugged gently and I open my eyes to her face looking warped in the pool light. We stare at each other then she giggles, and bubbles tickle our faces. We go up for air to start our friendship over again. I decide to slug Frankie's arm like we used to. She looks at me really surprised and then slugs back, harder. I slug back harder still, then she me. The whole time we are staring a challenge at each other, then pretty much at the same time, we both start to laugh, and just like in our younger swimming days, we both sink in the water to sit cross-legged on the bottom of the pool, still looking at each other. We both burst out laughing down there and rush up for air. I wish Frankie wasn't growing up faster than me, but at least she's still the same old slugger.

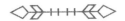

The day before I'm to take the train back home, we're in Frankie's room getting ready for an excursion with her mom. Frankie gives me the eye and says, "You've been wearing that braid since elementary school. Want me to fix up your hair?" She expects me to go along with her, so she starts taking out my braid before I answer.

She's all spiffed up and pink in the cheeks, and I suppose I'm about to be the same, even though I think it's silly to go to so much fuss for a picnic.

"We're not children anymore," Frankie says. "We're almost thirteen. Geez-a-mo, we can act like it!" She pulls the sides back into a barrette on the back of my head. "Like Peggy on *Lost In Space*," she says. I know what she means, because I have a beautiful Alexander doll named Katrina that has this hairstyle too.

Once I'm fixed up, we help Mrs. Halstead load picnic baskets in the car and we head out. We drive awhile in the direction of Wyoming, heading for a spot that's supposed to be quiet because tourists don't know about it, only the locals. We park along the side of the road and start down a narrow path towards the river. It's a bit steep but soon a path winds in and out of the Lodgepole pines along the upper bank of the river.

Mrs. Halstead whispers suddenly for us to stop. A dozen feet in front of us, right beside the path with his body partially hidden by the trees, is a buffalo. It's a giant of a beast, snorting his nostrils, and his eyes are right on us!

"Stand still," Mrs. Halstead whispers in awe. "This is the buffalo scout. He'll return to the herd and announce we're here. They aren't interested in us, the bison just like to know when people are near."

I think she is trying to reassure me, but I am already not afraid. I take a small step forward. Then another. The buffalo slowly steps out of the trees. His entire, massive body comes into view. His dark eyes watch me.

Mrs. Halstead scolds me to back away right now. She and Frankie duck behind the trees beside me.

I heard her and know I stand alone. I raise my arm, palm up, cautiously, as I would around a horse that doesn't know me. Mrs. Halstead hisses my name but I am somehow not at all afraid.

He regards me as I regard him. I keep my arm up without any idea why I reach for him. Perhaps this didn't last long, but to me it's eons of time before he backs into the forest, turns around and heads through the trees, away from us.

When my arm goes down I realize what I have done. Frankie and her mom rush out to hug me, mad and excited and then mad again. Mrs. Halstead is asking over and over why did I do that, why did I put myself in such danger? All I could say was that I saw he was a friend. Mrs. Halstead argues, and is once again angry at me for taking such a risk around an untamed animal. I tell her again that I seemed sure we recognized each other as friends.

Under her breath I hear her snip, "Now you're even talking like a crazy Indian." She starts down the trail going faster than before, still working off her steam. Frankie gives me a look, skeptical, with her mouth a bit twisted. She shakes her head and follows her mother.

I go to the place where the buffalo stood and I stand there. I bend to look for hoof prints. Seeing one, I lay a hand over it, wondering. I search the trees, in case he stopped to watch us, and I don't see him. Deeper into the forest, I see movement and spot him watching me. I stay where I am, keeping my eyes on him as he turns to go. Goodbye friend, I whisper.

Mrs. Halstead yells for me with exasperation in her voice so I yell back that I'm coming. The two of them are out of the trees and waiting.

Mrs. Halstead considers me with a serious expression. "You are a mystery. First it was the Indians at the train station, carrying on as if you knew them when I know you didn't, and now this standoff with a buffalo. Why are you doing these things?"

I shrug.

"You don't know why you are doing them?"

I shrug again. "No. I don't."

Mrs. Halstead regards me like the buffalo did but I don't stare back at her. What she said about Indians is still on my mind so I look stubbornly just past her daring her to say more. That buffalo must have given me some guts. Finally she says, "Well, okay. I'm used to antics with Frankie but yours take the cake!" She heads off again shaking her head. Frankie slugs my arm and I slug hers but neither packs a punch.

We continue on, and I'm relieved not to have to answer any more questions. I don't know why I do the things I do. Mrs. Halstead must be ready to move on too, because she goes back to teaching us again. "That buffalo scout is probably off to give his report about us being in their territory."

There is a steady, very high pitch along with a low one developing in the distance.

"Sh-h-h, listen," Mrs. Halstead says. "That's the herd."

The sounds become loud and high, sounding nothing at all like I imagine bison would sound. I feel pure wonder bursting in my heart. Meeting a buffalo, who could ever imagine? Hearing a herd of them? No way!

"If the bison have young calves," Mrs. Halstead explains quietly so we can still hear their sounds, "the adults will circle them and run off together like that, making a ring around the vulnerable. It's a beautiful sight, really shows how parents feel about protecting their children."

I smile. Being a buffalo 'young' sounds like a good gig to me.

◇⋙┼┼┼┼⋘◇

I have to go through missing Frankie again, now that the train's brought me home. I'd gotten used to her changes, I guess. But nothing beats returning to Chief. When I get home to him, the getting's good—the comfort of his head lying against my hip, the way he carefully licks something off my hand as if tasting where I've been. It's the best compliment from a dog, saying with a lick that I'm good enough to eat. When he gets to the heel of my hand, it sends a tickle up my arm, around my neck and down my back. Chief wins the prize of a giggle, looking up at me with dog-smile eyes. I'm a Chief's girl, not a daddy's girl.

I am so relieved to be back with him, that I stay with him in the backyard for a couple nights after my trip and find ways for him and me to go trekking together. His loyalty helps me find my way again. Chief is a seeker and a finder. He explores and conquers. His sure-footed race with me onto badland formations is movie-worthy. He's a natural poser, a star without trying. When he climbs to the top of almost any little knob, somehow he knows to hold his head high, spread his front feet, and puff out his chest to let the wind blow through his long, flowing hair. I can't take my eyes off him when he shines like that.

He's the light at the end of my tunnel.

9
HOBO

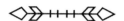

I didn't expect an adventure to happen right out of the gate when I got back from western Montana, especially since Hell Creek can be pretty dull without my imagination, but for once I didn't need it! When we came home from church we found a hobo from the rail yard asleep on our couch. This can happen I suppose, we've always had hobos around town. Why this one is here instead of at the ramshackle hotel the folks taught me to steer clear of is anybody's guess. Our not-so-good watchdog, Chief, lies along the couch looking real proud of his catch, his mouth open in a dog smile, while the hobo saws logs. Dad shoos Mom and us kids out to the front step and we hear him say, "Hey, buddy, nap's over. Clear on out of here."

Mom tries to chase us kids through the door of the mudroom since she's not keen on us being face to face with a real live hobo, but I crack the front door and keep listening. Before she catches me I hear the hobo say, "I know 'bout yer girl."

Dad sounds instantly mad. "I doubt you know a damn thing about my girl."

I only have a second to wonder whether I'm that girl before Mom drags me away from the door so the hobo can be kicked out of the house. She's scolding me, but I'm stuck in wonder about whether I might have picked up a clue to my adoption. Am I a hobo's daughter? My imagination flips cartwheels between being creeped-out and fascinated.

When Mom goes to get the scoop on the hobo from Dad I sneak off after him, dying to see where he goes, but I'm called back inside "this instant!" What was I thinking anyway? I would stick out like a sore thumb chasing a hobo while dressed in my short white gloves with pale pink beads on top and a smart-looking navy cape with matching dress and beret.

I'm detoured only as long as it takes to jump out of my Sunday best and into grubs, sneaking out to the backdoor into the yard for Chief and then down into the coulee to chase down this hobo. Will I never get enough of the trouble I cause myself? But there's no way I'm going to let this hobo go without asking him a question or two.

We take the coulee toward town . He could've gone in the opposite direction and into the badlands, I guess, but I'll bet he's headed for the railroad tracks that run right along Main Street. Up ahead, over the coulee, is an overpass for the road that leads to town. This section of the coulee hangs in shadow. As we enter, Chief barks his 'back-off bark', the one that makes the hair rise on the backs of both humans and animals. I stop. It takes a second for my eyes to adjust. Plus I'm working up some courage.

I don't see anybody at first so I keep going. When I see what Chief was barking at—the hobo we've been tracking—I'm almost within arms' reach of him. He's leaning against the concrete wall about half way in, his eyes popped wide-open looking at us.

I touch Chief's head to calm both of us down, which isn't working since I'm aware of the danger. Nobody moves, but I'm ready to turn around in my cowboy boots and run if he lunges at us. Meanwhile, I have questions knocking around in my head I'm dying to ask. The fight between having guts or fear flips my stomach. I gotta wonder if I've let my curiosity get me into trouble again. I search for something to do or say, "You lost?" is all I grab out of the blind spot in my brain.

"Don' think so," his voice is scratchy, needing oil.

Nerves clog my thoughts but I finally spit out, "You were in our house on the couch and my dog here didn't stop you." I trust Chief's instincts, but wonder if he wouldn't have been okay with a hobo coming into the house if I'd been in it. Maybe that was why he gave a warning bark when we first got to the overpass—the kind that means "My job is to protect this here girl, and I will!"—but doesn't seem too bothered by the hobo now. I'm not too sure what to make of Chief's mixed signals though, so I'm still treading carefully.

"That's a mighty fine animal ya got thar."

I nod once. "You hopping a freight?" My dumb question is a dead giveaway that I'm nerved up.

"Hopin' to." He answers without moving which is good. I haven't moved an inch and neither has Chief.

"Wanna come?" He says it, but doesn't mean it.

"I do, but I can't. I will some day, for fun." I'm surprised that I mean it.

"Ask for Ol' R & R Ernie, that's me, 'cause I know pert' near ever'thing 'n' ev'ryone."

"Pert' near ever'thing 'n' ev'ryone," I imitate under my breath, then boldly ask the question that drove me here. "Do you know me?"

He thinks for longer than most adults ever do about my questions and squints at me. "Think I might."

His answer makes me think longer than I ever do with adults. The high hope of finding my family on an ordinary sidewalk where I would be swung around in joy comes crashing down as if I am dropped hard on that sidewalk. I'm not looking for a hobo to lead me to them. How could they even know a hobo? What kind of person would that be? I don't think I want to know! But I do. What I want most of all is a happy story. I sure hope to heck I got one. But a hobo and a happy story don't seem to fit together too well. Chief lies down on his haunches, meaning he's sniffed this hobo out long enough to relax a little.

I don't think I want to know any more about this hobo and how he knows me, but I'm not sure. Just in case I do, I dig in my jeans pocket and take out my latest worry stone, a rock that fits well in my fingers with a smooth dip I rub with my thumb. "Here." I walk just far enough to stretch out long and drop it in his open hand. Chief is up and right close to my knee. We back up together.

"What's this fer?"

I shrug. "Anyone else that might know me."

Now he mumbles under his breath like I did him, "Anyone else that might know me," and out loud he says, "I know who it'll be."

I still wonder what he does know about me. I'm more curious than ever. But I can't muster the courage to ask this hobo what he knows. What good would it do me getting any hopes up with someone like this?

He seems to peel himself off the dank underbelly wall of the overpass. "Maybe catch ya on the fly," he says while digging in one of his pockets. "Don'cha ferget Ol' R & R Ernie now," and he reaches toward me without moving my way. I walk over and reach a hand out and a shiny silver dollar drops in my hand. I gasp. "I don' steal, so that's mine fer you."

"Thank you!"

"If'n ya need help with any kinda trouble, ask the hobos for Ol' R & R Ernie. Ev'ryone knows me."

He doesn't say goodbye, he just walks away, and somehow I know it'd be weird if he did. It might anchor our meeting in a way it should never be.

I pocket the coin that must be worth a lot to a hobo, because it's valuable to me. Now that he's gone, my fears and doubts aren't as strong anymore. I want to kick myself for not finding the guts to ask more questions about his knowing about me but I'm not running after him. I wish I hadn't been so afraid to find out more. I've been looking for truth so long, it never occurred to me how scary it might be to find it. But I feel comfort in this one thing: he's got something of mine and I've got something of his, and it's not just an old rock. What if he gave me this silver dollar because he thinks I'm valuable to people who might be my family? I'll never spend it until I know the truth. Maybe not even then. If I cough up the courage someday to ask him more he said he's not hard to find.

"Ol' R & R Er—nie, Ol' R & R Er—nie," I choo-choo in rhythm over and over as I walk the coulee home. Chief's tail dances like it's the engine of our train.

It's never that simple at home to pretend we are a train free to come and go. The moment I come through the mudroom door and into the kitchen I know I've caught trouble for good this time. Mom comes out of the hallway carrying a foot of rope and says, "Gothcha!" in sort of a teasing voice that doesn't match the scary look on her face. I cover my neck, I don't know why. They must've both been waiting for me, wanting to teach me a lesson for running after the hobo, because Dad comes into the kitchen from the living room, his eyes hard on me. The look on his face and the metal rod in his hand turn my blood cold. I don't know why they're carrying these things but what I think is, *Run! Hide! Get to where they can't find you!*

I bolt back out the mudroom door into the backyard and run around the back of the house. Chief lifts his head to watch me as he is sprawled out in the shade, but I hear them coming and see Chief look at them too. Dad tells Mom to go one way and he'll go the other, so I must get out the side gate and around to the front door before anyone sees me go in. Once inside I panic. It was stupid to come inside. But why am I so afraid of my parents? The basement door leads from the kitchen and I clomp down the stairs three at a time using the handrails and frantically look for someplace to hide and never be found. The storage area is packed with boxes, several of them huge yellow wardrobe boxes. I push through to the very back one and do a pull-up, kicking against another wardrobe box to dive in. It's jammed so full I have to dog paddle through clothes to hit bottom. Once I pull my feet under me, I move like an inchworm up to the opening to shut the cardboard flap.

I hear a muffled version of Mom sweet-calling, "Where did you get off to, you stinker? Mama was just kidding...you don't need to hide. I was just teasing you about your running off. You're not in trouble." I can tell by her voice she's walking around upstairs.

"She's gonna get it this time," I hear my dad say, low and dark.

"Shh! She might hear you."

I decide there is no way I'm coming out. Never, ever. I'm surprised by this, but I realize I'm scared to death of them and can never tell just what they'll do next.

After a while, I hear Mom's footsteps on the stairs and hear her yell out the front door for my brother to come look for me. It's not long before his search brings him downstairs. I hear his gallop down the steps, skipping to every third like I did, and he starts right off with threatening that Mom and Dad are really, really mad, so if I don't come out now, I'll be sorry. He's not a peacemaker. He bangs around in the dishes from the child-kitchen in the playroom, takes what sounds like some sort of mug, or knowing him, something precious of mine. He walks around, putting every cuss word he knows into it for an echo. He probably thinks this'll get me to jeer 'I'm te-lling', which sounds about right, because I tell on him as much as possible. But not this time! He gives up after giving me one heck of an earful and then in a minute I hear him trying some of the same tactics upstairs.

I stay for hours; past dinner, past them sounding frustrated and arguing with each other. Still looking for me, they're back to moving some of the boxes nearby. It's dark and stuffy, and the calling of my name sounds like my ears moved to the hollows above my collarbones. I get more and more light headed like I might be suffocating for real. This seems like a good idea. I'll go to sleep in here and die in peace.

"We aren't in here." I hear a playful, young voice say, seeming to come out of me but I didn't do any talking.

"Nobody is ho—ome," singsongs out of my mouth next, without any help from me. I'm wishing it hadn't so I hold my lips shut hoping this stops before I'm discovered.

Too late. Boxes start moving in a fury and Mom and Dad are both talking at once, flipping from anger to relief, then back again. They're getting close and I imagine the rope around my neck and something about that rod that was in Dad's hand makes me want to cover my crotch. I don't know why.

"Where are you? Cat got your tongue? Is Stormy George in there with you?" Mom forces a chuckle as if she's not fit to be tied. "Knock on the box you're in, Missy, until you feel us move it, and then yell out, okay?"

No answers come sneaking out of my mouth to help me now! I've been deserted. Now that the game is over, I'm on my own.

The box flap flips open wide and Mom yanks her face back in surprise since my nose is inches from hers in what would have been my upright coffin. Sweat is all through my hair, which is plastered to my scalp, and I am strangled by clothes with a face red from heat. Mom is scowling, but moves back so Dad can pull me out. It was stupid to hope they'd be happy to see me.

I wake the next morning, my body numb. I stroke my neck, still remembering that rope I saw when I got home, but I don't remember seeing it when I came out of the box. I don't actually remember coming out of the box. Last I remember is Dad reaching for me, then I woke up here in my bed, like usual. I must have used my pink eraser again without even knowing it and swept the shavings right out of my memory. I'm used to things like this so I don't need to think about it. Never does any good. I push the rope and rod to the back of my mind. Far, far back. It doesn't matter why they were carrying those things around. The only thing that matters right this instant is Chief and escaping with him into the badlands. Except I'm too tired to even move a muscle.

10
THE BOARDING HOUSE

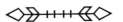

Watcher with Owl saw the revolving door swing around, bringing the two kids out to shout each of their quick sentences. Owl swooped with talons ready to grab them, but the boys knew better than to go too far and stayed in the revolving door, riding the triangle-shaped spaces back inside. They accomplished this trick in two seconds and went running back to their rooms.

As She is removed from the box and the other residents get to work doing their jobs, Watcher with Owl warns Knower, who was already aware of the boys' bad trick and is on to them. Since Katrina works with the kids she is asked to bring the culprits, Giggler and Name Schmame, to the vestibule for lessons. She knows to stand quietly in support of Knower as he works with the boys.

Giggler and Name Schmame are resident boys who do well at their jobs as deflectors and protectors. Giggler is nutty and wiggly. His job is to block tricky questions with his giggling. Name Schmame talks in riddles and repeats words, as his name implies, but he also has been known to use muscle when needed to save Her. They are both good lads, but they made a mistake, and mistakes are never allowed. Mistakes like this could make The Boarding House no longer a secret to the Outside, and more importantly, no longer a secret to Her.

Knower asks Giggler what he went out the revolving door to say.

"We aren't in here," Giggler confesses, struggling with all his might not to giggle.

"And you, Name Schmame, what did you say?" Knower asks.

"Nobody is ho—me." Name Schmame says.

"And why did you break every rule in The Boarding House to say these things?"

"To be funny," Giggler laughs but Name Schmame interrupts him.

"To give Her away! She wasn't safe in the wardrobe box full of clothes with hardly any air. I wanted to protect Her," he says.

"So you rushed the revolving door to protect Her? Boys oh boys oh boys," says Knower, pacing and wringing his hands.

Knower tries not to scold too harshly; after all they are children, overly responsible children doing jobs that save Her life. He draws a deep breath. "You confused Her. She heard you use Her voice knowing She did not say these things." Knower lets them think on this. "This is not funny, especially coming from two members of Her defense team."

The boys hang their heads, as they should.

"So let's go over a few essentials of The Boarding House." Knower goes to his desk and digs out a record book, flipping to the page explaining the inner workings. He tells the boys to take a seat on the hard floor and asks them to pay extra attention to his teachings of Articles 4 and 5:

4. Perfect timing is crucial to Her safety. As one resident goes out the revolving door She comes inside the revolving door at precisely the same time.

5. Her Safe Place, a room set up inside The Boarding House for Her alone, is a place of rest and comfort. She rests while a resident completes their job. When She is safe to resume Her life, She travels out the revolving door at exactly the same time as the resident returns inside.

Knower takes off his thick glasses and rubs his eyes with a thumb and third finger. He takes a deep breath and blows it out. "Name Schmame and Giggler, when you stormed the revolving door we didn't have time to bring Her into Her Safe Place. When She heard you use Her voice, it frightened and confused Her, because she wasn't safely inside.

"Remember boys, that above all... are you listening?... above all else, She is not to know we are here! The Boarding House will never work if our secret is out. We must always perfectly time the revolving door."

Knower is visibly upset because he cares so deeply about protecting Her, and the residents. "If this kind of mistake keeps happening, She will wonder if something is wrong. She and those on the Outside will think The Boarding House residents are here to play tricks, but we are not. We are here only to help Her survive."

Knower paces back and forth in front of the revolving door. Katrina knows not to interrupt. She is not impulsive. Knower stops in front of Name Schmame and Giggler. "Lastly, you alerted Watcher with Owl. Nothing could be more dangerous than that! Their job is to protect both Her and The Boarding House at all times and in all ways. Owl swooped to dig her talons into you, and that is what she is *meant* to do when any surprises take place." Knower's glasses have slipped to the bottom of his nose and in his frustration he roughly shoves them back onto his face. "That would have taught you both a very painful lesson, one I don't want you to have to learn that way."

Knower goes to his desk by the door and starts writing in a record book. "I am writing these events so we have a history on you two. Make sure the next thing I write about you is life-saving for Her."

Katrina knows it is time for her to intervene, so she sends the boys back to their rooms. Giggler is not giggling, at least not until he is out of sight.

11
GONE

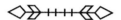

It's bath day for Chief, which means tons of brushing afterwards to keep him gorgeous. I'm tired from last night and I think Chief can tell because he's not fighting me like usual. He walks away for short spurts because brushing hurts, but circles back and lets me brush him some more, knowing he gets the treat of a knuckle bone when I'm done. After he's groomed, he prances around, jumps his front paws side to side all frisky, and takes laps around the short agility course he created in the backyard. This cheers me up some, which is why he's doing it. It's hard to believe, but this big dog can turn on a dime and shoot back fast so tight along the fence, around the crab apple tree, weaving around the posts of Dad's chin-up bars, leaping over the sandbox and across the yard at high speed. Man oh man, my chest bursts with pride over my hairy best friend.

Mom pops her head out of the house and thanks me for making him look so nice. Instead of responding to her praise I feel suspicious. Why does she care?

A couple days after the grooming, I end up throwing punches at my older brother because he globbed mud on Chief's coat and turned the hose on him. Collies hate water, so he was being cruel. My brother was getting even because I got him grounded by telling on him for sneaking out of the house in the middle of the night to see the girl all the boys like and call "fast," the one who wears black eyeliner and shimmery, silver-pink lipstick, too. The only reason I told is because someone told me and I don't think it's good for my brother or *anybody* to be seen with a girl like that. Dad elbowed him in a buddy-buddy way like he's proud of my brother, but Mom half-heartedly grounded him for a while.

After getting mud on Chief's coat, my brother is told to "go clean the dog up nice" but I yell "no way, he's not touching my dog" and the folks chime in together, "our dog."

I roll my eyes as I walk out to re-clean Chief. Right, as if he's *their* dog. My foot! My younger brother heard all the commotion and offers to hold Chief's leash while I clean him up again. At least *one* person in this family is nice. But I'm still mad so I'm not nice to him and I say su-ure.

When I come back inside I overhear Dad and Mom discussing Chief in hushed tones, and it brings on a serious case of nosiness. I can't help it. Chief is my business, my life. I am supposed to be seen and not heard in this family so when I dare interrupt Dad he says, "This is none of your cotton-pickin' business."

I probably shouldn't know this, but people with big ears do: Dad definitely didn't want us kids. And kids are something you can't erase. I think this is why sometimes trouble hangs in the air around Dad like an electric current aiming to zap me.

"Yes, sir," I say, "but what's a farmer going to do with Chief?"

The flat of Mom's hand smacks the tabletop. "Young lady, like your dad said, this is none of your business!" She chases this with her trademark I've-had-it-up-to-here sigh. I'm dead-ended. Or should be. But even though I know I'm crossing into a danger zone, I can't stop. They talked about Chief and a farmer, and shared a telling look that has me worried. I can't hardly bear to think it, but I fear they're giving my Chief to some dumb farmer. I don't care what they say, I'll run away with him before I will let them take him away!

Stupid tears shake up my voice, "Chief is my dog. He's mine!"

Dad pinches his face, squints his eyes, and says in a tone that makes me stop, "He's our dog and he's going to stay that way. Now get outside!"

I run to the backyard, not trusting my dad's words. I find Chief and let him lick my angry face. "They're gonna rip our hearts out and feed them to the wolves, Chief." Then I tackle him to the grass, only because he lets me. He can tell I'm not there to giggle. How does he know that? We wrestle until I feel better.

In bed, I fight through nightmares about Chief that wake me up, and I can't get back to sleep. The farmer thing has me worried, so I get up in the pitch black, get a flashlight from the knapsack in my closet, and comb the house in search of clues.

Papers with notes by the hall phone reveal nothing. I go back down the hallway to listen for Dad's snore, because I'm never allowed in his den without him. I go anyway. I find a paper with a rig number and directions where a broken down semi needs to be hauled out for repair, and another scrap that says 'Another dumbo in the gumbo. Need crane?' with information on where that poor sorry sucker got stuck. Dad says he capitalizes on gumbo in the summer, that it's his bread and butter. I crack gumbo like it's potato chips so it's food to me too.

After scrounging around some more, I find a note in Dad's capital-letter scribble:

JT OLSON—OLD HWY NORTHWEST FOR 12 M., 1 M.
SOUTH PAST TRIPLE T RANCH FOR JUST UNDER 4M.
AT CAR-BODY ON HUMP GO SOUTH 7 M. JUST SHORT
OF THE TRACKS. WEST 4.5 M THEN SOUTH AT 3 GRAIN
BINS FOR 1.2 M. DUE WEST 7 M, 2ND GRAVEL DRIVEWAY
ON LEFT, GAMBREL BARN, KENNELS, WHITE 2-STORY.
DON'T MISS DRIVEWAY AND ENTER REZ.

Kennels? I figure I've caught them. Barn might mean farmer. I copy it down because nothing else looks like this in all his piles of paper.

"Who's up?" Dad croaks from their bedroom.

"Just goin' to the bathroom, Dad." I lean against the bathroom door, eyes wide, hand over my heart. Lucky.

I hide these directions in my knapsack, just in case, but resolve to stay even closer to Chief than usual. I climb back in bed, but barely sleep.

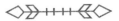

After a week of heavy downpours, the kind that changes our backyard coulee from a winding path to the badlands into a raging deathtrap of water, I wake up to a sunny Sunday and say a prayer that the sun will hot-bake the land faster than normal, then smile at the chance of maybe getting into the badlands tomorrow with Chief. I haven't heard any more about the farmer, and hope my parents changed their minds about whatever they had in mind to do with him, once they saw there'd be hell to pay if they tried to get rid of my dog.

A few hours after church, an old-timer's car pulls up. Dad calls to my mom and they go talk friendly with him by his car. He's very slight and dressed in a dark suit, so I'm thinking he must be some sort of insurance salesman. I stand by the front door, turning on my Indian eavesdropping ears while they ignore me. I only hear bits, not enough to make sense of whatever they're talking about. The farmer hands Dad some money, and my ears perk up when I hear him say Chief's name.

I start walking toward them, my heart thump-thump-thumping as I wonder if this fellow who looks like an insurance salesman is really a farmer. "Sounds good," Dad says, turning toward the back gate. "I'll go get him."

I run in front of him and cut him off, looking up at him. "Get who, Dad?"

He gives me a hard look and steps around me. "This is none of your business."

I run ahead and race to the gate. I turn and plaster myself against it. Dad hasn't slowed his stride at all. If anything, he only looks more determined. And angry. It's the kind of look that normally would send me scurrying, but my blood is pumping in fear for Chief and I can't stop. "Dad, NO!"

He stops short in front of me, exhaling sharply. Then he does something he almost never does: he explains. "Chief's just going out for breeding. He'll come back soon."

This does nothing to settle me down, partly because I think maybe my dad's just saying that to get me out of the way, but mostly because Chief is my dog and I need him more than some stupid farmer and I will not let him go.

"How soon?" I ask, testing, still blocking the gate.

Fed up, Dad grabs my upper arms and forces me away from the gate, placing me aside just as he'll place Chief aside. As he goes through the gate I lunge and wrap my arms around his waist, like I'm possessed with some child who's been raised in a completely different house. I've never been so defiant, but I'm too afraid of losing Chief to be afraid of what my dad might do. He only keeps walking, dragging me behind him as my cowboy boots rip clumps out of the grass.

Mom grabs me from behind and rips me off. Chief runs around the back corner of the house to my rescue, but I yell "No, Chief, No! Go! Run!" His tail wags, then stops, wags, then stops. "Run away, Chief! Run away! Noooo!" My yell turns into a scream as Dad gets a firm grip of his scruff. I'm still fighting against my mother, but I'm sobbing, already knowing a kid like me never wins.

Dad speaks firm and final, "Now that's enough, do you hear me? Chief will come home as soon as he's been bred."

"No, Dad! He won't."

"You are too young to understa—"

"NO, Dad!" I fall to my knees and Mom releases me at last. With hands folded in the praying position, I beg and plead with everything I've got. "Chief will think you're giving him away! He will. Please, Dad, he won't like it." Chief cocks his head at me, trying to figure out why I'm so upset. Oh what will Chief think if he's taken away from me?

"Chief will be fine," Dad says sharply, turning to lead my dog away.

"No!" I look up to Mom, hoping for an ally. "Please, Mommy, please. He won't stay. He won't! Chief will try to get back to me!"

"Get in the house now," she says, grabbing me by the arm and yanking me to my feet. "I mean it. You're confusing Chief."

She releases me, but I run after them.

"Oh, you're gonna get it, girl," I hear her mutter behind me, but I break away anyway. I catch up as they're going through the gate. I fling myself on Chief, wrapping my arms around him. Chief is whimpering now, understanding something's wrong, but I know he can't know just how bad it is.

Even though the farmer is not too far away, standing by his car with the back door open, Dad loses his cool in front of him. "Get in the goddamn house NOW!"

Mom pulls me off Chief again, even yanking my long braid to help move me. Dad hauls away Chief, who's starting to struggle too.

"No Dad! Noooooooooo!" I can't stop myself from screaming.

They lift him into the back seat but Chief tries to push past Dad to get out of the car as Dad tries to shut the door. They finally get the car door shut and Mom gives my arm a hard squeeze of warning. I'm helpless as I watch the car drive off with Chief's beautiful head looking out the back window, already too far away for me to chase.

Then he starts barking. If I could I would chase after the car until there's nothing left of me. I'd run until I died of asthma. Except Dad would catch me first. I fall to my knees again and cry hysterically.

I lost. I know deep down that I just lost the one thing I love the most in all the world.

Maybe that's why Dad doesn't come to teach me a lesson, but just gives me a disgusted look and goes into the house. Mom leaves me be too, only parting with irritated words, "Your dog will be back. So calm down and don't you dare take it out on the family."

She walks off in a huff, disappearing into the house too.

I stay where I am, paralyzed.

Come back, Chief! Come back!

That's it. I've had it with these people pretending to be a mom and dad. They don't care about me! I know I need help, but from who? Who would be on my side to help me get my dog back? Grandma Naomi, but what can she do from Minneapolis? Nothin'. The hobo? Yah, right. Frankie's Mom? Nope. She has no clout with Mom. Who? There isn't anyone at all that can help me? Nobody? I'm all alone.

I throw myself on the bed and clasp my hands together to pray with every single ounce of begging for God's help. I'm bold, telling God that if he cares at all, NOW is the time to show it. Chief being gone makes me so nervous I have to run down to the coulee to throw rocks—hard! They said Chief will be back, but adults lie too much for me to trust these words. Did the farmer buy my Chief for good, with no intention of returning him? Would my folks do this to me? Oh God, yes. Help me.

They have to call me three times before I come in from outside for dinner. That's daring on my part. I move the food around my plate and keep my eyes down. I'm not daring enough to let my eyes show my hate for them.

When the phone rings I know it's late for a call, so it's probably for Dad's business. Maybe it's a horrible disaster and people were killed. I don't care either way. Just goes to show how miserable I feel with Chief missing from my life.

"What'd you say there? Speak up, we've got a bad connection," Dad sounds gruff then listens.

"You opened the door and he just bolted?"

I stay around the corner but come closer to eavesdrop. This is my dog he is talking about!

"Dammit! You GOT to be kidding me!" Dad paces the distance of our extra-long phone cord. He's pushing his free hand through his tight buzz cut, sharing the hair grease. I step in front of him and he mows me over, cups his hand over the phone and growls down at me, "Get your butt to bed this minute." I see the glint in his eye that tells me he means business. I run to my bedroom, but keep an ear out in the hallway.

"I know you feel terrible, JT, I know. I appreciate you looking, of course."

I hear the name and remember that JT Olson is the name I copied from Dad's note.

"Do we have any direction to go on? Did you catch any sight of him?... None at all? Hey, who's rubbering in?"

Somebody must be joining in on the telephone party line. "Well, whoever's listening in, did you happen to see a large, sable and white collie running through the fields?"

I listen, getting my hopes up.

"Of course he's looked! He's been looking all afternoon until dark. Can you keep an eye out and let JT know?"

My heart sinks again. The farmer's been looking all afternoon? Chief isn't just wandering around. He's trying to head home for me, I just know it. Dad is quiet for a moment.

"I agree, JT. There's no point looking until sunup. Listen. I'll get a notice put on the radio for folks to keep an eye out for Chief, and then I'll head out your way in the morning. I just hope he doesn't try to cross... " Dad curses. "Yep, I know, I know... water is still awful high from the rains and spring runoff." My heart clenches. Is the farm on the other side of the Missouri? If it is, there's no way Chief could cross it, and no matter how much he wants to get back to me, there's no way he could. "I'll track the roads from town to your place in the morning."

He hangs up and I scream at the top of my lungs from the safety of my room, "I told you! I told you he'd run back for me!" slamming the door for a big finish.

There's a knock on my door. I'm surprised whoever it is doesn't just barge in, with all the trouble I'm causing them. "We'll find him," Mom says. "He can't just up and disappear."

"Leave me alone!" I'm mad and sobbing. They've done Chief wrong when Chief has done nothin' but right by us! I go to my knapsack and pull out the directions to the farm, to see if I can get a better idea about where Chief is. How far away is it? If Chief is coming back to me, how long would it take for him to get here? And is the Missouri really between here and there? I read through my notes but it doesn't help. I need the map in Dad's study, but I'm not leaving my room. I don't want them to know I know where they took Chief.

I wring my hands and throw myself on the bed only to pop right off to start fretting again. I can't survive here without Chief. I *can't*. I need him. And he needs me too. I hate to think of him wandering alone out there in the dark. Oh my poor Chief, what must he be thinking now?

After everyone's asleep, I take the note and go into Dad's study to see if I can figure things out on the map. I can place the first directions on the map well enough, since the note talks about the highway at first, going west. The rest gets a little tricky, taking farm roads that jigjag back and forth, but after looking at things for a while, I think I have the general idea. The farm is southwest of us, nearly in a diagonal line from my house. It's not far from where Big Sandy Creek marks the western border of the rez. Things get a little crazy over there, with the way that border runs. As the creek flows from Canada southward to where it dumps into the Missouri, it winds back and forth like a snake across the land. This meandering makes the rez bump up against and stretch into white territory like the two worlds are interlaced fingers, one hand white and the other hand red-brown. Or are we the ones stretching into their territory?

If this creek is the water Dad and JT were talking about instead of the Missouri River, like I'd assumed, that's even worse. Chief would never try to cross the Missouri, but Big Sandy Creek is something else. He could maybe get across that one and so might try it, but if the water's high, that could be dangerous.

That's not the only thing worrying me. Between town and the farm is a stretch of badlands I'm not familiar with, and Chief wouldn't be either. If he tried to get home that way, he could be facing gumbo mud and snakes and all kinds of danger without me there to keep him safe, or help him if he gets hurt.

My only comfort is this. Looking at the map, the best way to get from the farm to here on foot is by following the tracks that run next to the river to the south end of town, not far from my dad's shop. It's almost as direct a route as trying to cross the badlands, and a whole lot safer, but depending on where Chief took off from, it's hard to say for sure which way he'd go. I think if Chief follows his sense of direction, he'd know he could follow the river.

Wouldn't he?

I'm not so sure. It's easy for me to know which way to go, looking at this map, but what about Chief? He's got the Missouri and the railroad tracks along one side of the farm, and the Big Sandy Creek on the other. If he darted off to the west as he escaped, he'd hit the creek right away. If he made it clean across, he'd be on the rez for a while before crossing the creek again and finding himself in those foreign badlands.

Then there's this. Even if he made it through the creek a couple of times and through the badlands, once he hit the south end of town, he'd have to go north to our house. He'd have to cross the highway and most of Hell Creek to do it.

I get a mental image of Chief's body lying on the highway, hit by a car or a big ol' semi, but I push it aside.

No. Not my Chief.

My eyes scan the map again, looking at the routes Chief could take. He's a smart dog and I think he'd have a good general sense of direction to find his way home, but he doesn't have a map in front of him like I do. Which way would he go? Through the unfamiliar badlands, or along the tracks and the river?

I try to estimate how many miles it is between the farm and home. I can't tell for sure. The little finger of land I think the farm is on stretches on a ways, like a white finger poking deep into Indian territory. I can't tell from the directions exactly where the farm would be on that finger of land. But if I go by way of the river, it has to be somewhere between twenty-five and twenty-seven miles from home. I do some calculating. Yep.

Whew-ee. That's a mighty long stretch for my Chief to be going alone. I wonder how much of it he's crossed since this afternoon. If he didn't get into trouble somewhere.

And there's that panic I've been feeling without my Chief again.

In the time it takes me to walk from Dad's study to my room, it all comes to me as clear as a bell. To tell you the truth, it's as if God is answering my prayers and is whispering in my ear. And anyone who's heard God whisper in their ear knows what a big and powerful thing that is.

I know what to do now, and how I'm going to do it.

When the morning comes I know Dad will be shocked to find me gone. I figure they'll probably check on me sometime during the night, so I go to work on the first part of my plan, already feeling better in the doing of it. 'I'm coming, Chief, I'm coming.'

The scissors I'm allowed to keep in my room are junk, for babies, but they do the job. It isn't easy though, chomping through my braid. I clip along the nape of my neck. At that first snip of the scissors, though, I yelp just like Chief would. But I pay that no mind. I think only one thing: 'I'm coming, Chief, I'm coming.'

The brittle sound of the breaking hair and the feel of it slipping off my body tell how I feel with Chief gone—the braid slumps to the floor like a dead body. I stare at it. Then, as if the job isn't yet done, I grab chunks of hair still stuck to my scalp and hack away at them. It feels right, painful, to destroy something so beautiful and admired by my folks. I hope it hurts them.

I lump spare blankets under my covers, pushing them into a bended knee me-shape, then snake the long braid out from under my pillow and along the purple quilt, dropping the tail of it down the bedside. Sometimes when I sleep, this heavy hunk of hair seems to take on a life of its own and will tug to reach the floor at night, waking me to gather it and tell it to go to sleep. Seeing it now, lying there dead on the bed, I ache for Chief. Then I kiss the braid for luck and let a tear drop into its folds, regretting the loss before I've even left it. With this pain of a lost Chief, I've hurt myself more and more.

The knapsack is checked one more time as I look over what I'll need. I've packed it many times before, only this time I add what's in my piggy bank and extra food from the pantry. The note of directions to the farmer's place—along with my own notes added after looking at Dad's map—crinkles as I pat my jeans pocket, double-checking. I'm ready. Sneaking out the mudroom door is easier than I thought. Glad I didn't climb out my high bedroom window to drop onto the pokey evergreen bushes below.

Soon I'm running down our silent street. I pass our church and the stained glass window of Jesus sitting by the brook with his lambs nearby. "Help me," I plead.

I turn the corner and run over the bridge of the coulee, Chief's coulee, ours, ours, ours. I run past the snack hut at the little league field where the scent of sugar usually seeps through the cracks of the shoddy building. Nothing sweet hangs in the air tonight.

I run up the short hill into the neighborhood of small old houses, the sound of my panic echoing under the canopy of trees in a whimper-cry, "Chief, Chief." I've only gone a mile or so when the grip of locking lungs stops me in the middle of a four-way stop. I'm hunched over with hands on my knees, wheezing, gasping, and this attack by asthma wants to win the battle. There's not many cars out, but I hear one approach the stop. The driver honks friendly, prodding me to move out of the way. I'm busy trying to breathe and I can't move and I can't think of anything but Chief, my Chief. Out of the corner of my eye, I see the small grocery store that serves our neighborhood. I watch the feet of someone come out its door, heading my way, and a lady says, "Hey, sweetie, d'ya need some help here? Let's move you on out of the way, okee dokee?" People this friendly and helpful are always a marvel to me. With my hands still on my knees, she awkwardly pulls me out of the intersection. I've sucked in enough air to recover some, and her kindness raises my hope of finding Chief. I lurch away down the road, still wheezing, and crying. I'm heading for Main Street, but can't run. I realize no matter how badly I want to get to Chief NOW, my lungs will make me walk. I probably should stop and catch my breath, but I can't. I have to keep going. He's running towards me. I feel it.

I've heard songs of heartbreak, and read poems about heartbreak in school, but I didn't know the heart can actually break right down the middle and that I would feel it.

I push myself another three-quarters of a mile to the highway that runs through town. Even though I know he probably wouldn't have come this far yet, I've been keeping an eye out for Chief the whole time. Here at the highway I look extra hard, fearing I may see a lump of a furry body along the side of the road. My asthma's been dogging me the whole way, but I've been trying to ignore it. Just as I find a break in traffic and start to cross the highway, it gets back at me. My lungs seize up and I can't help but hunch way over, right there in the middle of the road, wheezing and gasping for air. This asthma's been trying to kill me for years and now it's finally going to do it. A semi-truck is charging toward me, but I can't move. I can't breathe.

My legs give out and I collapse. Gears grind and there's a screech that only scared tires can make. I squeeze my eyes shut tight knowing this is death and that death smells like my favorite cookie, a fresh-baked chocolate chip. It is comforting and I'm not afraid.

Then I smell a stinky rubber tire as it sinks slightly into my chest, rolling me onto my back.

I don't seem dead.

For a minute I'm lost, thinking I'm under a semi-truck jacked up in Dad's shop for repair—dark, oily, dirty.

Miraculously, the wind comes back into my lungs.

The hot truck bottom is close overhead, but when I realize I'm not stuck under here and can finally breathe, I make a frenzied scramble out from beneath it.

I stand in front of the semi, wobbling, looking all around.

The cab door slams, other tires squeal around us and people start yelling as I hobble up the weedy slope on the other side of the highway.

"Stupid, stupid goddamn kid!" the driver is yelling, and marching after me.

I want out of there fast, but feel like I'm moving without my body coming with me. I slowly make my way up the slope, and when I get to the top I turn to look back. I watch another great big fellow grab the trucker's sleeve, pulling his shoulder around saying, "Leave her be, mister. Just let her go. She ain't hurt and that's a good thing."

The trucker doesn't budge. "She could'a killed me right along with her! And you all too," sweeping a bulging arm over the small crowd.

"Come on, buddy," the big guy says in a chummy way, "let's get this road moving before another accident happens, ya know?"

The driver that almost killed me finally stomps back and jumps in his cab.

I disappear down the other side of the slope and start to shake all over, teeth chattering, working themselves into huge, uncontrollable chomps. Slumping to the ground, I feel like I'm revving like a hot rod. I have my wits about me more this time, so I do what I should've done all along but didn't, because I all could think about was getting to Chief. I take a pill from my medical bracelet and put it under my tongue to help settle down the asthma. My head's pounding. I might puke.

As I hunch over, my side where the truck tire had been is tender and makes me wince. I didn't realize how hard it had pinched me against the road. I can't help wishing that some nice lady from down at the accident would trudge up the hill to care for me. That won't happen, so I better care for myself. I get the canteen from my knapsack and take a long drink.

I squeeze my eyes shut so tight, patterns burst from behind my eyelids in colorful comets—dancing, wriggling, and being themselves—unguarded. I can't just stay hunched up here. I have to keep going. I'll have to be more careful though. If Chief is in trouble somewhere, I can't exactly help him if I get into trouble myself. I hope he's being careful too, so we can find each other somewhere in the middle, safe and happy.

My heart lifts at the thought of being with Chief again.

It gives me courage and strength. As my asthma settles down, I focus more on my plan. I'll head to the tracks that will take me south to the edge of town. I know the way because Dad's shop is nearby. From there I'll follow the tracks southwest along the river as far as I need to before I come across Chief.

I have to believe he's out there. I have to believe I'll find him, or that he'll find me. I just know he's looking for me as hard as I'm looking for him.

I'm not going back home. I'm going to Chief. 'I'm comin' Chief, I'm coming.'

12
THE BOARDING HOUSE

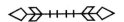

Watcher with Owl and Knower are on guard, watching everything as She drives Herself deeper into danger over Her love of The Dog. Knower never closes his eyes or ears to Her turmoil, always assessing whether a resident of The Boarding House should come to Her rescue.

It's a very fine line. She is supposed to live Her life. Knower is usually confident that he understands where the line is, though right now he is not so sure. This is a different kind of danger than the kind she usually faces.

Owl shrieks a frantic alarm for help as the truck comes straight at Her. Name Schmame starts pushing the brass bar of the revolving door ready to spin out. Knower says, "Stop!" just in time. Name Schmame lingers inside the revolving door and the residents watch as Archangel Michael arrives. Powerful wings blur in divine intervention as he covers Her, saving Her from near death. Knower says, "That was close." Owl hoots in agreement. The tension of the Truck Incident is felt among many of the residents.

As he has done before, Archangel Michael visits The Boarding House now that She is safe. Each resident smells their own favorite cookie, because the smell of Archangel Michael is fresh-baked cookies.

Watcher smells cinnamon snickerdoodles, and Knower smells gingersnaps. For Katrina it is sugar cookies, and for Name Schmame, the inviting smell of oatmeal raisin. Being around Archangel Michael is comforting, and The Boarding House residents unwind.

Katrina asks Archangel Michael to walk the halls of The Boarding House with her to comfort the children who are upset about The Dog being lost. Some of the children seem to love The Dog as much as She does, often wanting to watch out the windows when she is with The Dog. As the Angel passes the door of a child's room he hears giggling, then, "Hi Archangel Michael!" then more giggling. He is a very effective angel. Children smell the happy smell of cookies and know it's him.

On his return to the vestibule of The Boarding House, Archangel Michael commends the residents for their deep love of Her and their dedicated, consistent care. As he leaves, the residents know he will not go far. It is one of the many miracles of Archangel Michael, his nearness.

After Archangel Michael is gone, some of the residents discuss the angel's physical appearance. It seems that however a resident believes an angel of his great stature should look, that is what they see. As usual, Watcher with Owl communicates telepathically from his outside post saying the Archangel's wings are massive and owl-like. Knower says he looks like a brother of Jesus; only he has large wings on his back. To Name Schmame the Archangel is a muscular man with wings twice the size of his body. Katrina giggles behind her hand, reluctant to say that Archangel Michael has glorious purple wings with golden tips on his feathers, and that his body is a blurry, see-thru form. They go on to discuss what each of them smells when Archangel Michael is near, and this brings comfort.

Smell creates powerful memories and Archangel Michael knows it.

13
CAMPFIRES

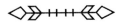

The railroad ties call me onto them with a calming rhythm as I reach out one foot after another, on... and-on... and-on... and-on, like rocking in a cradle, or the sweet repetition of a lullaby. I keep my eyes on the ties for comfort, and stumble in surprise when the track weaves into three under my feet. I keep myself from falling. I try walking the top of the winding licorice rail, but slip off it again and again. Seems my balance is stuck to the bottom of that truck tire.

Sometimes the tracks get close to a road, or cross over one, and sometimes I'm more on my own, with only the moonlight for company. It's getting ever later, so even when I come to a road, I usually don't see anyone about. If I do see a lone car pass, I drop onto rocks or pokey weeds. Lassie and Timmy taught me this, escaping some bad guy. Thinking of Lassie always leads to thoughts of Chief, and my solid belief that he's running towards me right now, same as I'm running toward him! I don't dare call out Chief's name here in town, I don't want to draw attention to myself, the bad kind, but I keep an eye for him everywhere I go, even though I still think he probably hasn't made it this far yet.

I've been walking a few hours and my body is threatening to delay my progress as much as my asthma was: I'm exhausted!

As I walk next to the dirt road that's running along this part of the tracks, I smell a fire. Not a chimney or a brush fire, but a campfire.

Smoke explains itself. I'm getting closer to Dad's shop and knowing this helps me not be afraid. I've been here many times before.

Oops, a passing truck! Get down and pay attention, I scold myself.

I continue on, and soon see the light pole in front of Dad's business, more yellowed at night than I knew. I've never cared much about his shop, or what's out here seven miles from my home. The yellow light helps me make out the bulk of the empty railcar that's on the side of the shop property. Dad has made it crystal clear to us kids to never to go near it. Never! But I never wanted to, so there.

Now I can smell food on that campfire, so maybe someone's camping down by the Missouri River. It's not far now. It smells like someone is catching fish in the river and frying them up. As I get closer, I get hungrier. It lures me in, and I have an idea something like this could lure in Chief as well, if he's made it this far. There's plenty of brush and tall trees to hide behind, so I sneak up to take a peek. It's my dad's property anyway, so it's not like I'm trespassing. Maybe this shouldn't make me so brave, but it does.

My first obstacle is a barbwire fence, but being a cowgirl I have lots of experience. This is the usual four-strand, so I go to the middle between two posts where it's the slackest, stick a leg over two strands, push down hard on them and bring my butt just above them, careful not to catch a barb in the rear. Next, I lean all the way over at the waist to slide under the upper barbed wire, but a barb catches on my knapsack so I have to start over, taking the sack off and throwing it over like I should've done in the first place. The knapsack lands kind of noisy, so I drop to the ground to hide in the high grasses for a listening minute. Nothing. Careful, nitwit!

It's awhile before I see the campfire, but before that, I hear voices. I'm not prepared for more than a couple campers, so I have to decide how stupid this'd be to show myself. Then I hear the whining cry of a child, a very young child, and a distinct bark of a dog. Chief! is my first thought, but it isn't his bark at all. This is some sort of hound.

The campfire is close to a railcar that's not on any tracks, which I don't understand. How'd that car get there? A woman with a toddler 'round her skirts lifts the logs bringing the flames up high. It seems late for a wee one to be awake, but maybe it's because she's coughing deep and sickly. Their scraggly long hair tells me this might be their home. The dog is chained on the far side of the fire, thank goodness; otherwise a good hound would have caught my scent. A moan and nonsense words draw my eyes to a ragged man hunched against a log with a dirty, long beard and filthy hand around the neck of a bottle. I don't see Chief, so I should move on. But what if they've seen him around? I'm tempted to ask. With a mom and a baby in the group, maybe it would be safe enough for me to approach them. But who can tell?

If only the hobo Ol' R & R Ernie would be looking out past the fire waiting for me. I'd feel safe going up to the fire then. He did give me a silver dollar and told me to ask for him. Since he said he knows "pert' near ever'thing 'n' ev'ryone" around the rail yard and the hobos, even if he hadn't seen Chief, he could maybe ask around.

Ol' R & R isn't here but I am, trying to make up my mind already. I'm crouching, and need to adjust so my legs don't fall asleep. Heck, I'm even trying not to fall asleep myself! It's been a long night, and I'm worn out. I wonder if Chief is sleeping somewhere, waiting for sunup like maybe I might have to do. The bush behind me rustles against my knapsack from losing my balance and almost falling down.

"Did ya hear that?" says a man's voice. I hadn't spotted him.

"Ya," says the lady with the child.

The man comes into view now, looking in my direction but not seeing me, that I can tell. He wears a tight, white T-shirt with a pack of smokes rolled in the short sleeve. "Prowler or a big animal... something sneaking up. GIT! GIT!" he yells, charging the foliage.

A small yelp escapes my mouth.

"What the hell? Who's out there? Come out and fight like a man!" he challenges, boxing fists up. Two other guys jump down now from the railcar. Uh-oh.

"He-l-lo?" My voice shakes. He straightens in surprise and drops his fists slightly as I walk out and into the firelight. Everybody freezes at the sight of me. I try to smile but it comes off lopsided and probably crazy-looking with my eyes popping out of my head and my hair to match. I clear my throat a couple times, but still croak as I ask, "I'm looking for Ol' R & R Ernie?" I'd rather ask about my dog, but figure I better make friends with them first. Ol' R & R is my ticket, so long as he does know everyone, like he says.

The woman picks up her clingy toddler and walks my way, her thin hair tucked behind large, sticking-out ears. She seems not much older than a teenager. "You lost?" she asks, softer than I'd expected.

"Um, no. No. I know where I am, I know exactly where I am." The guys shuffle around, coming a bit closer and I get scared. "But I've never been right here before, er, I mean... to this campfire... um, before."

With doubt in her voice she asks, "And you know Ol' R & R Ernie?"

"I do! He told me to ask for him. He said he knew 'pert near ev'ryone,'" I imitate him the best I can.

They seem to relax a bit.

"He ain't here, kid," the first guy says.

Apparently, they think our business here is done, because they go back to the fire. Finding my courage, I trail after them.

"How about my dog, Chief? I'm looking for him too." As I talk, the woman sets down her child and the man with the cigarette pack in his shirt looks back at me. "A large collie about this big," I say, showing with my hand.

"Eh," he says, taking a seat. "Ain't seen yer dog neither."

Right.

The weight of everything I've been through in this one, long night hits me hard. It's more than my worn-out body can take. I plunk down by the fire.

The man and woman look at one another, apparently not sure what to think about their uninvited guest. I should get up and move on, but I'm growing more tired by the second.

The toddler yanks my sleeve saying, "Ni-nigh, ni-nigh," over and over. The gal offers me a metal camp cup of water tasting tinny. My eyelids are heavy.

"Listen, li'l girl, you mean trouble fer us," she starts up.

"No," I say limply.

"You're a townie, prob'ly even went ta church t'day. Ya jus' can't be here."

"No, no. I have to..."

"I see ya had an accident, an' I'm sorry fer that. But ya had a bath too 'n that smells of home, which, fer us, smells like trouble."

"But... Ol' R &..."

"We'll be dead if townies find ya here. Dead. Ya hear me?"

I try to get up and she helps me. "Okay. Okay," I say, but I'm unsteady on my feet. "I'll head off."

The woman sighs. "Listen girl, is there any chance someone could track ya to here t'night?"

"No. Everyone who knows me knows me to be in my bed."

"You're sure no one is tracking?"

"Yes miss. Sure."

"Ah, such manners," says one of the guys.

A guy sitting on the ground off away from the fire slumps over and the movement makes me jump because I forgot about him. He could be sleeping, I suppose, but with that bottle still in his hand, I'm guessing he's passed out. "Don't mind him," the gal says. Then giving me a pitying look, she points to the other side of the fire. "You can go get yer stuff over to mine and get to sleepin', but you'll have to be off first thing in the mornin'."

I sleep so hard that I only wake up when the woman gives my shoulder a gentle shake. The sun's just barely broken over the horizon.

"Time to get up," she says gently. "Don' want no one seein' ya' now."

I nod and stretch the aches out of my body. Now that I'm awake, I'm eager to get going myself. I gotta find Chief.

Everyone else is still asleep, but she's got a fire going and something cooking on it. Whatever it is gets my stomach to growling. As I pack up my sleeping bag, she brings over a plate.

"Have somethin' to eat first," the young woman smiles nice, with only one missing tooth around the side.

"Thank you, ma'am." I take the plate with a fried fish on it, eyeballs, tail, bones. This isn't how it's served at home, so I give myself a talking to so I don't act spoiled. Besides, I have food but fresh fish is hard to beat. I take one of the thin leather gloves out of my knapsack to hold the tin plate since the bottom is hot under the fish. Then I take to picking out bones and rubbing them off my fingers into a pile. As I pull fish off the skin and into my mouth, it reminds me of my family.

Everybody has a first memory, and this one is mine. I've tried hard to remember something before this, but I don't. I'm not sure why. In this memory I'm 'no bigger than a minute,' Mom liked to say. I see myself sitting on a dock kicking my feet in the lake, toes barely reaching the freezing, blackish-green water and making the water drops fly up to sparkle in the sunshine. I'm wearing a crisscross bathing suit with a bloomer bottom, and am as happy as the sunny print on my suit: tiny bunches of orange, yellow and red flowers. It's just me and water and playing in the warm summer sun.

Dad runs down the hill from the log cabin in his bathing suit, hands holding a towel hanging around his neck and yells, "Get your toes out of the water or the fish will bite 'em off."

I screech and run, squealing up the high hill, far for my little legs, and into the cabin to the waiting leg of my mommy. She looks down at me, knife in hand, and continues making our picnic lunch with me holding tight to her leg, not letting go. There's no safe leg to hold onto now. Not even Chief's.

This memory makes part of me want to run on home. I'm like that kite again, pulling to be free and then changing my mind.

Only this time, I'm not changing my mind and I'm not going back, not without Chief. I can't survive there without him.

"So what were you wanting with Ol' R & R Ernie?" the woman asks.

"I'm not looking for trouble, Miss, just hoping Ol' R & R Ernie has either seen my dog or heard of someone who has."

She studies my eyes, looking back and forth between them. "Well, he camps upriver 'bout a mile or two if ya wanna trek there."

When I say thank you and goodbye and start walking toward the river, the gal calls after me, "Sometimes an Indian camps out with Ernie." I stop. "But he's all right," she says.

An Indian. But he's all right. I start off again.

She said the path is pretty clear to Ernie's camp. I skirt wide around the yard of Dad's company, far from the chain link fence. I don't need to be spotted before I find Chief. The engine of Dad's longest tow truck is running in the yard and another is pulling out onto the highway.

I take my mind off all of this bother and get it onto what I'm doing to find Chief. If I am right and he chooses to follow the river from the farm, we could find each other. He's been running longer than I have. If he bedded down for the night, he's half a day or more ahead of me. I've studied the map and know how far I've gone. I figure the farm is over twenty-five miles or so from where I am. Chief could have covered a lot of that land by now, hard to say.

Since I understood Dad to say the farmer searched all around until dark last night and didn't catch sight of him, it makes me wonder again if Chief got into trouble somewhere. What if he tried crossing that creek that winds so much it practically turns back on itself, or what if he got bit by a rattler? They're poisonous enough to kill a human, let alone a dog. If he tried to go home through the badlands instead of along the river, there's been so much rain, that gumbo is a real danger. Not to mention the gully washers. Animals have gotten stuck in those before. Then there's that mountain lion we saw in the badlands.

As my mind starts turning over the dangers Chief could have come across, I start to feel afraid something awful has happened. My armpits are wet from nerves. Is this helping? I make myself stop dwelling on it.

I'll find him! I know I will!

I just have to have faith like a mustard seed. That's all there is to it.

I must believe with all my heart that Chief is finding me as I am finding him. It is possible with as much as I love him and he loves me. I pray strong silent prayers to Jesus and then say over and over to comfort myself, 'I'm comin' Chief. I'm comin'.'

As I travel upriver, I keep a sharp eye out. Once I'm far enough from town, I start calling Chief's name and it feels real good. It seems farther than two miles upriver to Ol' R & R Ernie's to see if Chief has shown up around there. It's tough picking my way through the brush without splitting off on the many deer trails. It's beautiful though, wild asparagus starting to sprout and small ponds of tadpoles. Chief and I will check this out when we team up again. We've been looking for a new place to play. These thoughts feel good, like clover honey on the tongue, like hope wiggling in my belly. Last night's accident is walled off, gone, of no help to me today. 'I'm coming, Chief! I'm coming!' kicks into rhythm with my breathing.

The Missouri River roars before the path skirts nearby, massive tons of rolling water sounding a warning for me to turn away from its dangers.

Up ahead, bushes move and snap. I freeze, waiting. Is it an animal? I'm the stranger here, the hunted. I gather myself to not be afraid then keep walking.

"Ceta—n!" I hear a male voice call.

I know this word from the old Indian lady I met on the train. It means hawk. Up ahead of me, the caller rises from a crouch into a stand. The light on the river dances around a tall silhouette of a man standing on the riverbank with long, dark hair seeming to float downstream as it lifts in the wind.

I fall to my knees to grab the earth with my hands. Round river rocks scrape against each other, an ugly sound that grabs hold of me, keeping me grounded. I've seen many Indian visions while hiking the badlands, but they don't call out Indian words that I know and they don't look this real.

"Coca Joe Stratmore?" I'm stunned as he approaches and bends down to me, calling me by the name I gave him. As I look up at him, he gently pries open my fists and takes the rocks from my hands, brushing off the sharp pebbles imbedded in my palms. I'm dwarfed by the river and by seeing this Indian man again. This is the grandson of the old lady he called Unci. It is weirder than weird that he is here right now, but I won't be deterred from my plan.

"I'm in a hurry to find Ol' R & R Ernie to see if he's found a lost collie, my dog Chief. Have you seen him?"

"I have not seen your dog Chief, but maybe Ernie has." He turns and gestures me to follow. "This way."

I follow the Indian like he's a buffalo scout sent out to meet me, like the one I saw in western Montana with Frankie and her mom. I met this Indian on that same trip, not that long ago. Somehow the buffalo and this Indian seem like the same mystery.

I smell a smoky fire of drying fish and walk through smoke hanging low around the path. When I emerge on the other side, sure enough, I see a camp and Ol' R & R Ernie next to the fire. A quick glance is all it takes for me to see there's no Chief.

The men say a happy "Hau!" to one another and I smile, thinking that was only in the movies. Ol' R & R Ernie sees who's behind his Indian friend and can't believe his eyes. He hunches down to get a closer look and shakes his head, squeezing his eyes shut tight, and opening them wide to look at me again. I stand there smiling at his antics.

"Do ya see what I see?" he asks his friend.

The Indian says, "Coca Joe Stratmore, meet Ol' R & R Ernie. Ernie, meet Coca Joe Stratmore."

"Shee—ee—it!" says Ol' R & R, rubbing his eyes, "I already knows this girl!"

"What's your name?" I ask the Indian.

"Talks With Knees Quaking, but call me Hatch."

"Hatch? A bird egg or like Hatch-et?" The two of them laugh at me and I never get an answer.

"Coca Joe Stratmore," says Ol' R & R Ernie shaking his head. "I'm callin' you Ragamuffin from here on out! What 'n the heck happened to yer long hair?"

"I could tell you, but the only thing that matters is finding my dog named Chief. He's a big male collie," I say to Hatch, because Ernie's already seen him. "Sable colored, blonde and white and a few dark markings." I swing my eyes back to Ol' R & R. "Have you seen him?"

"I ain't seen 'im, but I'll keep my eyes peeled and ask 'round," Ol' R & R says. I didn't realize how high my hopes were that Ernie had seen Chief until I feel them let down just now. My shoulders slump as Ernie pours a cup of coffee and puts it in my hands. I take a whiff... Mom, home. I'd rather just get moving, but I sip out of politeness. Next second, I spray it all over the place and start apologizing. These guys laugh again, and Hatch takes the drink for himself.

Ernie says, still chuckling, "God-awful, ain't it? So... last I seen ya, which was the first I seen ya," he stops and strokes his scraggly beard, "you were talkin' 'bout riding the rails."

Hatch follows with, "Last I saw you, which was the first I saw you, you had ridden the rails across the seat from Unci, my grandmother."

I smile. "Right. Look, I gotta go, but quick tell me how you know each other 'cause it's weird that you do."

They tell me they go way back, meeting in the beet fields to work for extra money and at the Jungle, the hobo camp where people like them stay sometimes. Hatch says that Ol' R & R is a lot more than just a hobo, that he likes to help people, and that Ernie helped get him a basketball scholarship to a small college. I never met a hobo that gives that kind of help and have to wonder if they're pulling my leg or telling me the truth. Stranger things have happened, I guess. Hatch says that over the last twelve years Ernie has become one of his family up at the rez. Then Hatch says he wants to tell me a joke:

"You can't judge a book by its cover, just like you can't judge an Indian by his car."

I think if I laugh that'd be rude, knowing what my Dad always says about Indian wagons. He sees me frowning instead of laughing, but lets it go.

Ol' R & R Ernie rearranges the smoking fish.

I tell them about Chief being my savior in the mess of a life like mine, and that my parents gave him to a farmer for breeding. I say, "I heard my Dad on the phone and he got real upset because Chief bolted from the car when the farmer opened the door and they couldn't catch him and didn't find him after searching half a day before dark. Dad said he was going to go this morning to find Chief, but I don't know if that's true, so I left last night on my own, since I'm gonna find him on my own anyway."

Ol' R & R raises his eyebrows at my explaining. "Ya think?"

"Yes! Chief is trying to find me as hard as I'm trying to get to him," I say, tough and mouthy, as if it's their fault I'm in this tight spot. "You'll see."

"Coca Joe?" Hatch says softly, "We understand that you and Chief have been all over this area, and that Chief is by far the best dog in the world. And we see that you're a brave young girl." I know what it means when adults talk like this. He's building up to something, and here comes the sledgehammer, "But it's too dangerous."

"Not for me," I set my shoulders. "Chief and I have done lots of things that adults like you guys wouldn't approve of. Lots! And the thing is, I know Chief is headed my way. He's running back to me! Best thing I can do is meet him halfway and we'll go home together."

"Ragamuffin?" drawls Ernie. "Have ya considered ya might not find him?"

"Well that's just mean!" I yell, jumping to my feet. "A mean thing to say!"

The hobo says, "I care 'bout you finding Chief, but both a ya have a rough road ta' travel."

"Even a dog as great as Chief could have trouble crossing this land," Hatch says. "The sky is clear now but that can change quick and creeks will flow higher, flash floods can come out of nowhere, and mud will be a danger."

"I know, I know, and the rattlers can strike us dead. I didn't say it wasn't going to be dangerous! So what?"

I don't want to hear any of this. Me and Chief, we know how to fight dangers and I'm going to fight for my dog. I'm tired of talking to these two traitors and want to get going finding Chief.

"I know that I'm the one to find Chief, that it's up to me, and that all the looking of all the people in all the world will not find him. Only I can."

"Where do you get this stuff?" Hatch asks.

"Church."

This stops him cold.

"God... told you... to do this?"

Maybe, but not that exactly. "God understands why I'm doing it and He will help me."

"Well! We must not argue with God," says Hatch.

"You think I'm a joke? I invited Jesus into my heart when I was five years old 'cause I needed the help and figured he'd give it. From what I know about Jesus he doesn't seem like a wandering fool or the kind who gets disinterested in helping a kid."

I turn square to Ol R & R Ernie. "But *you* are everything my Dad has warned me to stay away from."

Ol' R & R frowns as he looks at the ground.

"And you should know," I yell at Hatch, "that my dad hates Indians! He'd rather shoot you than see you come anywhere near me."

A loud pop on the campfire causes me to jump out of my skin. It would be funny if I wasn't so serious. It's only oil dripping out of the fish but it made me grab my heart.

"Your father believes he has reasons for his hate," says Hatch before drawing in a breath and squinting into the coals of the fire.

"But they are not your reasons. It's you that made friends with us, Coca Joe Stratmore."

I shrug my shoulders blowing him off, and put my mouth off kilter. It's hard to fight with people who won't fight back. Their gentle ways remind me I like them and make me suspect they're not the ones I'm mad at. "Well actually, I'm not Coca Joe Stratmore at all," I say, as a peace offering.

Ernie and Hatch look at me, waiting. My mind chases the stories and gnashes the truth around until I'm ready to spit it out. "I just call myself that. I made the name up out of nothing, because I like it. It doesn't mean anything."

Hatch looks at Ernie as Ernie looks at him. Ol' R & R shrugs his shoulders and looks away. Hatch has to take this one. "You made it up out of nothing?"

"Yeah, well, my parents, they adopted me, you know, after I didn't belong to anybody. So, I'm theirs now. They named me Jane Louisa Rose, which they like but I don't so I made up a new one. I call myself Coca Joe Stratmore."

This shuts them up for a minute. Kids must seem confusing if you aren't one.

"Coca Joe Stratmore, whoev'r you is and whatev'r yer called's okay by me, got it?"

I shine pale blue eyes into his and smile, close-mouthed. Seems done enough.

"Ya know, yer folks'll be out lookin' fer you instead of Chief. But if'n ya go on home, all ya all could go lookin' for Chief together. Might'n get the job done quicker."

My heart is starting to pound again and I twist my fingers. I can see this old hobo and this Indian are my friends, but I won't let them make me go home. They think they know what will happen there, but they don't.

"Home without Chief isn't home, so I'm not heading anywhere except to him. I can take care of myself out here without anyone's help. And there's nothing you can say to make me go back!" I'll bolt on out of here if I have to.

Ol' R & R Ernie frowns as he looks at me, real deep, like he really sees me. "Ragamuffin, what's makin' ya so rough and ready, so stubborn and wantin' to scare yerself runnin' around at all hours like this? It's like ya wanna run off from home. Like Chief's giv'n you a reason, and off ya go."

Something about this cools me down. "I might not be tough, really. I just need Chief like I need..." My voice starts to quiver, but I talk with power because I need them to understand. "Like I need my legs taking me to the badlands, I need him. And to go home, and to be at home..." my emotions are coming out more than I mean them to, but I can't help it. "I *need* a dog like Chief. I need him!"

"All right," Hatch says in a gentle voice and holding up his hand like he's soothing a skittish colt. "Calm down. We will figure this out."

Finally the guys start to take me serious, wanting to know what my plan is. I pull out the directions to the farm and the notes I took while studying Dad's maps, and for the first time I think it may not have been a waste of time talking to them after all, because Hatch says he knows just where that farm is. "It's just across the creek from the rez." I figure it's good to know where Chief came from, but I think I'll probably find him before I ever get to the farm, because Chief has been on his way to me.

Unless he's in trouble.

But I can't think about that.

Hatch asks what I'll do if I don't find Chief. I shrug my shoulders, because to me that's answer enough. They look at one another for a moment, then say they can help me and describe how. Hatch will travel with me, since Ol' R & R Ernie is a freight-hopper and not a trekker. Ol' R & R says something about them being irresponsible to let me go off alone, which I don't care about, but that Hatch is a good tracker and can probably help me find Chief quicker, which I do care about. I agree to let Hatch come, but don't tell them I'll just run off on my own anyway if I change my mind later or if he tries to trick me and turn me in.

I'm not going home without my dog. I'm not.

So it's decided. Hatch packs up, then the two of them shake hands, or more like hold arms like I've seen in the movies, each gripping the other's inside forearm. I make a mental note to practice this with Hatch. I like that.

"I'll go to the Jungle and have a word with him," Ol' R & R says to Hatch. They don't explain who the 'him' is and I don't care. I'm itching to go find my dog. "I'll call over later and let you know how things go."

Hatch nods solemnly, apparently knowing this business they have between them that has nothing to do with me.

Ol' R & R Ernie gives me a squeeze. Nothing could be stinkier than a real hobo, but I surprise myself and hug him tight for as long as he lets me. "Trust yer instincts, Kiddo. Ya got 'em, so use 'em."

"Okay. And keep your eyes out for Chief!" I say.

"Will do. Not to worry, Ragamuffin, not to worry." He holds me at arm's length and my nose says thank you. "Ol' Injun scout knows what he's doin' out there, ya hear? Work t'gether an' you'll be alright. We'll watch for Chief here, 'round the tracks and river. People 'r comin' and goin' and we'll get word out, promise. Now, GO! Find your Chief!"

14
SEARCH

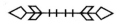

Hatch and I spend the morning covering the flat land between the river and the tracks, land that has seen plenty of water. Wild asparagus is sprouting up and ponds are edged with reeds and cattails. We are calling for Chief and looking for signs of him because this land is thick with cottonwoods, willows, and thickets of bushes like wild roses where animals can safely hide as they come to the river to drink, and we don't want to miss Chief. It feels good to know I've come far enough to find him any minute! If he's coming this way, and if he hasn't gotten himself into some trouble. But I'm not going to think about that. And I'm not going to think about my folks waking up to find me gone. I'm not. I'm not going to start being afraid they will find me. I'm finding Chief first and when I do, if they threaten me with their anger, I will show them that Chief and I are not afraid to leave again. I will show them that I was right and they were wrong and should never have sent him away in the first place. I will show them. I will show them.

Hatch is a good tracker. There's been rabbit tracks and deer tracks, and even a line that means snake, but no tracks that look like dog. This scares me some. What if Chief went a different way? But I decide it just means Chief hasn't come this far yet, so that means we're heading in his direction and that's good!

Hatch is a quiet walker and I try to copy him, but can't. In between us calling for Chief, he teaches me about spotting the dangers we talked about. I try not to worry about whether Chief knows the dangers of the land. We keep moving and calling for him and I keep pushing away the long list of things I'm not going to think about.

I'm comin' Chief! I'm comin'!

I get back to answering Hatch about spotting the dangers, "When Chief is beside me or out front, I know where I am and have a sense of the dangers. On my own without Chief, it's people I don't trust, like someone stupid who might take Chief for themselves and tie him up to keep him from..."

He covers his ears. "Hey, hey! Your worrying hurts my ears."

This doesn't stop me. My worries have taken over talking for me. "Well if your parents gave your dog away..."

Hatch mumbles to himself, "I was that dog my parents were forced to give away."

"What?" I heard him even though he wasn't really saying it to me. He called himself a dog that was given away.

"Never mind Coca Joe. Nobody wants to hear what I have to say."

I'm relieved that I don't have to think about him being a dog. "That's what kids say. You're not a kid."

"I am still trying to become the thirty-year-old man I am supposed to be. Growing up Indian on a reservation is like a bad dad throwing you into your room to keep you quiet, then yanking you out to be stolen and thrown again into a boarding school that treats you like they want to kill you, then throwing you back into your room saying, 'Never mind. You are not worth it.'"

"What kind of bad dad does all that?"

"You are probably too young to understand all this, but people have been pretty confused about whether Indians qualify as real people or not. We have mostly been treated as subhuman. Like dogs."

Is this when he was a dog? I talk about Chief like he's human, and I seem to need Chief like he's human. And now a human is saying he's been treated like a dog. I'm not sure what to think, so I say, "Well as a person or a dog, I think you would be one of the real good ones."

Hatch chuckles quietly.

I have instincts for people and I can smell a rat if I get close enough. Sure, Hatch is handsome and nice, but I can spot a handsome rat—it looks slippery. What bothers me about Hatch is the opposite. He seems familiar, and how would I be familiar with an Indian?

"Hey Hatch, something I'm worried about, or, I mean, wondering, is why you are out here with me? I mean, I'm not... well, grown-ups ignore me and that's what I'm used to. But you and Ol' R & R Ernie pay attention to me and it's weird that you do. Like, it's not normal."

He grunts and comes back fast with, "Look at you! You are talking of normal?" He chuckles at teasing me and then stops walking again, takes a deep breath and picks his words as carefully as searching for ripe berries. "Well, okay. You are right, especially for an Indian man." I stew for a second waiting for the rest. "Ernie and I have an ulterior motive, do you know what that is?"

"Something good for you and bad for me?" I take a guess.

"Hah!" Hatch laughs in one loud spurt. "You think just like a white man, Coca Joe Stratmore."

I squint fiercely at him, wrinkling my lips like an old apple doll. I slide into being a toughie, slumping my shoulders and striding around him down the path like a regular bully, saying as mean as spit, "You better go on back to Ernie. I'm not interested in your ulterior motive."

I'm pushing fast down the trail. Hatch keeps up with legs to spare, but I've written him out of this search for Chief. "Coca Joe, my ulterior motives are not bad for you. Come here. I'll show you."

I stop and scowl at him, folding my arms. He stops too, and says softly. "Ernie and I already told you we want to make sure you're safe, and that's true. But..."

He pauses and I squint up at him. His expression softens me, though I don't know that I want to be soft. I can't seem to help it though. I keep trusting Hatch like something inside me knows it's okay.

Hatch digs in his pocket to hold out the worry stone I recognize as my own, saying that Ol' R & R Ernie gave it to him because I had told Ernie that it was for anyone else that might know me.

I think about this.

Sure, Hatch knows me because he met me at the train depot in Livingston.

I say in my bully voice, with hands on my hips and legs planted wide, "I'd like to know about your ulterior motive." It hasn't been explained by the worry stone, and I know it. "You better talk fast, or start walking yourself back to Ol' R & R." I'm proud of myself for talking tough.

He nods, agreeing. "It is all right to have two names, Coca Joe, and a face with two halves."

"Well," is all I can say, and it comes out like 'wool' in a low grunt pulled deep from the back of the throat, common for us in Hell Creek. I slice a look at Hatch from the bottom corner of my eyes hoping it's knife-like, threatening him to stop talking in riddles.

He continues, "Because... Coca Joe is short for something, right?"

"No. Not that I know of. I made it up." I kick at a clump of dirt at my feet.

"Constance Josephine?" he asks soft and gentle.

I don't blink, don't look up. "I never heard any name like that before," I say. My mind takes off, runs around a tight corner, gains distance and ends up imagining what Chester would say on Gunsmoke. In his whining, nasal wind of a voice he'd say, "Don't know as I know, Marshall."

I think about it again, Constance Josephine. Nope, don't know it.

Hatch digs into his back jeans pocket and pulls out a wallet. From this, he pulls out an old photograph. "Yes, Coca Joe," he says, looking at the picture, "I'm sure about this. I'm sure it's you. Do you want to see this?"

I'm sure it's you sends sound waves through my body like a skipping stone over water. He's become giant-sized by what's in his hand. Lumps in my throat always come at the wrong time, choking me like a pair of thick hands, keeping me quiet. I close my eyes to stinging tears behind my lids. Ouch. Clearly his ulterior motive is bad for me, and good for him.

I force myself into being tough again. "Not that I care, but I guess I'll take a look."

He hands it to me and I take it. A little bitty piece of paper never felt so heavy in my hands before. It's a photo of a baby being held in the arms of a young Indian woman that looks a lot like Hatch and a young white man with his arm around her and eyes the color of mine. "He looks familiar," I say.

"Does he?"

"Sorta."

"That's my twin sister Josephine, we called her Jo. That's her husband Tim Stratmore."

"Stratmore?" I say, my ears full of a funny ringing. "That's weird, isn't it?"

"Yes."

"What's this got to do with me and an ulterior motive?"

"That baby in the picture is you."

I suck in a breath so fast I choke myself, and go right into having a coughing fit. I give him back the picture and shut the trap door I'm about to fall into. I shut it fast and start running down the trail.

What if that's the truth? My mom is an Indian? What kind of saving can Indians do?

I don't turn around and I don't look back. I run faster.

This isn't like climbing through the badlands with sparse plant life, this is river drainage. Sticker bushes attack and won't let go, dead fallen trees block the path and need climbing over, and I duck under low-hanging branches that sometimes skim my head. There are puddles to jump over and piles of dried river wood wriggling underfoot, trying to twist an ankle.

Hatch is yelling for me, but I yell for Chief. Finally Hatch stops yelling and only follows me, but I don't stop at all. I yell over and over: "Chief! Chief! Chief!"

With each call it seems I chase that picture a bit farther from memory. I open the trap door and throw it in.

I finally start to slow but stay in the lead and he lets me. I don't mind that he's behind me, for now. I push hard until there is a need to rest since asthma and wheezing has kicked up strong and I'm not going to ignore that again. I take the asthma pills out of my knapsack and drink some down with my canteen.

I let Hatch catch up with me. I decide it's not his fault if he thinks I'm the baby in the picture, and will let him stay with me so long as he leaves me alone about it. He sits down and I sit down next to him. He brings out some Slim Jims and peanuts, and I lighten up, asking Hatch if he robbed a bar for food. He thinks I shouldn't know about bars. I smile an all-knowing smile. I take out a bruised banana and small crackers to share. Hatch asks if I robbed a monkey.

Then Hatch turns serious. "We are concealed here, which is good and bad," he says.

"Bad because Chief can't find me?" I ask.

"Right. But I figure your parents will have a very large posse out looking for you by now. Did you think of that? They got up this morning and all that is left of you is a mile of hair."

I picture the hair on the bed in my beautiful purple room. I feel bad. This makes my memory go to the purple color of the crumpled dead body of the friend that was scooped from the icy water and Mom saying that the child's poor parents can't live with themselves now that she is gone, that the grief is killing them. My heart sinks. Everybody loses until I find Chief and we go home together, but I have no home without Chief. This I know.

"Would anyone know which direction you would go?" Hatch asks.

I'm pretty sure it's a no and say so, since I think they would guess that I'm still really mad at them and I ran away into my badlands.

"You are still a young girl and people get real serious when a little girl goes missing. There will be bulletins on the radio and television, and tomorrow it will be in the newspapers. The wind is sure kicking up some dust over your running away. The whole county will be combed by all manner of law enforcement, and civilians will volunteer from all over to help look for you." The fear of this turns me cold.

Hatch reads my face but goes on to scare me further. "So we do not have much more time to be out here looking for Chief, Coca Joe. If anyone finds you with an Indian, especially your Dad, I will not live to tell about it."

I'm still frozen. If Dad finds me before I find Chief, that will be bad news for everyone. I've done a good job not worrying about the fact that we haven't found Chief yet, but this is making me more than afraid. We've gone more than half way to the farm. If Chief is on his way back to me, why haven't we found him yet?

We've seen a few trains on the tracks this morning, and here comes another one, coming up on us. Even though it is a freighter, there are still engineers on board who could spot us and remember an Indian and a white girl if they were asked. As before, Hatch has us hide out of sight until it's passed, then we get to our feet. "We can head farther into the fields," Hatch says, nodding his head in that direction. The fields are on the other side of the tracks, away from the river. "Chief might have done the same. He might come to the water to drink and follow the river into town. Or he might have found a watering hole and stayed in the fields. We are guessing, either way. What do you think? How would you and Chief do it?"

I think about this. Focusing on a plan is helping me push my fear away. I just have to have faith like a mustard seed. I'm going to find Chief! I must!

"Let's go into the fields," I say in a confident voice that's still a little bit of pretend. "If Chief is by the river, he'll still hear us when we call."

15
THE BOARDING HOUSE

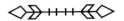

"The photograph, the photograph," Knower says, searching through the record books frantically. "I don't remember any photograph."

Every resident is still staring out the revolving door windows hoping to see it again.

"When She blocks something from her mind, She is stubborn about it," Katrina says in her matter-of-fact tone.

Lonely is standing snuggled close to Katrina, her hands in fists under her chin, her arms hugging herself, the hope in her voice clear, "A baby. I saw a baby in the picture."

Gangster resets the Fedora on his head. "How could She be an Indian baby?"

The Babe sighs, "*Those* parents looked happy to have her."

Watcher with Owl says telepathically from outside the brass revolving door, "Should I have Owl try to pry open the trapdoor?"

"Only if you want us residents to fall down inside it," Knower calls out from his desk by the revolving door. "We should wait and see if this is Her family. Until then, we must trust Her to know if She is ready to let it back into Her mind. Let's everyone return to their rooms. She is under enough stress. She doesn't need all of us pushing from the inside."

16
HORSES

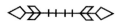

We haven't gone far when Hatch says, "Too bad we haven't seen any wild horses yet. That would speed up our search."

My eyes bug out. "Are you from a horse tribe?"

"Horse tribe? Ha!" He snorts. "The Sioux Indians are famous for their horse riding skills. Imagine this, galloping in a herd of very fast-moving buffalo, you are riding bareback and guiding your horse with just your knees because you have a taut bow ready to fire an arrow in a precise place to kill a buffalo."

I stare at Hatch, wondering if he's managed this feat.

He laughs at the look on my face. "Not the answer you were looking for? Yes, I can ride a horse, Coca Joe, if that is what you mean. Bareback." Then he teases, talking slow and broken like Indians in the movies, "We of 'Horse Tribe' taught you of 'Saddle Sores' to ride bareback." I squeal with laughter, the first fun he's heard from me since the photo. I smile up at the dollops of sunlight dropping down the leaves on the cottonwood trees, believing this joy means Chief will be found soon.

On the far side of the field is an old farm road, and I spot a road sign to the side. "I'll crawl low to the ground near the road until I can read that mile marker.

"Your eagle eyes cannot see it from here?"

"No. Hawk, remember? I am Ceta—n!" I yell, and run ahead with my arms in wing formation, then pretend to dive to the ground for cover.

"Save your strength, Cetan." Hatch yells after me.

After I read the sign and return to report to Hatch, I realize we're not far from where we'd already figured we were, but that doesn't make me happy. Where is Chief? Where is he! After about another half mile of walking through prairie grasses calling for Chief, we come up on a band of grazing horses. It's as if Hatch's wish conjured them up out of thin air. I've seen horses like this from time to time, but these are show-stopping, and my heart lifts at the sight of them. I'm a horseless cowgirl, through no fault of my own, who's watched a lot of rodeo.

Hatch takes to walking extra quiet, drawing close to the nearest horse, a palomino. I've never even imagined what I see next: Hatch bounces as if off a trampoline over the rear end of the horse, who rears in surprise, then bucks, twisting in a circle to pop Hatch off his back. I scramble back and watch in shock, waiting for Hatch to be dumped. Instead, he rides over to me, reaching down with one arm as if I would fly up to straddle the horse's back. In great shock and wonder I do it! With my right arm hooked to his left and a jump with a scissor kick just like a circus performer, I'm on the horse!

A cowgirl like me needs a horse, not a cow like the name implies. Whitey was that horse, and to tell the truth, I never got over her, never-ever stopped wanting another horse, and I'm still as horse-crazy today as anyone could ever be. Riding on the back of one is an answer to hours of prayers.

Feeling such turmoil over Chief being gone, then such happiness to be on a horse is a lot to handle, and tears roll down my cheeks. Hatch spurs the horse on, spurless, and I hold tight around his back as the horse gallops across the prairie like a burr is on his underbelly. Hatch leans forward taking me with, glued to him, as his hair flies up with the horse, then whips my face when it comes back to earth.

The combo of the slapping hair and my boney bottom slamming with each stride almost ruins the fun. I try, but don't have the strength to float on the horse. Several other horses flank us; a buckskin, a sorrel, and the white, like the horse I once had.

We keep a sharp eye out for any sign of Chief, and I manage to call for him even with me and my lungs bouncing along. Montanans can own huge spreads—as wide as the Montana sky, we say—so Hatch and I ride over many sections of land before a barbed wire fence stops us, and still, not a soul has been seen, no houses, barns or roads, just one owner's land ending and another's beginning. We hear a large herd of cattle now that we're sitting still. They're talking, mooing, as if there's something to say. "Chief!" I yell up to the sky. "Chief, you over there? I'm coming, Chief! I'm coming!" I yell his name again and again but hear no happy bark in reply.

We sit still awhile and the heat off the sweating horse soaks through my jeans. The palomino shakes his head many times, and swishes his long white tail up along his back and across me to shoo off the flies. Hatch turns the horse in a tight circle to give us a full view of the land, to get our bearings. The trees along the river are far off now, and the badlands in the distance blow me a kiss on the breeze. I smile their way, as if the rock formations standing upright are my people.

We continue on, and it's late afternoon when we catch our first sight of Big Sandy Creek. We're not far from the bottom of the "U" shape it makes as it winds back and forth. We keep going deeper into the long, wide finger of land that reaches in toward the farm and the rez, until the creek is some distance to the right of us. On the other side of the creek is rez territory. I know if the farmer was looking for Chief, he wouldn't have looked there. But Chief doesn't care about boundaries like that. If he crossed the creek on his way toward home, he could be in Indian territory. And here I am with an Indian, hunting for him!

To our left, far on the other side of the field we're in, the railroad tracks break into a Y. The lower arm will head into southern Montana, but the upper arm will keep going straight through this finger of land, like us, then right on through the rez, not like us. There's no need to go past the farm. I'm already closer to it than I thought I'd get before finding Chief. This thought brings a knot of worry into my heart, but I stomp it down. I just have to have faith like a mustard seed. I know Chief won't give up looking for me, and I sure won't give up looking for him.

Soon we start to feel the squeeze of the land, with the creek and a road getting close on one side, and the tracks close on the other. We're in fields again, but these aren't as broad, and we can see houses spotting the landscape in the distance. We've crossed a lot of distance thanks to the palomino, but Hatch says it's time to get low again. We don't want to be spotted.

We dismount and, since I don't know this horse, I step backwards and away. The horse stomps his front foot twice and shakes his head. His loose lips fling slobber on my chest and neck, as if scolding us before he turns tail and trots off with the other horses.

Not far away he stops, turns sideways and rears up, pawing at the air. Hatch cups his hands around his mouth and yells, "Hi-Yo, Silver, AWAY!" I bend over laughing hard and long and right into an asthmatic wheeze, which is the saddest problem with asthma, it can bring on an attack from laughing. Hatch gets nervous as he watches me wheeze violently.

"Way to go... Kemo Sabe," I choke out, waving him off as if he's using up my air. Finally, I sit hunching over my lungs to take the emergency pills from my bracelet. After that, when I can breathe enough to swallow, I take the longer-lasting tablets that are supposed to keep asthma stable.

"My sister had asthma... my twin," Hatch says a bit sadly. I throw this down the trap door with the photo, focusing on sucking in air. Between the asthma trying to kill me and worry that the sun will go down before I find my dog, I don't have room to think about anything else. I keep a foot on that trap door forcing it closed, because right now Chief needs me and I need him. He and I are on the run, and we better be running towards each other.

Hatch sits with me and offers more water. Once I'm breathing better, he pulls out some food next, and I do the same, wanting to make my own contribution to our dinner. But I'm not ready to eat yet and I guess he isn't either. He walks away, more of him disappearing beyond the grass with each long, quick stride. He's gone a long while and doesn't look at me when he gets back. He's hiding his face behind his long hair. I know that trick, and miss it with my hair chopped off.

Hatch has gone quiet. I don't know which I can't bear, the idea of sitting when I still don't have Chief, or sitting with Hatch when he's serious like this, but either way, my legs get me to moving. I walk along the fence a ways off from where we've stopped for a rest, and rub against several of the posts. "Catch my scent, Chief," I whisper, and then rub low on a fence post. "Here I am, Chief. I'll find you! You find me too!"

The evening sun lights the seed heads of the Tallgrass, turning them into pale golden wicks of candlelight. I wish they could light the way to Chief. If the sun is going to go down, how can it go down on another day without Chief? I burst into tears and cry real tears of deep longing. I was supposed to find Chief by now. I've had so much faith I'd find him, I can't see what's gone wrong. Maybe that photograph under the trap door hints at finding somebody but what is it worth without finding *my* family, my Chief?

I know sometimes God is a mystery and makes us wait, but I sure don't feel like I have time to wait. I know I need to keep on having faith, though. I'll find him, I will!

"I'm comin' Chief!" I holler so loud I figure even the wind will take notice, so I hope it's good enough for God. "I'm comin'!"

Hatch is friendly when I get back, his private thinking over, but he's serious too. "It is getting late, Coca Joe."

"You can go on home if you want to, but I'm not going home," I say firmly, guessing where he might be going with this.

"I cannot leave you out here alone."

I shrug. I'm not budging on this and I think he knows it. After what he's told me, I don't think he'll try to turn me in either. That would make him seen with a little lost white girl, and that's bad news for this Indian.

"Maybe Chief made it home and is there wishing for you," Hatch says carefully.

I think about this. What if Chief *is* home without me? What if he went home through the badlands instead of along the river like I thought he might? I admit to Hatch that Chief may have gone that way, then say, "If he's not by the breeder's farm, I'll just have to turn around and track him in the badlands." I don't think about what kind of trouble Chief might be in if he's not here and he's not home either. Instead I focus on what I'm supposed to focus on: finding him!

I consider I might need to cross the creek to see if Chief's on that side of it, but don't say so. Hatch is already nervous enough about the idea of me going through the badlands, I can tell, and might tell me I'm not allowed on rez land either.

I want to put all this thinking in a funnel believing it would drain out, soak into the dirt and dry up, turning to nothing.

On the other side of the field, another freight train is heading west toward the rez. We watch it in silence until it disappears. After a day of walking and riding and calling and not enough resting, my body is starting to betray me again like it did last night. I feel I could curl into a ball on the ground right here, close my eyes, and sleep hard until morning. But I don't want to stop while there's still light out. I stand. "Let's get going."

Hatch stands too, still willing to go along, at least for now. "You think Chief will still be so close to the farm, after all this time?"

If Chief got turned around when he left the farm but has since found his direction, maybe he's still up ahead. And maybe we're farther than he is because of riding that horse. Or maybe he crossed the creek but has since crossed back. I don't know, but I feel like I need to keep going, and say so.

We discover it's a short distance to the county road. Up ahead, dust rises off it thick and curly. From the direction we're headed, the direction we imagine is JT's farm, several cars are flying down the road. The sound of their big engines mean business. Their headlights cut through the dusky evening light. It'll be dark in less than half an hour. This many cars all together makes me wonder what they're up to, and I can't help but worry it's something to do with me.

Hatch and I hurry away from the road. There's a ditch and a clumpy line of trees ahead we could hide in, but it's too far to get to without being seen first so we nosedive into the crops. I'm breathing wheezy and I have to take the time to take my medicine, but I'm careful to stay low. It's bad timing, but my asthma is threatening enough to kill me anytime.

"Coca Joe?" Hatch asks, briefly taking his eyes off the line of cars. "Is your asthma okay?"

"It will be," I say into the dirt under my face.

"We are really on the run, you understand that? They aim to find you."

I won't go back alone. I won't! "Chief is counting on me!" I say. "I can feel him." I look toward the first car, passing us now, and see a man sitting in the passenger seat, scanning the fields. Even though he doesn't seem to have spotted us, the sight of his searching scares me. But not as much as seeing my dad's car, three cars back.

I soon see it's my mom driving, not my dad, but I don't have a spare thought to figure out why. My fear spikes into panic at the sight of her and I start scrambling backwards on all fours. "I can't go back, Hatch. I can't!"

"Coca Joe, wait!" he says. "Stay still!"

I hear another engine then, but this time not from a car. I follow the sound to our left and up into the sky. There's a little silver Cessna, far off still but heading in our direction.

"My dad's plane!" It's going to fly right over us! "He's gonna see me!"

I scramble to my feet and start sprinting toward the ditch.

"Coca Joe!" Hatch says. "No!"

I'm beyond reason. An animal cornered. All I can think to do is run and hide. The ditch feels like a million miles away and like I will never get to it. The plane is getting closer and it seems the engine is like a monster roaring in my ear. A car horn sounds somewhere behind me and tires scrape against the dirt road as the posse comes to an abrupt halt. A train whistle sounds in the distance. "Run!" it says, and I do!

I run down into the ditch, which has a thick line of trees on either side of it. The trees on one side block me from the road. Hatch is right behind me. "Coca Joe! Wait, listen!"

I spot a fan of low-hanging branches and duck under them, crouching low and hugging my knees. Hatch comes up next to me.

"It's over," he says gently but urgently. "You need to go on out there so they can take you home."

I whimper and shake my head hard. *No, no, no.*

The plane is getting louder and I back against the dirt side of the ditch, roots from the tree above sticking out and sticking into me. Stomach juices push into my mouth so that I taste puke.

"No, Hatch, no!" I whimper in a panic. "My dad can't get me! Don't let him get me!"

"Coca Joe, he is not going to hurt you," Hatch says, but he doesn't sound so sure. He says it more like a question.

I hold my hands to my ears and shake my head and curl into a ball. "No, no, no." I say again. "Don't let him get me. Please, Hatch, please."

"Okay, okay, sh-hhh," he says, bringing me close to him and holding me against his chest.

My name is yelled through a bullhorn and I flinch. I even think I hear Mom yelling for me to come back, but I'm not sure. The plane roars above, passing over us.

"We have to get away. Please, please," I say, still panicking. I can't go home without Chief. I can't go home. I can't.

Hatch lifts my chin and makes me look him in the eye. His strong gaze shushes me more than his shushing did. He says low and firm, "I will keep you safe, Coca Joe. I promise you that. Do you hear?"

I nod once, still looking into his eyes as if they're the only lifeline I have, and right now without Chief, maybe they are. The plane is getting quieter, but the voices from the posse are getting louder. Even the train I heard earlier is getting louder. All this noise just makes me want to run more. "Don't let them get me," I plead.

"I will not," he says, still holding my eyes firmly, "but we have to be quick and you have to do what I tell you. Do you trust me?"

I nod. I'll do anything he says so long as he gets me out of here!

"Stay close," he says, and I do. We climb out the other side of the ditch, and through the trees on that side. I'm glad for the growing darkness now as we run for the opposite side of the field, where the tracks run. We must be heading for the other side of them, but I don't know where on earth we can go from there. Plus, the train is finally coming through and is blocking our way. It's not going too fast either, so if we have to wait for it to pass, we'll be caught.

"This is our train," Hatch says.

"What?" I breathe, glancing up at him as we run along. We're getting *on* the train?

"That open car down there," Hatch says, pointing toward the end of the train. "That's the one we want." We drop down into a drainage ditch by the tracks and have to stop and wait. We take a quick look behind to see who might be coming.

I can tell from the sounds that the posse has made it into the tree-lined ditch. We'd better be quick or they'll see us. Hatch is busy digging something out of his bag, but I don't know what because my eyes are on my dad's plane. He's still flying away from us, but he's starting to bank and turn back around, the orange light from the setting sun glinting off the sides like angry monster eyes saying, "I'm going to get you!"

"Hatch!" I whimper.

He pulls a cap out of his sack and plops it on my head. "Pull it down low. If there's hobos on the train, you'll be a boy, got it?" He sees the fear in my eyes and puts an arm around me, but there's no time for much comfort. His eyes are on the open car coming our way. "I know what I am doing, so do exactly as I say. You're going to get on this train like you got on that horse." For one moment my knees start to give out, but I make them hold. I have to get away, and even I can see this is my only chance. "You can do it!" Hatch says urgently, taking my hand and starting to run in the same direction the train is going. "Now forget everything except riding that palomino, Coca Joe. You will get on this train the same way as you got on that horse." Boxcars go by close to my face, with none of their doors open. "When I yell 'JUMP' throw a leg into the open boxcar just like on that tall horse! I will have a hold of you!" I begin to panic just as Hatch says, "Here it comes! This is it, here we go!" I forget fear for excitement. He reaches for an outside ladder and has hold of my arm, yelling, "Ju-mp!" I do it, throwing a leg up in the boxcar as he pulls me up, then the other leg, and then Hatch scoops me like a jellyroll and rolls me inside.

17
FOUND

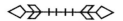

I hear voices saying, "Way to go!" and "Get on in here, sonny." Hatch pats my back as raking sobs overcome my body. I hide my face in folded arms and weep in front of the hobos huddled inside the boxcar. One of them asks, "Tough day at the office?"

I hear chuckling.

"Is that you there, Hatch?"

"It is," he says, putting an arm around me as I yank the cap to cover my face. "This is my friend Tommy. He will recover. Make room for us back there."

Hatch leads us to an empty corner. Once we settle down and I realize we're safe from the posse, and even the other hobos seem content to leave us be, I flip like a light switch from total tears to joy. I've hopped a freighter! I once told Ol' R & R Ernie I would and I did. He was my very first hobo, and now I'm sitting in a boxcar full of them!

I grin up at Hatch. It's a bit dark in here but I can see his face well enough. He doesn't look as recovered as I am. He's still panting and giving me a concerned expression. I'm distracted by a hobo coming up to us.

"Want some vittles?" The guy asks. I look to Hatch for his nodding okay.

I grab a hard roll and a fried chicken leg, a little too frazzled yet to eat, but grateful.

"Headin' home?" he asks Hatch.

"Yep. We have been out looking for Tommy's lost dog. Hey," he says louder, "anybody here see this dog, a large male collie, blond colored?"

"Maybe," comes an answer from the dark on the far side of the boxcar. My heart sings 'Yes!' and my chest rises toward the speaker.

"No joshing now, Ruby. This kid is lost without that dog and is sure he cannot live without it," Hatch scolds. "Anybody else? This dog is special, and Chief, that's the dog's name, is trying to get back to Tommy."

Nobody answers for serious and the hobo goes back to his own spot, leaving us alone.

My heart sinks, getting dark like the sky outside.

Hatch asks, real quiet, "Are you going to tell me the real reason why you don't want to go home?"

I don't answer right away, thinking while I gnaw the cold chicken bone. Then I say, simple as you please, "I need to find Chief first."

He only looks at me like that's no kind of answer, but it's the only answer I've got.

"You still gonna help me find him?"

He nods. "We will go to my house, and make a plan from there. That alright?"

"How far is it?"

"Not quite twenty miles into the rez, once we cross the border at Big Sandy Creek, which we probably crossed already."

I nod, agreeing. I might be excited about where we're going but I'm not sure. What I am sure about is being tired, so I slump against Hatch. He rearranges me, putting my head on his thigh and I curl up like a cat. Maybe I look like one too, because Hatch tells me we only have time for a catnap, but it will be better than nothing.

The rough floor churns at my hip and I slip back to a time with Jesus reaching down to lift me into his arms, saving me from being trapped outside between the railcars on a moving train. I can see him clearly, his gleaming dark skin and kind brown eyes. It's not so different now. I'm trapped again between looking for Chief while hiding from a posse. A handsome brown man with kind brown eyes is rescuing me this time too.

I'm almost asleep when I hear myself say, all dreamy-creamy, "You're handsome and…" the tired takes over, exhausted from being over-brave for too long.

"Lot of good it does me," Hatch answers in a sleepy voice.

I wake up a little, and peek up to see him leaning into the corner, his eyes closed. "What'd ya mean?"

He looks down at me. "You know what word comes before Indian? It isn't handsome."

"Yes." But I won't say it out loud.

"Damn. Damn Indian." He could have said this angrily, but instead he says it sad. "That is what white people call me so they do not have to give me a chance. Just a damn Indian."

"I know that word. I'm just a damn kid."

"Yes, but you will outgrow it, Coca Joe. I will always be Lakota."

I answer him with a quiet confidence, "But you're still young, Hatch. You might outgrow it too."

"I am young, but old too." He gives me a concerned look, the same as the one he gave me before. He sighs and puts his head against the wall, closing his eyes again. I close my eyes too, then hear him say softly, "Young or old, Coca Joe, I think I have a chance right now to make good medicine out of bad."

Sleeping isn't easy in a boxcar with the stench of hobos circling in the wind. It brings dreams: the fly-over of the silver Cessna turns into our cat, Susie, hissing as she flies off the power pole to land on the back of my neck, tearing my flesh with her claws. Teepees are blowing around in the sky like in a twister, with one floating down towards me, hovering too high for me to get in, and I hear high, loud screams of women and children.

It's the train braking.

Hatch pushes me up saying, "We need to jump out now, before we arrive, so let's go." I'm fogged by sleep and glad of it because the ground looks much farther down than it would be from that floating teepee. Hatch tells me to jump and roll like a black bear when I hit the ground. I do, but wish I had the cushioning of a bear. I roll smack dab into sagebrush and come to a stop.

Hatch grabs under my arms and pulls me up. I want to brush off and shake my head to clear it but Hatch grabs my hand saying that our running isn't over yet. We head toward the caboose of the train still coming at us. My legs seem asleep as I struggle to run, not even tingling to wake up, but Hatch is solid as a totem pole and keeps me steady. The caboose passes and we leap over rail after rail and race around sleeping trains. They look peaceful until I hear men yelling in the distance, aiming large spotlights and running our way.

"It's Dad!" Dad did see me from the plane, and he and his posse aim to catch me!

"No, those are the bulls. They don't want to catch us. They're just doing their job."

That's crazy, what is he talking about? Of course they want to catch me! My legs wake up at this thought and run faster.

We leave the tracks behind but still run. Hatch turns to look for our pursuers just before we disappear over the edge of the railroad ditch. We scramble down and I'm lucky to have practiced this half-gallop in my coulee and badlands, keeping my weight on the upper leg.

"STOP! NOW!" I hear through a loud megaphone. Hatch is wrong. They want us.

A large culvert is to our left. It makes the one in my coulee look like a toy. Hatch hugs me to his side as we step into its darkness to catch our breath. He feels me pulling back outside to run and says, "Whoa there. Almost home now."

"They saw that it's me and want me back! I can't get caught! I can't! Please, let's keep running!"

"Hush, Coca Joe," he whispers. I'm pulling away from him but Hatch contains me. "Sh-h-h, now. That's not them. Those are bulls. The railroad police," he says. "They want to scare us from hopping trains because it is against the law now. But we're okay. They never run down here."

I slump to my knees. Bad mistake. Wet mud soaks through to the skin. I reach for his hands and he helps pull me up and, like a good big brother, lets me rest against him. "Are we almost there?" I sniffle into his chest.

"We are, we are," he soothes, patting my back.

We don't wait long; the bulls don't come.

Once we are walking away from the tracks, I ask Hatch how we're going to find Chief now that we're so far away. We talk about it as we walk. He says Chief could have crossed Big Sandy Creek and gone across rez land on his way to the badlands, which is what I'd thought before too. He suggests that tomorrow we first call home to see if Chief's made it back, and if not, we can get some people with cars to check the rez land that runs close to and past the breeding farm, in the direction of Hell Creek.

"We'll do that first, and go from there alright?"

"He's not home yet," I say miserably. "If he was, mom would've had him in the car with her so I'd come to her."

Hatch is kind, putting a light arm around my shoulder. "You may be right, but he may turn up there yet tonight, or may have when they were out looking for you."

I don't ask what we'll do next if Chief isn't on the rez land. Seems like in this search, I can only think one or two steps ahead of where I am. And right now, where I am is heading for Hatch's, exhausted.

Finally Hatch turns up a dirt road so rutted, driving on it would feel like the stomach flu. Prairie grass and weeds are mowed down on the center hump. "Is your tepee close?" I ask, relaxing into my tired body.

"Did you think I live in teepee?"

"Why wouldn't you?"

"We live in houses, Coca Joe, just like you, roofs and doors. Except ours are worn out, flimsy, and cold— a little like a teepee I guess— but we cannot make a warm fire in the center without burning them down, or move them to our favorite hunting grounds." Pretty soon small box houses, tarpaper shacks, and tiny log cabins line the road, some with hulks of old cars guarding them like sleeping lions in the fading light. As we pass, I can hear inside these houses better than at home. Dogs argue under the open sky and my ears tune to Chief out of habit and hope. A generator's hum sings no song.

He turns up a path toward one of the houses. I hear a loud radio or television. Hatch opens the door calling, "Unci!"

I wait at the threshold, peeking into a small living room with a few Indians watching a small black and white television. This surprises me. Hatch leans over a ragged, stuffed chair to hug the old Indian woman I recognize from the train—his unci—while a huge man and a younger, round woman get up from the couch, and a girl about my size sits up from a large worn, overstuffed chair when she spots me at the door. "Hi," she says shyly, and lazy-waves a hand at me. I smile, but shrink back a bit. After so much running, I forgot how to enter a room.

The men hug and backslap, saying "Brother" to each other. Then Hatch speaks to his grandmother in their language, and gestures toward me. My feet are glued to the porch. He has to come and bring me to her. Because she is so old, she struggles to get out of her worn, large, stuffed chair and is helped by the big man who looks at me funny. Hatch pulls me inside the house and says in English. "Coca Joe, this is my brother Nathan, his wife Sue," he says, gesturing to the round woman, "and their daughter Teenci." I nod hello and practice the girl's name in my head since I've never heard of it before, Teenchee, Teen-chee. Nathan is very tall and pockmarked, and his features and build do not resemble Hatch.

"Family, this is Coca Joe Stratmore."

The woman named Sue repeats, "Stratmore?" and covers her throat. I smile like I have learned to do when I'm nervous, big and hopeful. With a slight shake of her head 'no', she walks into the little kitchen. I feel the trap door trying to open, but I push-push-push against it.

The girl, Teenci, comes a little closer. She is pretty in all the ways I will never be—warm brown skin, cheekbones that underline eyes of dark beauty, and straight black hair left to grow long. I can see she and Hatch are related, because of their likeness. She tucks her head in shyness as she notices me staring at her. Dressed like any other American girl, she wears sneakers, not moccasins. I know I frowned when I noticed.

Sue comes back from the kitchen and wraps arms around Teenci from behind, as if protecting her child from me. I back towards the door, aware that I'm filthy from head to toe and wondering if this is her reason for keeping the girl away.

After talking more to his grandmother in their native language Hatch walks her carefully over to me. I look into the loving old eyes on the ancient face that I remember from the train. She holds my face in her gnarled hands and speaks softly in her language while touching each part of my face: my cheekbones, nose, and chin, ending with my mouth. Hatch smiles at me and I smile back so that Unci's knuckles scrape my teeth. She laughs in a gentle grunt. My shoulders drop from their nervous perch. Hmm... .

Hatch's grandmother places my hands over her heart and covers them with her hands. She looks at me with fierce love and says, "Cetan Maka Sichu," as tears pour down her cheeks. We remain this way for some time and then Hatch guides his unci to her chair. Sue frowns and moves to the kitchen and uncovers two large bowls with dough rising over the top. She punches the dough as hunger punches me in the stomach.

I'm ready to eat, but first things first, I'm told. Hatch shows me the small bathroom, gives me a thin towel, and starts the bath before leaving. Sweet joy travels through my body. After several minutes of waiting for the slow-filling tub there is a soft knock on the door and the girl Teenci hands me a full set of her clothes. We giggle together, timid, and I hold my nose and point at myself. She laughs, "Ya, you stink. Good thing you get a bath," she says, talking in Hatch's rhythm, a lowering and lifting of syllables, sometimes with a soft chop and a slowing of some words, like the Big Muddy Creek taught them to speak. I have to be careful not to imitate because my tongue always wants to. She and I study each other and laugh harder, especially me at myself, for doing sign language when she speaks English. I didn't know.

I hadn't looked in a mirror since before I chopped off my hair and ran down the dark road. What I see is ridiculous. All that's missing on me is a red clown nose. It's hard to imagine how anyone kept a straight face when they talked to me! And the dirt—thick smudges covering my face and neck like the art of a toddler.

After the bath, I try hard to match my cleanliness with looking nice. The accident-on-my-head called hair does not calm down with brushing. No amount of water helps. When I get one area settled, it springs back to life as I work the other side. It reminds me of the boys in Sunday school who try to slick down their hair for this one day of the week out of respect for Jesus. It doesn't work on them, either. I give up and shake my hair crazy-looking like before. I shrug. I guess it's my run-away style.

Hatch's brother Nathan, Nathan's wife Sue, their daughter Teenci, and Unci sit at the kitchen table and nod their approval when I come out clean from the bathroom. Each of them drop their eyes right afterwards and keep them down. I blush anyway. I don't see Hatch and I look for him. His brother Nathan sees me looking and says, "Talks With Knees Quaking went over to our house to shower. One bath maximum here." I feel guilty for taking it.

But just that quick, Hatch comes in the house and takes my breath away. Really. I'm a tomboy and young, but I'm not blind. I've noticed being around him that he is handsome, but now that he's all cleaned up and wearing his body like someone happy to be home with those he loves, Hollywood should be calling. Even his family stops to stare, making him break into a wide, joyful smile that shifts everything back to normal. He's like my dog Chief—stunning—only human.

We gather at the kitchen table and I give myself a talking to about not attacking the food. It might help that I don't recognize some of it. There's a tall stack of bumpy but flat dough-like things as big around as the plate. They smell a little like donuts. Hatch eyes these like they're a birthday cake with candles. Must be good! My empty stomach growls loud and long, so it has the effect of a long-winded prayer.

Unci sits beside me hardly taking up a whole chair, with the girl on my other side, and Hatch across the table. He winks at me as we all dive in. "Fry bread is the best!" the girl Teenci says as the pile shrinks fast. Hatch and the grown-ups sprinkle a little meat and lettuce on their fry bread, but the girl spreads honey over hers and scoots the tub to me with a sly smile. They speak what I think is a Sioux language when they include Grandma, and mostly English to each other. I'm content and quiet, eating and listening. I feel comfortable with these laughing, teasing people.

Even though they mostly speak English, I noticed Teenci calls her mother Ina. Mother.

"Ina... Ina," rolls off my tongue in the midst of their talking, so quiet that no one could have heard. Except every fork stops in mid-bite. "Cetan," the words keep coming, maybe influenced by hearing their language. "Ina, Ina." I put down my fork and place my hands in my lap.

The trap door flings wide open.

The photograph of the baby and the Indian mother and white father comes into my mind. I look around the table and can see that this is her family. Hatch's eyes well with tears as he watches me with a face of tenderness. "Ina... Mother, Ina... Mother," I say. I start to cry, "Ina, Ina, Ina... !" I run from the table into the bathroom, the only room I know. Silence holds the others. Then everyone starts speaking at once in a blur of languages.

I throw myself to the floor and scamper to curl my back against the wall. Tears burn hot and my chest tightens in pain. I wail without stopping, rocking my back against the wall so that it hurts like the rest of me. The trap door won't close, and I try to make it, but it won't.

Hatch comes in and lifts me, arms encircling the tight ball-shape, and easily carries me into the front room and to a chair to rock me. My fantasies of my dumb, made-up parents are wiped away and these kind Indians are taking their place, but none of them are my mom and dad in the picture and I'm afraid to ask where they are. Hatch is whispering, "Coca Joe, little one, sh-h, sh-h." I do not stop wailing. Sometimes the babies in people take a long time to quiet.

After a long while, I settle down enough to realize I'm being held in Hatch's arms, and I don't struggle to get out of them or pull out the toughie in me to push away his caring. I stay. It's a big deal for me to stay. A tiredness heavier than the semi-truck tire that pushed into my chest takes over, and I finally give in to sleep.

I wake in the morning under blankets that don't smell like me, my body still curled around its tender heart. There's salt on my lips and a dried crust over my face as if the sandman tripped and dumped his bag. I peek out from under the blankets, looking for Hatch and see him sleeping on the couch that looks child-sized under him. I am on the large, overstuffed chair Teenci was in when I first arrived. Quiet shuffling is heard in the kitchen, a slow waltz, and bubbling sounds bring ideas of more fry bread before bacon smells tell the real story. Bacon reminds me of Mom at home. Her frying pans must sound dry, and her whistling still.

"Hatch. Hatch." I shake his shoulder. "Wake up. Wake up! I need to call home and tell them I'm okay."

Hatch doesn't open his eyes, just rubs and rubs them, finally saying, "Good, Coca Joe, good. Okay. Let me wake up."

I wait impatiently for him to open his eyes and sit up. Once I get an idea in my head, I'm not too keen on waiting. But I can see already Hatch doesn't intend to be rushed. He's giving me a careful, studying kind of look, like he wants to know what's inside my head. As if anyone could figure that out! Half the time I don't even know. Soon he has that same look of concern he gave me on the train after we ran away from Dad, but I don't want to talk about that, so I say, "And maybe Chief is home."

His searching look lets me go then and he nods, stretching. "Okay, Coca Joe. Let me see what time it is, and you can make the call."

We go to the public phone at the Trading Post. I haven't been in one place before with so many Indians. I notice the wide variety of people here just like I see anywhere else; some striking, some plain, some beautiful, some with darker skin, some lighter, but nobody in here like me right now. One man has a missing eye and I try not to stare. Hatch goes to shop for a few groceries while I dial home. Mom answers instead of Dad and I'm glad about that. I'm not as brave with my Dad. He might trick me into saying where I am. Mom is her public self on the phone, nice and fussy and crying at first. I ask Mom about Chief. She says she won't tell me unless I tell her where I am. Dad must have coached her on this. I tell her I'm at a family's house, but I'm not going to tell her who. She says she won't tell me about Chief then and goes off, madder than hell. I hang up as she's screaming, "Exactly where the hell are you, young lady?" Mom is overheard by anyone even close to the phone. Indians close by look at me with mouths in straight lines.

I know I'm playing with fire, making my folks more and more mad at me, but how was I to know I'd be gone this long? I thought I'd have Chief with me by now. I try not to think of the worst as I report to Hatch, "Chief's not there, Hatch. He's not there! If he was she'd tell me so I'd come home too, but instead she tried to find out where I am." Where is he? What if he's hurt? I know I have to stay strong so I can keep looking for him, but my worry is starting to grow bigger.

Hatch leaves his few groceries and hugs me saying, "We will find him. We will. We continue our search today, soon." He keeps holding me and that helps the worry get small again. I just need to have faith. I'll find Chief. I will! I open my eyes to see people watching us. When they see my eyes on them they look away. They must wonder who the heck I am.

As we walk back to Unci's, Hatch tells me that after I went to sleep last night, he made some calls at Sue and Nathan's, and there will be people coming by after breakfast to help us look for Chief. At the yard in front of Unci's, Hatch says he needs to head over to Nathan's again for a quick minute while I get myself ready for the day. I head inside to my knapsack and find my clothes on top all clean. I don't see anybody around to thank so I go into the bathroom to change.

I am eager to look for Chief, but I realize my mind is pulled just as strongly in another direction now. Talking to my Hell Creek mother on the phone makes me wonder even more about my Ina and what kind of mother she might be. I am still afraid to ask where she is. I guess I expect her to just show up, to walk into Unci's as easily as the rest of the family that I hear now outside the bathroom door. What will happen once my Ina arrives? Will we run to each other like I always imagined? Will she grab me into a bear hug and swing me around and around? Will joy so grand enter this hovel that it shakes the very walls?

I get to the breakfast table before Hatch and I'm quiet right along with the others, as if my outburst last night still rings in my ears. I eye a tall plate of fry bread over by the stove. The only word spoken before Hatch comes in to sit down is Sue saying to me, "Later," because she noticed me eyeing the bread, but she says it with a smile that dimples her big round cheeks. I smile back, shy.

When Hatch settles in, we get to eating. What he has to share between bites is that last night Ol' R & R Ernie called over at Nathan's to say he was at the Vagabond Hotel getting himself and an important friend all spiffed up. I know this place in Hell Creek. It's a rundown brick building beside the train depot that my folks always say to steer clear of, since they allow riff-raff in there. This time they are right. I squint at Hatch. He studies me for a long moment.

Nathan breaks the silence by reporting that cars will arrive in about an hour to start searching for Chief. Hatch says I'll be in his good friend Henry's car with Teenci, and that we will search one part of the rez near the breeding farm. Sue adds that she made several calls alerting friends who live in that part of the rez to be on the lookout for Chief. Now I am beaming.

Nathan's family leaves after the meal, and Hatch directs me to the couch. He moves Unci's chair near the coffee table that has a few photos on it and some papers, and sits me between him and his grandmother to look at them. A teenage girl, a look-alike to Hatch, radiant and gorgeous, looks out at me from the first photo. Another picture shows her with a young white man, both looking very happy. These are the same two I saw in the small picture Hatch showed me from his wallet. I can't stop staring at Hatch's twin. Grandmother points as best she can with her crippled fingers to the picture of the couple. She touches the girl's tummy and says, "Niye. Niye."

"That means 'you' in Lakota, our Sioux language," Hatch nudges me with an elbow.

"How do you know?" I ask, suddenly wondering if Hatch doesn't have it all wrong. "Have you looked at me? I stick out like a sore thumb around your kitchen table. I'm no Indian baby." I cover my heart, devouring the young couple with the baby but still doubtful and protective.

"Half of you is Lakota, and maybe even more shines through your true nature. Do you know what I mean?"

"I know what you mean, but a picture of a baby with black sticky-uppie hair doesn't mean that's me."

Hatch pulls over what looks to be a senior portrait of the white boy. He covers the photo of Tim with a piece of paper just beneath his eyes. "You inherited this part of him. I think that's why you said he looks familiar." Then he sets a portrait of Josephine next to it and covers from the eyes up. "It may be harder to tell with her dark features, but you inherited Jo's cheekbones, nose, mouth and chin. So you have the best of both parents." I stare at the bottom half of her face.

"I guess I can sorta see my face in them," I say, but something is fluttering around inside my chest. I've never resembled anyone before, not even just the bottom half of them, and it's a fragile feeling of belonging I'm afraid to hold too tightly.

I study the larger photo of Josephine. Her eyes are twinkly, and give me hope she might be the saving kind after all. Hatch says, "Beautiful inside and out, everybody loved Jo."

Loved? I throw that down the trap door.

"Tim was so in love with Jo and her with him they seemed to hang the moon. There was nothing that could come between them."

"I don't know why I'm not darker," I say, a safer subject.

"You can never guess how a baby is going to turn out. In one family, two sisters close in age can look like the difference between you and Teenci." I look at him shocked. "True." Hatch says. "Our family has married white people before your mother Jo. Unci had a good marriage to a French trapper, Pierre Angevine."

Unci hears this and smiles sweetly saying, "Pierre," with her Lakota accent.

"Listen Coca Joe, nobody can say how we are going to turn out. You may marry a Lakota boy, and your baby could turn out as Indian-looking as possible, or just like you!"

I poke Hatch in the ribs, smiling. Then, I drop the smile. I ping pong off this warm feeling and have an attack of guilt for sitting here wanting to listen to all this instead of searching for the family I already have, my Chief. My real family has fur, not this brown-red skin that will get us all in trouble if I am seen with them. But ... I want to know more. I've wanted to know my whole life.

I give myself time to recover and start piecing things together again, saying to Hatch, "Your twin sister," letting a tiny smile back on my face.

He picks up a piece of paper and sets it on his lap. "Last night you spoke your mother's name. It flowed from your lips, Cetan." He smiles at me after calling me hawk in Lakota, then takes a breath that expands his chest and keeps going. "My sister's full Lakota name was Cetan Maka Sichu Winyan, meaning Bad Lands Hawk Woman, referring to the hawk-like screeching of her breathing with asthma. Mostly we called her 'Jo' short for Josephine."

He gives me a minute to roll these around on my tongue.

"You were saying Ina, which you know means Mother in Lakota." Hatch will make a good daddy someday. He lets me think about this for as long as I need, practicing and studying the pictures of Jo, Josephine. Ina. Cetan Maka Sichu Winyan. The trap door pops up a bit, knocking against me as I think each of my mother's names.

Somehow he guesses I need a break so he shows the other few photos they have. In the first he wears a uniform of short shorts, a tank top with a big number 7, and a basketball under his arm. His legs are spread and planted. He is frowning at the camera looking tough, hard to do when you are young and handsome. Another photograph shows him in a white dinner jacket and bow tie with a gorgeous blonde date on his arm. "This is Karen Carter. She lives in her home country of England, but she came to America and studied our indigenous culture as part of her university degree. I consider Karen one of my truest friends. She knows Ol' R & R Ernie too!"

I giggle and lean into him teasing, "Love Birds, tweet tweet."

He smiles and says, "Not exactly, but she is a great person. Karen and I are still in touch because we care about each other. She is a television reporter for the United Kingdom, and she travels the globe to bring news stories about difficult situations." I catch him really studying her and nudge him again. He laughs.

I'm ready for more about me.

Hatch brings out a paper next, reading from the top, *Montana State Certificate of Live Birth* and slowly walks me through it. I notice Grandmother has been leaning over staring at me for quite some time.

She interrupts Hatch speaking in Lakota, pointing back and forth between her and me. Hatch nods 'yes' and takes a deep breath.

"Grandmother wants me to tell you that she saw Josephine in your face when she was seated across from you on the train going to Livingston. You had asthma, she said, just like Jo. She saw cetan over the prairie and believed the hawk was a sign that you could be Jo's daughter. Grandmother said your mother's Indian name to you, Cetan Maka Sichu."

"Wait! Wait!" I let the trap door fling wide open now as the realization of everything hits me, this time with joy instead of guilt or tears. "Oh, oh!" I jump up, squeeze past him and run around. "She is MY great grandmother. You are MY great grandmother? Mine!" I yell in joy.

"Yes Coca Joe, she is Tanka Unci," Hatch points to her, "which means your Great Grandmother."

"You are my uncle!" I bounce and jump around, pointing back and forth to them. "You are my family!" I start figuring the rest of it out, telling Hatch that Teenci is my cousin; Nathan and Sue are my uncle and aunt. They are laughing and smiling and Hatch howls like a wolf. "You are something else, Coca Joe."

I smile and sit right next to him, my handsome uncle, and look down at that piece of paper, indicating I'm ready for more.

Hatch laughs and puts his arm around me, giving me a squeeze. Then he picks up the paper and takes a deep breath ready to explain.

"Wait!" I interrupt again. "How did MY great-grandma know I would be on that train? How did we sit across from each other? And how did I get to meet you at the depot, Hatch, when you are my uncle?"

"OK, OK, slow down, just slo-w down. That is a mystery, and a blessing. As a traditional Lakota, I believe it was a gift from Wakan Tanka, the Great Spirit. Perhaps you would say it was a miracle from God. Either way, Indian people do not normally get one of our own back once she becomes lost to us."

"Lost?" My face falls. "You... lost me?"

This hurts Hatch. He furrows his brow, takes a deep breath and says, "There is much to tell you. I will tell it all, but it must be in order. Do you trust me?"

I don't want order. I want to understand everything right now. At the same time, I am afraid to know too much, just like that day when I chased down Ol' R & R Ernie for answers, but didn't have the courage to ask too many questions. I am pulled back and forth between these two wants, just like I'm pulled back and forth between wanting to know more about this new family and wanting to find the one I've always had, Chief. All this tugging inside is a lot to handle. Maybe Hatch realizes this and I should trust him to tell me things the way he wants. Still, being the stubborn girl I am, I don't answer right away. When I'm darn good and ready, I nod my okay.

"First look at this paper, Coca Joe, are you ready?" I nod again and he begins pointing at the names. "My twin sister, Josephine, or Jo, your mommy who gave birth to you, fell in love with this young man when they were both seventeen years old," he points, "Tim Stratmore. Look right here. See this? This is your name."

He points and I read silently, Constance Josephine Stratmore. Hatch lets me look at the paper and read all the names and the dates, mouthing them over and over, especially my own name.

"Constance Josephine Stratmore. Coca Joe Stratmore?" I whisper.

"Your father Tim Stratmore, nicknamed you Coca Joe when you were a newborn, and since you were such a cutie and a little pistol, we all called you that. It just seemed to fit! And there was never a baby more loved than you."

I love the sound of that. "I knew that!" My real family loved me! "That's what I always believed."

"You knew the truth then. Everybody loves you... here." There's that look of concern again, but then Hatch continues with my story. "Tim met Jo when she and I worked at a convenience store in a border town on the edge of the reservation. I watched the whole courtship right before my eyes and it was sweet and powerful; there was no stopping it. My sister had everything a young man would dream of,

like I said, beautiful inside and out, and way smarter than anyone I
know. Tim couldn't help himself. He fell head over heels in love with
her and there was no turning back. Jo had tons of admirers, but he
was the most persistent. And I liked him too, which helped, since he
was not from the reservation." He stops, probably so I can think about
this. I do, but I have not forgotten what he said. I'm waiting to hear
how they lost me.

He starts again. "Tim wanted to learn our Lakota ways because he
seemed to love Jo deeply, and he was at home with us, doing everything
he could to be part of our family. He did many things to make our lives
better and promised to never take Jo away from us. He told me he
wanted to live as part of the tribe and he studied our traditional Lakota
spirit-way. Tim had a special love for Unci and enjoyed practicing
Lakota with her. They were sweet together—he never arrived home
empty-handed—always trying to make Unci giggle. His part-time
job at a lumber store went to full-time and he did well there because
he had a knack for construction. He even bought Grandmother that
television all those many years ago."

He pauses to check in with me. I am still waiting, waiting for the
lost part.

"What I'm telling you, Coca Joe, is that we loved your daddy, all
of us did. He was a friend and we welcomed him as family. He was a
brother to me. It wasn't until right before the wedding... "

"Hatch! Stop!" Because now I need to know. "Where are my
mommy and daddy? What happened to them? How could they
lose me?"

"Shh, Shh, Shh. We'll get through this," he says.

Great-grandmother reaches over and rubs my back, singing a soft
Indian lullaby that is sweet on her voice, even though she's old. It can't
be that I know it, but it seems that maybe I might, there it is... so, so
far back.

Hatch says, "I am going to tell you everything, I promise, but I
need to tell you other things first." I take a deep breath and nod my
head yes. I give him my hand so I can be more patient as he finishes

the story. "Just before the wedding ceremony we found out Tim had kept his parents from knowing about the wedding, because they hate Indians. He was sure they would try to stop him from marrying Jo. But, Tim and Jo were young and believed in love, believed this love could change his parents' minds, and they believed the birth of their first grandchild—you—would turn them towards love."

"So, I have even more grandparents? But they hate me?"

"They wouldn't hate you if they knew you, Coca Joe, that's for sure. Nobody could hate you." I don't tell him that I know different.

"My sister and Tim were just eighteen when you were born. So was I, of course, being her twin." He smiles goofy. "That may sound pretty old to you right now, with so much schooling ahead, but in six years from now you'll be that age. Can you imagine that, Coca Joe?"

I roll my eyes. "Not really, I don't even like boys. And marrying one gives me the heebie-jeebies."

"Right. Well, what I mean is, we were just kids too, not that much older than you. And one thing about older teenagers is that it is hard to change their mind on things."

He pauses to let me think about it. Finally I ask, "So are my Hell Creek parents teaching me right about my adoption, that it took Jo and Tim more love to give me away than to keep me?"

"Nobody here ever gave you away. Never. I loved little-baby-you enough to keep you myself! I promised my family and myself that somehow I would find you. But listen, I am going to tell you everything, I promise I will not leave anything out, but it will be best to tell you bit by bit. You guessed right, there is hard news yet to share, but I do not want to weigh you down with a heavy burden. Yes, there is more to your story, but the most important piece of all is that you were loved so much and now you have been found! Coca Joe Stratmore, you have found your real family and this family is so happy! Be happy over this for a while."

I nod my head slowly, thinking on what he has said. If I am going to take things bit by bit, what is the bit I have? I see he is right. I don't know everything yet, but the part I know is what I've always wanted.

I had a family who loves me and they still love me. I smile first a little and then a lot, grinning from ear to ear. It's not the fake Happy Face either, it's real, real, real.

Hatch says, "You found us, and we found you. So to me Coca Joe, you were never lost, you were waiting to be found."

Warmth settles my tightened middle, releases the clinching. I've carried these hard things around inside me a long time. I've worried that those with 'more love' threw me away somehow, like trash, like a leftover. But I'm learning that 'more love' never stopped looking for me, never stopped wanting me. I didn't do anything wrong. I'm innocent. What if for a moment, I really stop struggling and try to trust Hatch? I can always take it back later. But right now, what if I let myself be... what if I am... Waiting To Be Found? That could have been my Indian name. Coca Joe Waiting-To-Be-Found. Except now it could be shortened to Coca Joe Found.

I let myself go then and snuggle into Hatch. I breathe in found. Found. Found.

18
GRAVEYARD

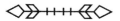

"It sounds like our search party is arriving."

Cars pull up outside and Hatch tells me it's time to go searching for Chief. He says he has a clear plan to finish my story later, if that would be all right with me. I decide it will be a lot easier to hear with Chief by my side, and I am so hopeful and eager that I hop up. "Let's go find Chief! If you can find me, we can find him!"

Hatch smiles and pats me on the back.

When I get to the front door, I'm surprised to see how many cars and people have gathered there. I stop in the doorway, with Hatch behind me.

"Are all these people helping us look?" I ask. I can't imagine so many strangers taking the time to help me look for my dog. They don't even know me. "Why?"

"Chief is your family," Hatch answers, "and is more important than anything to you. To the Lakota, our four-leggeds are family too. We will always take the time to help find a missing family member."

I chew on this as I start walking again. This makes me feel like I must have Indian in me, even more than the resemblances I saw in the photographs. My adopted family never understood just how important Chief is to me, but the Indians seem to know this just as well as I do.

Out at the cars I'm introduced, and Hatch has me give a detailed description of Chief. I can go on and on about him, so Hatch has to help me wrap it up. He leads me to a car where Teenci is already in the backseat. He introduces me to the driver, Henry, saying that nobody is a more reliable friend—with a car—than Henry. They smile at the joke, and Henry teases back, saying that if Hatch had any clue what was under the hood he could have his own car too. They are obvious friends, with Henry seeming about Hatch's age. His wry smile looks like he can be quite a joker and his wiry build seems like he'd be comfortable working under the hood of a car. Henry and Hatch slap each other's back and laugh as I join Teenci in the back seat. She and I smile at each other.

Henry's car doesn't purr as it takes off, it coughs. Riding in a car on rez roads is so bumpy, I scold myself for dreading this long ride back to the border area where we're going to search, because it will be worth it. I just know we are going to find Chief.

After many miles I spot a brown and white Pinto horse with an Indian rider seeming to fly. Teenci says excitedly that it's Tommy White Hawk, and Henry honks, saying Tommy corrals some of their horses not too far from here. He stops the car, calling Tommy over to his window. Tommy's smile is wide as he trots our way and his looks are not even fair to normal guys. Maybe other girls wouldn't like him, but I do, and I blush. Teenci leans out her open window smiling back. I'm on the far side, and he doesn't seem to notice I'm here.

He comes right up next to the car and stops. Thank God Tommy is at Henry's window and high enough on the horse that I can't see his face anymore. I suspect he can't see me either, and I'm glad because I'm dying of embarrassment. His shirt isn't on! And he's got quite a build for a kid. After Tommy says hello, Henry says that we are looking for a lost collie dog. Tommy says he heard about that from Sue and was told the collie belongs to a girl he used to know.

Teenci notices my nervous antics and bright red cheeks but keeps quiet. I'm back here with a crush the size that can kill you. I slink to the floor to hide behind the seat back.

Henry notices me, chuckles, and asks Tommy how he knew the girl Coca Joe Stratmore. Oh, these prying, teasing Indians!

Tommy admits that he fell in love with my pale blue eyes when he was a little toddler and that he used to stare at them wondering how the sky got in there. I cover my face but keep listening. Tommy laughs, saying to Teenci that she was there too as a baby and that it all sounds like a silly story now. Henry coaxes him to tell it, no doubt egging Tommy on because Tommy still doesn't know I'm in the car. He continues, saying that he never stopped wanting to see those blue eyes again, and that he blames his parents and Hatch for their non-stop teasing and even encouragement to never forget Coca Joe Stratmore and her sky blue eyes. The next thing Tommy says makes me almost speak up, that Hatch told him he saw Coca Joe at the Livingston train depot and that everyone was trying to figure out how to get her back to the family again.

Henry turns around to see I am redder than any beet. He asks Tommy, did you know she's on the rez?

Tommy responds by yanking the reins back, maybe by accident but the Pinto slightly rears and tosses its head. "Whoa! Well I hope to be the one to find her dog then!" and he leans into the horse that is already taking off. I crane my neck to watch the rider who is so easy-going on that horse. They leave a beautiful impression that still has me blushing.

"Was he pulling our leg? Doesn't he know I am on the rez?" I croak. Henry and Teenci are still laughing at Tommy's reaction and quick departure and laugh again at me. As he starts driving again, Henry says that Tommy's parents are well known for their sense of humor and that Tommy sure takes after them. Teenci giggles. Then he adjusts the rearview mirror on Teenci and asks her jokingly if Tommy seems a bit love struck if he believes he'll find the dog around here.

Teenci answers yep, then studies me, taking in my ragamuffin hairdo and my shirt still twisted from hiding behind the seat. "Are you going to be okay?"

My flush returns and I hide my face in my hands, avoiding her question. "Where do you think his shirt is?" She says that it's common for guys not to wear shirts around here. I keep my face covered until I think it's a normal color.

We finally reach the long fingers of rez land that stretch into white territory, following the path of that windy, windy Big Sandy Creek. Now that we're close to where Chief may have gone, Henry slows down and we all call out our windows for Chief. Calling for him helps me feel like myself again. Henry keeps the pace pretty slow, but it's hard to search for Chief without reaming my neck or bonking my head. At least calling for him feels good because my stomach doesn't like the ride.

My nerves don't much care for it either. After more miles and different roads with no sign of Chief, I have a nagging feeling that won't go away. Henry turns the car around, saying that Hatch requested everyone to return to Unci's by lunch to see if Chief has been found. I'm afraid to know if he has or not. I don't know how much longer I can go on without finding him. I force myself to think of something else, and my mind lands on Tommy. I beg Teenci and Henry to keep their mouths shut about him, especially to Hatch. They giggle, both agreeing that Hatch knows all about Tommy's feelings for the blue-eyed-baby and that Tommy is right, Hatch is part of the reason Tommy has feelings for me. I'm embarrassed again but think I might be a little excited too. Teenci says that pretty much every girl on the rez knows that Tommy hasn't had eyes for anyone else. Yet.

"That's stupid. I was a baby when I was adopted."

"Almost a year old, I remember," Henry says, "but anyway, sometimes love can't be stopped at any age."

"Love? What is this, some sort of ancient Indian romance for babies?"

They laugh as Henry says, "Pretty much!" But they swear they won't say a word.

We go from Henry's car into a house full of Indian men, many of them big compared to the men I'm used to. I catch Hatch's eyes and give him an obvious questioning look of hope. He shakes his head no.

My head drops as I go to the kitchen table to listen since all the space is taken in the main room. Different men give their report. They talked to quite a few citizens near the border, but they have no leads so far. The nagging feeling that I felt in the car grows stronger. Chief isn't here. He wasn't near the farm or along the river. He hasn't shown up at home. Oh where is my Chief?

Then I realize something. If he's made his way back home, but isn't at home, well then there's only one other place he would be.

Hatch tells the group that at least we aren't getting word that Chief has been found dead and that as long as we don't get that, we can still have hope.

"We will keep looking," a short-haired, bespectacled man says.

"No," I say, because I think I know where he is. "Chief is in the badlands near Hell Creek."

Hatch blinks at me. "You think?"

"Yes," I say, feeling more and more sure the more I think about it. "Since no one is seeing him around I think he went to our home away from home in the badlands."

Hatch says, "Well, we don't know for sure. He could have ended up in the badlands between the farm and Hell Creek. I wonder if he would know the difference."

I don't want to argue with him in front of his friends, but I feel a strong pull to my badlands home. "He'll know. I want to look there next." Somehow I have the faith of the mustard seed, that nothing is impossible, even in finding Chief. My badlands home makes me think of how Chief and I would get there by jumping into the backyard coulee from my family at home. I push the thought away. I am not going to think about that family. Not now.

"Well," Hatch says, thinking. "That'll take a bit more planning, but we'll come up with something. You may be right."

Hatch invites everyone to some stew and bread that Aunt Sue made. It sounds good. I eat until I hear that it's rabbit stew, then I don't. I'm not used to that.

The people don't linger. Hatch says he's got a few important things to do before he can arrange our search for Chief in the badlands. I grab his sleeve and look in his eyes. "Promise we will be searching soon?" I ask.

"Promise," he says, and the way he says it settles me. Unlike the adult promises I'm used to, I know Hatch will keep this one. I remember I've decided to trust him and think that's still a good plan. Besides, if Chief is in our badlands waiting for me, I'm not as worried he'll get into trouble. He'll be there for me. I know it.

Hatch says he needs to run over to Nathan's for a quick minute, and that when he gets back he wants to take me somewhere important. This gives me some time to show that I have been raised with some manners, and I get to washing and drying the dishes with Teenci. When Sue sees that we have the dishes under control, she says to Teenci, "See you later Daughter. I better go act like I have a job, since I do." From the door, Sue turns to smile, and she includes me in her gaze.

Teenci and I don't say much, but she does like to flip soap bubbles at me to get a response so I give her one, scooping a handful and blowing bubbles in her face. When Hatch returns from Nathan's he sees us playing and I watch as his entire body relaxes on the spot. I guess I hadn't noticed the toll all this is taking on him.

Since our talk about Jo and Tim, my mom and dad, and since seeing my birth certificate, I've had things rolling around the back of my mind waiting for the rest of the truth of where they are. Now Hatch is walking me somewhere important. At first I wonder if it's to see my Ina at last until he says we're going to a special place to talk through the rest of my beginning. I'm a little disappointed, but still glad I'll get to hear more about my story, now that I'm feeling ready again, and I'm relieved to be moving on the land. Tanka Unci sent us off with a Lakota prayer and venison jerky.

We walk away from the hubbub of reservation life, which goes from quiet to noisy, back and forth like a fat fly buzzing around a house.

The breeze feels like it does at home, always there, soft or strong. Songs from a meadowlark sing over the other bird songs around us. The meadowlark is my favorite. We climb to the top of a bluff, scooped like a wave near the top. Hatch turns around to point out a large, forked body of water. I close my eyes to take the beauty into memory. I can still see it with my eyes closed.

Hatch says, "There is the dam. Most reservations have a dam."

I open my eyes to look. "Why?"

"To revoke what was promised to Indians in the U.S. treaties of the 1800s, which said this land is our Indian land as long as the river flows and the eagle flies. A dam causes the river not to flow. In this way treaties are broken and new treaties are written so more land can be taken. It was our land to begin with, so treaties of old made little sense anyway.

"Look around at the sky, the clouds, the river, the prairie as far as your eye can see. You can even make out the badlands on the south-eastern border of the rez."

I'm listening but out of habit when he says the word badlands I catch myself patting my leg for Chief to come to me. He's not coming. I'm gonna go to him. I am!

Hatch continues, "To me, as an Indian, the land is my very skin, and my blood is in the rock, not because my ancestors died here, which they did, but because I am alive here on this land. I think you understand this and already know these words to be true."

I think about what I learned about Indians in school, not much, which means I didn't learn much about me, about the Indian me. My schooling has taught me about only one Indian, Sacagawea, who traveled these very waters with her baby Pomp to help Lewis and Clark, long before the dam. Now I'm traveling this same land to discover the history of baby-me, an Indian of mixed blood just like baby Pomp, who had an Indian mother and a white father.

We cross more of the bluff before Hatch speaks again. "After Tim and Jo married, they settled into the house with Grandmother. You were born and were the pride and joy of our family. We would all fight to hold you! We watched your thick black hair go fair and your eyes turn from gray to pale blue. Like I showed you, you look just like your daddy on the top part of your face but the rest of your face is from your mommy Jo. Your build and the way you move is all her too. And before you chopped it off, you had the thick, long hair of your mama in the color of your papa's. Great Creator gave you all the best parts of your parents."

I smile. I never paid that much attention to myself. I've never been this interesting to anybody else before. I'm just me, a regular girl.

"I am getting to the sad part now, okay, because we are close to where I want to take you."

I don't know if I'm ready to hear. I thought I'd have Chief with me for this part, whatever it's going to be.

Hatch explains that one day long ago Jo's asthma wound tighter than a drum and it wouldn't respond to any of the medicine.

I stop and grab Hatch's forearm, letting out a small whimper. I don't want to hear the rest of what's coming! I know all about asthma not responding to medicine. Hatch takes both of my hands and holds them to his chest. This brings me close to him, so instead of panicking and running away I rest my head on him, ready to burst into tears. He continues the story in a whisper above my head.

"Yellow Bird, the Wichasha Wakan, the holy medicine man, blended the plants and teas that always healed her before. He held a purifying sweat and pipe ceremony with our family to unwind the lungs and put the wind back in them. Jo was also taking her medicine from the health clinic. For reasons nobody can understand, nothing worked to stop the asthma from growing worse. In the middle of the night, after she was wheezing so hard nobody in the house could sleep, they called an ambulance. Sometimes they are slow about coming to the reservation, but eventually they did come to rush her to the hospital."

Hatch stops, lets go of my hands, and wraps his arms around me. "I am sorry to have to tell you this Coca Joe. She died before they could save her."

"I—eee!" I cry out, shoving Hatch's chest but he doesn't let go. "No! No! No!"

No! No! I need her to save me! I need her! She loved me and now she's gone and can't help me. For reasons I can't understand, I'm mad at Hatch. I beat on his chest with both fists, crying out like a wild animal. I shove him and he drops his arms and lets me push him back again and again. "It's your fault!" I scream in his face. "You should have saved her!"

This gives him a pained look that makes me feel badly, but I can't stop.

"I need my mother! I need her! I need her!" And then the anger runs clean out of me and I am nothing but heartache. I drop to my knees and bury my face in my hands on this land so used to tears.

Hatch sits cross-legged beside me and gently strokes my back saying words of comfort. I let him and I let myself cry out a river for my lost mother.

It takes awhile before I sit up and for the ragged breaths to settle. Hatch doesn't hurry me. I take a deep breath and let my eyes travel over the land. In the close distance, in the middle of this wide prairie bluff, with no signs, or paths, or even a fence around it, is a grouping of graves.

The sight makes me lean against Hatch and cry some more, because now I know we were going to see my Ina after all.

"When you are ready I'll show you where your mother is buried," Hatch says, warm and kind. "It does not have to be today." I'm not the kind that wants to get anywhere near graves. Hatch senses my hesitation and says I don't need to get any nearer to be with her ancestor spirit. That scares me a bit but I'm with Hatch, so I know I don't need to be afraid. That's a real good thing to know about someone.

We sit there for a while longer, and I like that Hatch lets me be silent and thinking. When I tell him I want to see my mother, he gets up, offers his hand, and leads me into the plain graveyard. When we get to the simple cross that marks her grave, Hatch explains that the tribe felt it could have built a large stone memorial, but nothing would ever be enough to show the love and respect felt for her. She was a young woman rich with gifts in spirit, mind, and heart. She was unique in young women because she followed the traditional ways of the Lakota as best she could, even though it was dangerous, and she honored her elders, but she was also a modern day Indian. Hatch says, "We were both raised like this and I still straddle both worlds."

We take time to talk about how she loved me and how much she would love the girl I turned out to be, and about how much fun we would have had. And then, after all that, there's more disappointment coming. Because now I ask about my daddy, Tim, whose name sounds funny coming through my plugged nose from all this crying..

"I am going to take you to meet him." I'm surprised by this and must look it too because Hatch nods to assure me what he's saying is true. "Right, Coca Joe. This is something I've planned to tell you today. Ol' R & R Ernie has gotten him ready."

After learning the hard truth about my mother, I'm afraid to know the truth about my daddy. But I've discovered Hatch is a strong, safe person to tell me hard truths and I trust him more and more all the time. "Ready? Is he … is he sick too?"

"In a way, that is a good way to think of it. He never recovered when Jo died. And he has had a tough go of it since losing you too."

"You can't just lose a baby!" I still don't understand this, but there is just so much a person can take at once. If Hatch feels he has to wait to explain it to me, maybe I don't want to know the answers right now.

"It doesn't seem like you can, but we did. You disappeared from our lives."

Hatch tells me that after Jo died, Tim couldn't handle living with himself. For some reason he blamed himself for her death even though it was not his fault, and he turned his face away from everything, even from me, his baby. Unci and the other mothers, especially Aunt Sue, made sure I was cared for and loved. Hatch says that in many ways it was like both my daddy and mommy died together.

"But he isn't dead?"

"No. He is alive and you will meet him soon."

"But he is sick?"

"Coca Joe, you might not know this but for some people when problems come, or pain, or the circumstances of life hurts them, they turn against their own self and hurt themselves even worse. Like, when things go bad, and then more things go bad, they stop believing that good things will ever come again. Does that make sense to you?"

"You mean, like, when things are bad you think you're bad?" I ask.

"Yes. You think you are bad. And you live like you are bad."

"Oh no! He did a very, very bad thing? What did he do?" I'm frightened enough to plug my ears to not hear what he says. Hatch was right to tell me my story in bits. I'm finding even the small bites hard to swallow.

Hatch gently brings my hands down and into his. I mutter, "He's in jail, isn't he?" I talk to the ground, guessing the worst thing I can think of.

"No. He is a drunk. He became someone with nothing left to live for."

"But didn't he have me?"

Hatch nods. "I will explain." He tells me that after Jo died Tim saw how people swooned over me, seeming charmed by his baby, and he got the idea that his parents would do the same. Tim decided that since I didn't look Indian since the thick black hair I was born with had faded, and my skin was warm cream, and my eyes were pale blue like his—like his own father's—maybe his parent's hearts would open again to loving Tim and his almost one-year-old daughter. He believed they would welcome their son back home since his Lakota wife had passed away and because he had their grandbaby. And they did.

Hatch suggests we start walking back to the house since we'll be leaving for the badlands soon to look for Chief. As we walk Hatch says that Tim and I went to live at his parents' house and that he brought me to the reservation for visits. "Do you remember anything from that time in your life, Coca Joe? I know you were just a baby, but I was wondering if you have any memories?"

I think about being a baby. So far I have remembered the Lakota word for Mother—Ina—and think I might have remembered the lullaby Unci sang. All of a sudden I am attacked by fear. I back up and this fear shows.

"What's wrong Coca Joe?" Hatch says.

"I'm scared."

"I see that. Did you remember something?"

"No. I'm just really, really scared."

"Come here." And I disappear in his big arms.

"Hatch. Something's wrong. Something bad is going to happen!"

"It already did, Coca Joe." He holds me but my fear keeps building.

Hatch says from a worn out, sad place in his voice, "I'm so sorry, Coca Joe."

"Wha-t, Hatch? Tell me."

"Somehow Coca Joe—" He chokes up, then starts again. "You were stolen." A cold chill climbs my back to my neck. "One day Tim stopped at the convenience store to buy something and he says he only left you for a couple minutes in the car, but in those minutes you were taken. Tim did not know who took you, he had no idea."

Still in his arms, I look up and stare at Hatch with red eyes itching under puffy lids.

"So, I was just... gone? Forever?"

I'm trying to understand. I think maybe I could if that baby wasn't me.

"Didn't anybody try to get me back?" I push away from him, mad again, and tearing. "You just lost me and that's that?"

"Oh Coca Joe, of course we did. And if we thought we could take a war party out to get you back we would have! We did do everything we could, we searched for you, talked to everyone we knew about how you could have disappeared, we sought wisdom from our tribal council and our medicine men and women, and we had ceremonies to receive visions to see where you might have gone. Our family and much of the tribe grieved over you. Tanka Unci never stopped watching for you in that special spirit-way that she sees."

They did search, just like I'm searching for Chief now. But they didn't find me. I feel real fear that I might not find my dog, but even that is not enough to overpower the fear from knowing I was stolen. Stolen. Who stole me? Why would they do that? It seems too horrible to believe and I want to push it away, but it stays and stays.

"Couldn't *anyone* find out where I went?"

With all my might I'm looking for a hero.

"Nothing for sure could be found out even with the help of a lawyer within the white man legal system. Indian children have been abducted and adopted out from the reservation for nearly a hundred years and with adoptions of any kind nobody messes around. Babies are protected. Adoption records are sealed tight, never to be opened again. And they rewrite your birth certificate."

Hatch takes a deep breath and we walk a few paces in silence. "After all that, Tim became someone with nothing left to live for. He was a young man, a kid really, who lost his wife and his baby. Because he was my sister's husband and a friend to the tribe, we welcomed him back to us. But we were all angry, very angry, and terribly heartbroken at not having you with us. You and Jo, both gone so quickly. Tim turned to alcohol to hide from his sadness, and now he's sick from it. Very sick, drunk a lot of the time."

I stare at the ground, all the fight gone out of me.

"I am sorry, Coca Joe," Hatch says again. "But we are so grateful to have you back at last."

"You were looking for me." I state facts that better be true. It is the only comfort I have in the sad story of my adoption.

"Always."

The wind blows through and we listen for a while as we walk, then Hatch says, "Tim is coming to the reservation now with Ernie. He would like to meet you if that is all right?"

"Um, I guess." What saving can a drunk daddy do? None of this has gone as I thought it would. I am comforted that I have Hatch, at least, but I need Chief now more than ever. All of a sudden, I'm impatient to get back to searching for him. He's waiting for me in our badlands, I know it. I need to hurry up and get there!

"I spoke with Ernie on the phone last time I was at Nathan's," Hatch says, "and not just about him driving Tim up here…"

"Driving? That ol' hobo has a car?" Yes, I'm feeling ornery now. I don't like my story and it's coming out.

"I told you that ol' hobo is not just a hobo, he is more than…"

"Anyway, so?" I interrupt feeling irritated about all these talks going on behind my back. I don't like it. Not one bit!

"Anyway, I needed to talk to Ernie to get his help to search for Chief in the badlands around Hell Creek. It won't be safe for you to be seen with an Indian so close to town, understand?"

"Well, who says you have to be with me? Who says anyone does? I can search all by myself and you can't stop me! You have no right to keep me here or anywhere."

"No," Hatch says soberly, "we will never keep you anywhere against your will. It will always be your choice."

"You're darn right it will."

Hatch is wise to me though. He lets me try to cool down. It takes going almost all the way to the end of the bluff to do it, too. He starts to talk again, explaining their plan to find Chief. He actually asks me if I will agree to their plan of having Ernie drive me to the badlands and help me look. I'm glad he's figured out who's boss!

I make sure Hatch can't see me rolling my eyes, though. Sure, Ernie can take me, but I'll be leaving Ernie in the dust first chance I get. Just watch me. I'm feeling hot under the collar again. All of a sudden, I know why. Now that I have it figured out, I really start to boil. "But Hatch, when you first saw me at the depot and I *told* you my name was Coca Joe Stratmore, why didn't you try to get me back then?"

Hatch kneels down, places his gentle hands on my shoulders, and says fervently, "Every single part of me wanted to grab you and *run*. Finally after all these years we had you right there talking to us! But we could not make even the slightest inappropriate suggestion or move your way or we three Indians probably would have been jailed right then! I don't want to add burden to you Coca Joe, but we felt terrible not to be able to bring you home with us. And it was not easy to find out where you lived. We did not know where you boarded the train and we had no real name for you. But with Ernie's help, we started figuring your whereabouts. He went to where you lived to find out for sure if that was your home."

I think of the Ol' R & R Ernie, the old hobo on the couch in our home, and I remember what he said to my dad, that he knew about his girl. I still have his silver dollar in my pocket. I feel myself almost getting blown over from all this truth. Instead I catch myself and take some deep breaths until I stand strong.

"You know what Hatch?" I say forcefully, "I'm gonna find Chief today and I'm gonna *blow* you guys off like dust! And I'm calling myself Sister of the Wind when I do. That's gonna be my new name, my Indian name, and you all better watch out."

"The wind has no sisters," Hatch says simply, trying to take the wind out of me.

"Well the wind has a sister now!" I need to start gusting to make it through this big heap of trouble.

"Tate Tanksi, huh?"

"Tah-tay Tunk-shee? What's that?"

"Sister Wind in Lakota. But really Coca Joe, there is no such thing in our stories."

"There is now."

I blow at him with all my might. He pretends to be blown backwards onto the ground, letting all his air out and his face faking fear.

I stand over him hands on my hips. "See? Sister of the Wind blew you over. Don't cross me."

He sits up and rubs the smile off his face. "I see, Tate Tanksi, I see. Nobody will cross you."

19
THE BOARDING HOUSE

Knower has his nose in the record books. He's looking for Her earliest years when She was a newborn baby. There aren't any records of the Lakota or any other tribe of Indians. There's no record of Her first year at all. Somehow a book has been misplaced! Knower puts the record books in order from the beginning to now, doesn't find it, then looks in all the nooks and crannies of his desk to see if somehow there could be a record book missing. Where are Jo and Tim, Hatch and Unci?

Knower was the first resident of The Boarding House. As the historian he keeps track of every resident and every job they accomplish, but he also keeps impeccable records of everything that has ever happened in Her life. The Indians are missing. How can that be?

He could talk to Katrina about it because she is wise for her age, but Katrina wasn't around when She was a baby. Katrina came into being after She got a special doll.

Other essential residents in The Boarding House are deeply wise, or extraordinary negotiators, or protectors of Her spiritual core, and each one is key to Her survival against the horrors, but they must not be disturbed. One resident is so ancient and has such a crucial job, he has a wife to care for him. His knowledge is vast, so he would know the answer to Knower's question. But he must not be awakened.

Quite a few of the residents have been watching along with Knower and Katrina. Watcher With Owl seem a bit on guard. Owl keeps fluttering her wings but not taking off from Watcher's shoulder. Name Schmame is pacing in front of the revolving door and listening closely. Even though there are not the usual reasons to spring into action, Her tensions and emotions have stirred up The Boarding House. Gangster and The Babe have come up from their room under the house and are taking an interest in hearing about Her early beginnings, but the Tommy Gun is not cocked and ready. There is no need.

While the residents don't expect to be needed for their usual jobs, they sense changes are happening and are not sure what to make of them.

Knower reaches exasperation. He feels he needs to understand things. He asks Jesus into The Boarding House from his place of peace and prayer under the weeping willow beside the brook. A white horse grazes nearby and Jesus runs a hand along him as he walks past. The horse lifts his head and shakes his luxurious mane, a thing of beauty catching the sunlight.

Once Jesus is inside, Knower asks him, "Why are the Lakota Indians not in the record books?"

Jesus asks, "Are you worried She doesn't belong to them?"

"Yes! Yes! I rely on the historical records of Her life and the Lakota are not in here!" Knower is embarrassed that he's so worked up but he feels someone should protect Her from any untruths about Her early beginnings.

Jesus says, "I am Her first family. She is of me. I adopted Her first, so most importantly She is mine."

"Yes, yes, I know," Knower says anxiously, "but I have no record of the Indians. I have no record of her first year at all." Knower is ashamed to admit this failing of his duties, but Jesus answers gently.

"Have you considered it is because I didn't create The Boarding House until after She was taken and given to Them?"

"That would make sense," Knower says thoughtfully, considering for the first time that there may truly be things he does not Know.

"Maybe that is why there are no Indians living in The Boarding House."

Jesus answers simply, "There is. When She is resting in Her Safe Place."

20
DRUNKARD

Hatch and I have been walking away from the graveyard and are now in view of their small village. We both leap off the curling wave-shaped bluff above the houses. Nimble feet land like Indians—like me! We chuckle at this shared grace. It seems a month of talking has passed since this morning so it's good to act light-hearted.

Once we are in the neighborhood, Hatch sees an old Indian man outside a one-room log cabin. He walks towards him and says, "Zitkala Zi," dropping his head in respect. I imagine I can see a spirit form within the man's body, which is weird because I can't. They speak in Lakota, serious sounding and long-winded.

As if just noticing me, the old Indian turns to give me his full attention and my knees buckle. Not just saying that either, they buckle for real! Hatch reaches to hold me upright, but the old Indian motions a gentle no and somehow I am still standing. His dark brown eyes travel deep into mine, not like he's searching for something, more like he's found it and is paying it a long visit. I don't feel frightened, even though this is new to me. He places a hand on my shoulder. When he removes it I'm leaning forward as if into a strong wind.

Then just like nothing happened at all, Hatch shakes his hand and we walk onward. Hatch explains that Yellow Bird, or Zitkala Zi, is a revered holy man, not only for the Lakota, but to many tribes. He is

Tanka Unci's brother and great uncle to my mother Jo and Hatch, so I am related to Yellow Bird by blood also. He is my great-great Uncle. I feel especially blessed right now, which is good timing. I stood against his strong wind so maybe I am this new name I call myself, Sister of the Wind.

Once we are at Unci's house and I see Ol' R & R Ernie and Tim Stratmore haven't arrived yet, I ask Hatch if we have to wait for them, wanting to go find Chief now with no more stupid delays! I'm agitated and pushy again but Hatch is kind and won't budge. I remind him that I am prepared to head out on my own and he reminds me that I'll get to Chief much faster in a car that will be arriving soon.

I huff. Hatch is a good match for me, but I won't tell him that. Since I'm stuck waiting anyway, I ask Hatch more about my dad. He says Tim lives mostly at the Jungle, the hobo camp, and that he sobers up for a while to plant or hoe the beet fields. He explains that's where he found him again after many years when Hatch posed as a migrant worker to earn some cash in the fields too.

Hatch says, "Tim got used to thinking the bottle is his only friend."

"I'll bet it is," I say, bitter.

Hatch quiets his voice. "When he stops drinking he cannot stop the memories of you and Jo."

I grumble, "I probably saw him that first night I ran away to find Chief."

"Did you?"

"Maybe. At the Jungle. Scruffy. Filthy. He wouldn't know I was there. The others seemed used to him. He toppled over from drunkenness." I feel blown over myself when I think a guy like this might be my dad. I'm nothing like Sister of the Wind now.

"Sounds like one of the ways Tim can be."

"If I'm finding a new dad, I don't want that one!"

Hatch doesn't let me pick this fight so I try another one, asking Hatch why Nathan has a phone but he doesn't, saying that everyone in Hell Creek has a phone. I don't ruffle so much as one feather though because, as calm as can be, Hatch explains that since Sue is a nurse on the rez people need to get a hold of her. Not done yet, I ask why we used the Trading Post phone before instead of Sue's, and Hatch says because Sue's phone is not his and besides he needed groceries. I say he should get his own phone but he says since he lives at Unci's house she has to be someone who wants a phone but Unci is not someone who wants a telephone ringing. Hatch explains very few people on the reservation have telephones, they have horses or cars to ride over to talk to whoever they want. I don't see that Hatch has a horse, or a car, or a phone, so what's he talking about?

Tanka Unci, my great-grandmother—*mine!*—slowly shuffles from her room down the short hallway and over to me. In the time that it took her to do this, and as I watch her sweet, old face, the hardness I was trying to place over my heart melts away. She looks at me as deeply as Yellow Bird. I place her gnarled hand in mine and caress it, feeling fresh tears stream down my face. No, I am not Sister of the Wind at all now. My shoulders heave from a cry that makes no sound. All these feelings roll into one gigantic ball and I'm afraid it might crush me. As I stand there all tucked into her love, here and now, everything starts to settle down inside me. I let her lead me to the couch and she sits with me patting my hand. I am grateful we speak this heart language since we don't share each other's words.

"Tommy!" Hatch says as I jump out of my skin. He hurries to the door and they greet with the one-arm man hug around the back, squeezing and jostling each other's shoulders.

"Coca Joe Stratmore, this is my tonska, my nephew, Tommy Cetan Ska, or Tommy White Hawk. Tommy, this is the blue-eyed baby that has come home to us!"

I've popped up from the couch but I don't leave it in case my knees go weak.

Tommy's face matches mine, eyes wide with a blush that makes his red-brown skin red-red. We're both stuck this way until he says under his breath, "Coca Joe Stratmore."

"You're wearing your shirt," my nerves blurt out. Somehow my boy-crazy best friend Frankie has taken over my body and is making it tingle in weird places.

He laughs a surprised laugh, "Have we met?"

"Sorta." He looks puzzled. "Saw you on your horse when we were looking for my dog Chief. So, is Hatch your uncle?" I gotta ask. It's every which way of wrong to have a crush this size on a relative.

"No. Hatch is my honorary uncle in the Lakota way," Tommy says. "He's been a good teacher and he's like family to me, so I call him uncle and he calls me nephew." I never heard of this before—so much new Indian stuff. Hatch watches us intently. I drag fingers through my hair to hope to make a difference and press them down my shirt, tucking the loose parts into my jeans.

Thankfully Hatch draws Tommy's attention by turning to talk to him. Whew! This brings new meaning to the phrase "ending my time in the hot seat." I fall back on the couch again with Unci. She leans forward to study my face but I look the other way. She nudges me with her elbow. My eyes fly open giving her a warning and she giggles quietly.

To my relief Tommy doesn't stay long. At the door he turns to say, "Mitakuye Oyasin," something Hatch taught me means we are all related. We hear this a lot on the rez. I try to say it back to Tommy as best I can.

He looks right at me and smiles that same big smile I saw when he was sitting on his beautiful horse. "Hope to see you around, Blue-eyes." He is so flirty I don't even respond. I can't. I'm tongue tied for the first time since my life began.

Once he shuts the door, I grab my stomach of butterflies and slump over. How will I live through these reactions I can't control? Will my cheeks light on fire? Will my stomach fly off? I'm grateful when Hatch turns to business, asking me to get my knapsack ready for the trip into the badlands because he imagines Ernie and Tim will be here soon to pick us up.

I've got my hopes pinned on finding Chief today, and as I pack, another set of mixed signals start showing up in my body. I can't wait to get out the door. I can't wait! But finding my dog means I've got to meet my real dad first. I'm getting colder and colder feet about him. Another fear pops in. I'm getting cold feet about going home to Hell Creek, even with Chief going home with me. Seems stupid. Why would that be? I do feel comfort being here with Hatch and Unci, my relatives, my new-old family. Even the idea of seeing my old hobo friend Ol' R & R Ernie is a comfort. I take the silver dollar from my pocket and study its beauty. There's something special about Ernie that can't be explained, at least not by me. I've gotten all turned around on this short journey. People I've been taught to hate or stay clean away from, like hobos and Indians, are now my friends. And even family.

My thoughts are interrupted by the sound of a car pulling up. I go out into the living room, a ball of nerves, and stand next to Hatch for strength. But instead of seeing Ol' R & R like I expected, it's *another* set of strangers arriving at the house. Now what? I duck behind Hatch to keep me from mowing them over out of impatience to get to my dog!

"Hey, Ol' R & R! You are a handsome sight!" exclaims Hatch.

Huh? I didn't see my hobo friend. I'm about to peek around Hatch when I'm the one mowed over and into the arms of a stranger with familiar laughing eyes. I pull my face back and struggle out of his arms.

"It's me, Coca Joe! It's yer ol' buddy Ernie!"

I'm speechless. Ernie is clean-shaven and shorn, wearing a nice suit and good shoes. He doesn't even look as old! I join them in a laugh even though mine is tinny from nerves.

Ernie straightens up tall. "Coca Joe, I got som'un special for ya ta meet," says Ernie, who steps away so I'm looking at the other stranger. I can see now that I'm looking at an older Tim Stratmore from the photograph. He gives me a shy smile. I gawk. He walks toward me holding out a hand to shake mine. I don't move. We stare at each other. I'm still in shock. He drops his hand.

Everybody seems frozen in time. Tim smiles sweetly. "Hi Coca Joe."

I keep staring trying to think of what to do or say. Finally I say, "H-ha-hand-some." I meant to say hi, it wasn't what I planned, but this breaks the ice into chuckles.

There he is. This is my dad. *My Dad.* All those years of wondering, searching city sidewalks, and longing for my parents and here he is. All those times I told the made up story about my dad being a big, burly miner who was nice but dumb, this dad is not him. And this dad isn't the hunched over drunk I saw before either. I figured dirt and grime would still be stuck on him, and I guess I figured he'd look like death warmed over, but he's scrubbed clean and even nice looking. He's well-groomed, wearing new clothes, nothing fancy like Ernie, but nice gentlemen's clothes.

And there they are—right in front of me, staring—my pale blue eyes. I don't know how people who belong to each other ever get used to seeing something of theirs on another person.

I always wanted to know how it feels to see someone you belong to in real life. It feels weird. Really weird. I take Hatch's hand, pulling into him as my protector.

My face hasn't changed. I'm still staring. Tim shrinks, pulling his shoulders in and head down. Wanting your real daddy is one thing. Getting him is a whole 'nother.

Tim puts his head in his hands and weeps. I look at Hatch like I've done something bad and worrisome, my forehead is scrunched and my mouth turns down. Ernie moves to Tim to put a hand on his shoulder. What can be said? I'm feeling terrible.

"I loved you," Tim says between sobs. "You were the best thing to ever happen to me and Jo. And you always will be—the very best thing—ever. And I see... ." Ernie shoves a handkerchief into Tim's hand, and he blows his nose and dries his eyes. Tim takes a shuddery breath. "I sure do see your mother in you."

I can't think of what to say. I have the excuse of being a kid.

I offer up one word: "Chief!"

This breaks the guys into laughter when it shouldn't, but it does. I move to the door. I'm not waiting a minute longer. It's already more than I can handle without my dog. That ping pong back and forth I've been feeling between this new family and my old one—Chief—drops to the ground and stays there. I'm ashamed of myself for getting distracted by this family I don't even know and abandoning the one I know and love best: Chief. Well, I'm not doing anything else but finding my dog, and that's that. They can talk me a new ear if they want to afterward, if I'm of a mind to let them. Right now, the only thing I'll let myself care about is Chief.

I go out and wait on the porch. Parked out front is a nice Oldsmobile, not a rez car, not a hobo car. If I knew how to drive I'd be taking the car myself. Through the open door I expect to hear the men shuffling to get on out after me quick-like but instead I can hear Ernie talking to Hatch. He's telling him to get his best suit and tie on and grab the real birth certificate because he has scheduled a meeting with a lawyer in Hell Creek for this afternoon. He is saying there is no time like the present to begin proceedings that will protect Coca Joe and bring her safely back home.

Protect Coca Joe? From who? Safely back home? And what about finding my dog like Hatch promised? We're not going to find Chief at any dumb meeting.

I pop right up and head in their direction. "Wha-t?" I ask in warning.

Hatch catches me as I come charging through the door. He must know what I'm fussed about because he says, "Ernie will help you search for Chief as soon as this meeting is over. It won't last long."

I push my way out of his arms steaming with anger and run back out to the porch. "No! You promised, Hatch. You said we could find Chief but you lied."

"Coca Joe—"

"NO! You said, but we're just wasting time with stories and meetings and I don't care about any of it. I need Chief and I'm done waiting on you. I'll go it alone, if I have to. I don't need you."

Hatch comes closer, ready to comfort me I can tell, but I take a step back and fold my arms because I mean business. "This is an important meeting, Coca Joe," Hatch says gently.

"You can go to all the important meetings you want. I don't have to be there. Drop me off in the badlands and I'll go get Chief myself."

"We can't let you go off alone—"

"I go in the badlands alone all the time," I say, not even caring that I'm interrupting a grown up. "Nope, I want to go alone. I wasn't planning on anyone coming anyway." I sound put out because I am. Maybe I was hoping for Hatch, even though he is an Indian, but now I want to take my knapsack and head out right from the car and forget all these people. I can do whatever I want. I'll be in my country soon.

"Coca Joe, what if Chief is in trouble and you need someone's help?"

He may have a point, but I'm not budging. "I'm not waiting for any stinking meeting to get over." And I'm not, but what I'm also thinking is that I am not climbing with any old hobo deep into the badlands. He may be spry for an old man but not spry enough. "Maybe I'll take him," I nod my head towards Tim without bothering to look at him, "but you can't make me."

Hatch looks at Tim thoughtfully but I keep my eyes on Hatch. All I need him to do is agree to drop me off in the badlands then I can go get Chief without any more stupid delays. I've had enough of this.

Hatch looks back at me. "What if you don't find him there and need to look in the badlands between the farm and Hell Creek? And how will we know if you find him or not?"

I shrug. I don't care. I just want to go get my dog.

He's thinking though, I can see it. "Is there a place we could drop you and Tim off and then meet up with you again before dark, so we know if you find him?"

I'm still scowling, not answering. I'm thinking about what he's saying, but I don't want to show it. I'm deciding if I can trust him or if this is a trick.

"That way we can help you keep looking if you don't find him," Hatch says.

"Is this one of your ulterior motives?" I ask.

He gives me a small grin. "My ulterior motives are not bad for you Coca Joe, but I will take you and Tim to the badlands if you promise to meet me somewhere later."

I chew on this a minute.

"You can trust me," he says. "Can I trust you?"

I can see this is as good as things are going to get, so I may as well give in. "There's a lean-to at the Shooting Range right by the badlands. The lean-to is off the road, so no one will see me meeting you there." Meaning, no one will see a little white girl with an Indian, but I don't need to say that since we all know it.

Hatch extends his hand. "Deal. We'll drop you off and wait for you after the meeting."

I shake his hand and grin, proud of myself for being a toughie since it got me what I want. This never happens with my family in Hell Creek. I spin and run off the porch, ready to go find Chief.

I get in the front passenger seat, Tim gets in back, and Ernie climbs behind the wheel. While we're waiting for Hatch to change, he gets the long thing turned around on the one lane road with the huge hump in the middle. As we go over the hump, I grip the dash to not bump my head. Hatch runs out quick and I scoot along the front seat over to Ernie so Hatch will get in beside me. That means Tim Stratmore is in the backseat on his own but I am not caring. From now on I am only going to be caring about Chief. We drive in silence for quite some time. I gotta admit, it feels good, heading right where I want to be. For once!

It won't take us long to cover the miles, since there's no speed limit in Montana, and Ernie cruises, like most other drivers, between ninety and ninety-five miles per hour once he gets out on the open road.

When we hit Hell Creek both Hatch and I ride low on the seat to not be seen. I give Ernie directions to the badlands entrance near my home, but I don't have to make him drive by our house. I breathe a sigh of relief at that.

I think again about how strange it is that I don't feel right about going home even with Chief, but once I have him, home is where I'll have to go.

I'm comin' Chief. You are my home.

I direct Ernie to the lean-to at the Shooting Range, which is not far into the badlands.

Once we get out of the car Hatch gets real stern. He holds my shoulders and says, "Remember what you promised me, Coca Joe. Get back here before dark, with Chief or without him."

"I promise," and hope I mean it, because I'd hate to break a promise to Hatch.

He surprises me, grabbing me into a bear hug. He doesn't let go right away. I squint up at him. I realize I don't like this feeling of saying goodbye to Hatch. He's the twin of my mother! I'm his family! He's mine. I'm his. I am relieved now that I am not saying goodbye to him, because I did make a promise, so instead I say, "See ya soon Uncle Hatch."

We both smile at my calling him uncle.

Ernie presses a bag of hard candy into my hand and says that this is to go with the sweetness of finding Chief. I hug him for real too and tell him thanks for the ride and see you back here soon.

I stand in front of Tim with my hands on my hips not sure what to do. Being the ornery girl I am I think about just taking off without him. He must be smart. He keeps his eyes on my boots.

Finally I ask him, "You comin'?"

21
DEAD

I am a stranger to my real daddy and he is even stranger to me. I wish the invitation to come along with me hadn't fallen out of my mouth but there are no take-backs with words like that. Nothing could make me miss the easy old life—cracking mud and singing at the top of my lungs to the prairie dogs—like this big dose of new relatives. Geez, it makes me want to run. I have my very own daddy named Tim Stratmore, a buried mom called Jo, an ancient great-grandmother, Uncle Hatch, Nathan, Sue, Teenci, even Ol' R & R Ernie is a relative in the Indian way.

All I have ever wanted was Chief, and now look what losing him has brought me. Maybe I would be happier if I had Hatch with me instead, but it's just me and Tim, and that's got me feeling cross.

I know where I'm headed, over to drop into the coulee and then start our way deeper into the badlands. I start yelling Chief's name and Tim joins in every now and then. Going from hiking with a Lakota Indian to a sobered-up drunk is not even fair. I'm trying to get the bee out of my bonnet. I tell Tim I'm pretty sure I saw him at the Jungle the first night I ran away. I tell him he wouldn't have known I was there on account of him being passed out. He's quiet like he didn't hear me for a long, long time, then he says he's sorry that I had to see him like that, real, real sorry. I tell him that it's okay and he says, no it isn't.

He doesn't say any more for a while and neither do I. We've wound back and forth through the coulee and into the area of mounded hills when a sound like the noisy click of grasshoppers makes me stop. I'm snake smart, familiar with their sounds, dens, and what time they tend to be stretched out sunning or cooling. But I'm dumb today! It wasn't grasshoppers I heard. An adult prairie rattlesnake coils six feet from my thigh, an easy mark. I freeze in fear. Its poison will kill me and if it decides to strike, and I can't outrun it!

I hear only the slightest noise behind me, then a brown blur of something flies past my ear and right onto the rattler as I'm crabbed sideways into Tim's chest. The brown blur was a section of hollow log the length of my arm, and is enough to startle the snake away from us, but not kill it. Still against Tim's chest, I'm shaking violently as we watch the snake move off. He pats my back like a guy not used to contact. I step away, sparing him.

We laugh nervously first. Then, I don't know why, but soon we're laughing full strength. I'm laughing so hard, my guts ache, just like when Chief was licking that peanut butter off my stomach.

"Stop! Stop now," I say, but I'm still laughing. I don't even know what's so funny! "I can't breathe. My asthma!" I giggle a little more, but suddenly Tim's face is stricken and his head juts forward and he turns white as a sheet.

"Breathe! Breathe!" he yells.

"I'm breathing!" I say, startled, my laughter gone in an instant. He looks like he sees the ghost of my mother on me and I guess he does. "I'm all right! Settle down, Tim."

He blinks and straightens, taking a big, shaky breath and shifting away. He puts his hands in his hair and is trying to catch his breath from his fright. His face is still drained of color.

"I'm sorry. I'm so sorry," he says.

I am sorry too. It was a bad idea that he's come along. I want to be thinking on Chief, and not all this.

We start off again.

I'm grateful for something to lighten my mood and make me feel like me again, because I turn Indian once we get up into the many formations. The Indian part of me loves every sandy-bottomed step, every dried-gumbo slope, every teeny tiny flower, every warm breeze. It all comes together—I am Tate Tanksi—I am Sister of the Wind!

Tim struggles but is steady, and needs more water than I do, but at least it's not the hard stuff. I haven't spoken to him much. He's a tag-along for now, and later we'll see what he can become for me.

I stop at the bottom of Big Elephant to call Chief's name over its wall. A wind kicks up not allowing me to hear him bark. I tell Tim to rest as I scramble Big Elephant's side. Once at the top, I touch the embedded fossil as always for luck, saying a prayer that God help me find Chief. I pray longer than usual, reminding God that he is the reason I believe I will find Chief. I suppose God remembers, but I figure it never hurts to tell God again why I am here and who I expect him to help me find. I don't imagine God would roll his eyes like I do when I'm told something again and again. It feels good to be here where I have come so many times with Chief. This is our place, and I think he'd want to be here waiting for me. He's here somewhere. I know it. I call his name, and each time I yell it into our land of sandstone, I start to imagine that even this land wants me to find him. I am warmed by this idea. Even our badlands playground will be pulling for Chief and me!

As I straddle Big Elephant's sandstone hide I decide to slide down to the Sand Circle to check every nook and cranny. When my feet hit the ground I have a powerful vision that knocks me against the wall. Warrior Indians are gathered around a flaming fire but they are not celebrating. I can feel their forceful nature. They paint their faces as a drum beats a powerful rhythm. Language that sounds similar to Lakota is spoken loud and serious. They paint their chests, legs, and arms. Horses move into view and they paint them in different patterns and dots and lightning bolts, white, red, yellow, black.

I am frozen, even my mouth. I try to tell them, "Chief! Chief!" but it is almost like there is a stone on my throat, a pressure, not allowing me to speak. The vision of these warriors is so powerful my back is still pressed against the side of Big Elephant. I use my arms to push myself away from the wall and I head for the opening. As I sneak past,

I feel like I bump into them. Really feel it! I cry out in fear but they do not look at me. A chill drops through my body but I start running until I'm clear out the only opening to the Sand Circle.

When I'm some twenty feet away, I stop and look back at the entrance. I hear pounding, but it's not Indian drums, it's the pounding of my own heart. I don't know what to think about getting a vision like that, and decide to tuck that away and chew on it later along with all the other bones I'll have to gnaw: *after* I find Chief.

I have to cover more ground, winding around misshapen mounds to get back to Tim. When I do he's struggling to make his way up Big Elephant.

"Here I am!" I say.

"Ar—gh," he says, falling on his face and sliding down the slope. "You made that look so easy!"

He scrambles to his feet and hurries to me. "I heard you cry out and it scared me. Are you alright?"

"Of course!" I say, feeling strangely bold.

He gives me a look like he's just now seeing me. "You're a strong girl, aren't you, Coca Joe? I don't know if I will be of help to you today."

The warrior spirits must have influenced me because I say firmly, "No! Don't say that and don't ever give up." I shake my head to clear it of whatever's influencing me but nothing changes so I stand tall with hands on my hips. "Come! Let's get Chief!"

"Coca Jo—e?" Tim calls.

I stop running. I hadn't realized I'd started! I take this driving force back down to him, running and jumping off boulders, around large sagebrush and leaping the knobs of small formations.

"Wow!" he says proudly. "You really know this place!"

"It's my home."

"Can we stop to rest, have something to eat?"

"Now?" I gape.

"Never mind. You seem to know where you're going."

"Chief is here somewhere. I just know it."

"Oh, Coca Joe... don't get your hopes up. You can't know that," then he adds a rusty "honey," to soften the blow, but it doesn't soften.

I will try to ignore what he said; he's just trying to help, but this kind of help isn't helpful.

I decide seeing the warriors might be a sign, so I head to the right aiming to climb all the way to Indian Brave, a hill shaped like the face of an Indian at the top, with a dense red sandstone rock jutting from the back, symbolizing a feather. I am going to search all the places where Chief and I spend time, especially if they have good vantage points like Indian Brave. I am calling for Chief, and get sidetracked on my quest to Indian Brave to check a tight canyon with a hard-to-travel sandy bottom. It winds deep back into the badlands, and there are small caves in the walls on the way, but Chief could be here. He could. Tim helps me call as a panicking sound starts showing up in my voice. At the canyon end is a wall that makes us turn back and go out the way we came. I pass Tim and he reaches toward me to pat my back in reassurance but I pull away telling him to keep up. Like he's my problem. "Chief! Chief!" I call out, almost in Tim's face. He looks shocked, pulling his face to the side like I slapped him. I stomp off, hard to do in loose sand. It's not Tim's fault I am growing frightened that I won't find Chief but I'm going to take it out on him anyway.

It takes time to get to Indian Brave and climb up. Whenever I know Tim can see me, I hurry. When I lose sight of him, I wait until he can see where I am climbing again. At the top I catch myself looking for those warrior Indians. Didn't you lead me here? I tell them out loud to go find Chief. I tell them to show me where he is. I search thoroughly off each direction from the top of Indian Brave, and I call my dog's name and listen for his bark that always gives my heart an extra beat. I notice Tim is resting part way down. Good. I wrap my arms around the rock that isn't really a feather shape and I squeeze. "Help me God, help me God!" I pray. I remember the mustard seed and I pray, "I have faith! I have faith!" I yell Chief's name a few more times really expecting to hear his bark because I have prayed and God is known for answering prayers. I yell a few more times with even more expectation. I look at the sun and threaten, don't you dare go down on me! I start my way back down the big hill knowing I am getting more worried than I think I can handle.

By the time I get to Tim, I tell him we are going deeper into the badlands to a place called Sleeping Lion. He stares at me. I snip, "Chief is there." He gets up and starts to follow. One good thing about not knowing each other is there is not much to say.

It takes a little time to get to Sleeping Lion and on the way I realize how frightened I am becoming about not finding Chief. This hill doesn't have as steep a climb, but there is a lot of sagebrush to go around. Tim tries to keep up and does as much calling for Chief as I do. He lets me walk out on the lion's outstretched paws of sandstone, and from there I can see into three steep canyons, but I do not see Chief, and he doesn't answer. I make a deal with God. I tell him that I am going to go up on the lion's back, and because people at church say that you, God, are the lion of Judah, you will show me where Chief is. I tell God, "You gave me Chief to love. And you gave me to Chief to save." I start to cry. "Find him!" I plead. Then, because I want to show I have faith, I wipe my tears and climb up onto the back of Sleeping Lion and search over all the mounded hill and formations. As I do, I get my answer.

I stride off down the slope expecting Tim to be coming behind me and he is. I slow down for his sake to prepare him for the rest of the journey. "We're heading to an old cabin where Chief and I would go together. It's the only building I've ever found in the badlands. There are roads but I want to go as Chief and I always did, as the crow flies, up the washes and hills, onto a wide sandstone pass, then down the other side and upwards to the right through a juniper forest. From there we'll be in sight of the cabin."

Alone from here this would take me less than an hour. With tag-along Tim, who knows? I get it in my head that Chief is there! How do I not run full out towards him?

He's looking pretty flushed, but hasn't complained. He's not Hatch by a long shot, but he's handling this pretty well, getting used to how you have to move on this land, quick-footed.

I decide to take a quick rest and give Tim some food like he's asked, so I choose a large, flat boulder under a smidgen of shade. We get out some good things to eat, but I don't take any. I'm way too worried to eat. To my surprise he gets up first, saying, "Coca Joe, we need to turn back now, before it gets dark." Then he does his best to keep up with me as I hurry off. Maybe he wants to talk some sense into me, but I won't listen and he can't make me.

"I know we'll be losing our light," I say to prove he doesn't need to tell me things I already know. And I know it's getting too late to go all the way to the cabin and still make it back in time to meet Ernie and Hatch like I promised. I don't want to break my promise with Hatch just like I didn't want him to break his promise to me. Which he did not and that's why I'm here ready to find Chief. But I can't turn around now. I will not go back until I find my dog.

Tim hikes for quite awhile behind me before he says that he understands I want to check the cabin but wonders how Chief could be there since we haven't seen any signs.

He's got a point, but it doesn't matter, and maybe he's just trying to trick me into going back anyway, since he can't be a dad and make me. I keep moving up the pass.

"Please Coca Joe. We told Hatch and Ernie we would meet them before dark."

"You go back if you want. Tell them where I went. I'll see you later. I don't need your help, you can see that."

"No. I don't want to leave you. Come back with me so they'll know you are safe. Tomorrow we'll all come looking for Chief when we have plenty of daylight."

Tomorrow? He's gotta be kidding. "Just go if you want. I knew I shouldn't have brought you up here. I knew you'd be too slow!"

I'm angry. I'm not going to slow down anymore for him. When I hit the top of the pass I have a good view of him coming up it. He didn't turn back. I got to give him credit for that. Maybe he's not so bad. I regret being harsh with him and telling him to go back, so I yell, "Keep coming Tim-Daddy."

I stop. Why did I call him that?

What do I think of that title? It'll do.

"We're almost there," I yell down to him. I point and yell out directions as I start on my way. "Go down this steep pass into the draw," I holler, pointing, "and then up through the juniper forest to the right and you'll run into the cabin. I can't wait for you now that I know you won't get lost. I gotta go!"

I'm coming, Chief, I'm coming!

"Wait, Coca Joe!"

But I'm done waiting. Then I remember something that proves he's the one who needs looking after, not me. I better warn him. "I've been watching out for the mountain lion, so now that we're parting, keep your eye out! He's shy and will want to avoid you so make a bit of noise. "

Then I turn and start running. Free at last, hope is on the rise and joy is in my heart. Chief is there. I know it! I'm already weaving through the trees of the forest and nearing the cabin. When I pop out of the junipers, I spot something flying over the ravine that makes my heart jump into my throat.

"No!" I groan, running toward the buzzards flying overhead. "No!" I yell, flapping my arms to let the birds see their enemy has arrived.

I see what they're circling over, something on the ground not far from the water pump. It's pretty close to dusk so from here I can see dirt and mud in matted hair and tail, and ribs sticking out of this poor beast. I see the pool of blood under it. I feel sorry for the pitiful animal. Could be a coyote, I decide, but you are not Chief, you are not! A predator bird drops from the sky to hop close to the body and I run up to chase it off.

When I look at the animal this time something in me breaks wide open and I shriek loud and long *No! No! No—o!* Then I fall beside Chief.

He is barely recognizable. His tongue is out and it's dried. Ants crawl on it. I take my canteen and pour water on it, sweep the ants away and massage it, trying to tuck it back into the long collie muzzle.

All the time I am panting and saying, *no, no, no, no* over and over because he's not dead, he is *not*.

I put water into my cupped hand and wash the dry nose, and breathe into it. With each breath I call on God, on Jesus, on Great Spirit, on Angels, on all power that is real to me, as real as my breath! I trust Them. I must. I breathe in my great love for Chief with each breath, pushing his tongue into his mouth and then holding it shut. It stays.

I pump with both hands on his rib cage like I have seen in war movies, where I hope his mighty heart is, pumping and then breathing into his nose. I don't know what I'm doing but it doesn't matter because I will try everything, and God will bring him back to life. I feel the power, convincing Grandmother Earth to give up on trying to take Chief away from me in death, and trusting Wakan Tanka knows how to bring life to one of her most mighty four-leggeds.

I pray over and over in my mind the prayer that came on my mustard seed bracelet given to me by Grandma Naomi, someone powerful with love: I have faith as the mustard seed and I say MOVE to the mountain, and it will move! And I say MOVE to Chief, and he will move!

I will not be tired. I will not be doubtful. My Chief waited for me like I knew he would and now I'm here, and he will *live* for me.

He will come back...

for me...

The tears well in me but I will not pay them any mind. Tim-Daddy kneels at my side saying, "Let me try to help, Coca Joe, let me."

I growl and shove his hands off my Chief.

His eyes flash fear after seeing my crazed eyes look at him.

I keep pumping the rib cage and keep begging God to save him. And I beg and I beg and I beg and nothing changes. He doesn't breathe. He doesn't move. His happy-wagging tail is still as death.

That is when I see the dead dog before me. My beloved Chief. And seeing my Chief dead crumples my shoulders down and yanks a sob out from somewhere deep in my soul. Tim starts to put a hand on my back but in the instant he touches me something wild rages up and I shove him with all my strength. I shove him hard, away from the love of my life, away from the family who was with me all while Tim was off somewhere else. He topples over and I scream at him, "Go away! Get away! Go far, far away from me!"

"Calm down, Coca Joe," he says gently, hands raised and eyes pleading. "I'm here for you—"

"I don't need you!" I scream. I scream it so hard and loud my throat strains. "Get away from me!"

"I can't leave you," he says weakly and I know how to make him go. "I don't need you! I can get home by myself. My *real* home with my *real* dad." I watch his face crumble as I tell this lie, because that dad and that home never felt real to me, but I don't care. I knew my words would make him leave and I was right. His shoulders curl under and that drunk who isn't much of a real dad either gets to his feet and stumbles away. He leaves me and I am glad because he has no right to be here with me and my Chief.

Death has no right to be here either, and I will tell it what I think of it stealing Chief when I needed him so.

Sobbing, I press my fingertips hard into the bloody earth in front of me and join the Sioux warriors I saw preparing for war at the Sand Circle. I prepare for my own war, with death. I smear my face for battle, bloody stripes across my cheekbones, down my nose, across my forehead, over my eyelids. I remember how the warriors painted their bodies and I grab up the blood mixed with dirt and I smear it on my chest and down my arms. I scream at the circling birds, "Chief is mine! Mine! Mine!"

I look behind me and see my dad is not gone yet. He waits on the edge of the ravine.

"I'll go get help, Coca Joe. I love you like you love Chief," he pleads.

I rise and charge up the slope like a bull. "Go! Go! Get away from me!" I scream, sounding raw. Like I am.

He looks at me like I have lost my mind, and maybe I have. "Get. Away. From. Us!"

Tim stumbles backwards and disappears at last.

I cry in wailing gasps, stumbling back to Chief and falling to my knees. "It's too late. Too late! I'm too late!"

I lie over my Chief and bury my face into his chest, winding my fingers into his fur. All I want to do is hear his heartbeat one more time. I tell him I will never ever leave him. Just as he is my life and my helper, I will now be his. I tell him, "I am here. I am here. I am yours forever and ever."

Far in the distance he barks three times. Is that Chief saying goodbye from the spirit world? *Don't go, Chief! Don't leave without me!*

I struggle to grab Chief up, to wrap my arms around him for our journey to heaven.

But he is gone and I am left behind. Jesus! Jesus! How could you have needed Chief more than I do?

I cry out desperately, until I am here no more.

22
THE BOARDING HOUSE

"Couldn't you have made it your job to save The Dog?" Knower wrings his hands and paces back and forth with heavy feet in front of the revolving door.

Jesus, who has prevented the residents from using the revolving door, takes no offense; it's not his nature. He understands Knower's deep caring for Her and his strong sense of responsibility.

Knower keeps challenging. "Losing The Dog will effect everything. The Dog is Her life. The Dog is like Jesus to Her." Knower winces at saying this to Jesus.

Undisturbed about being challenged, Jesus says, "Bless you dear Knower," and Knower experiences the peace that comes from being truly blessed. Jesus continues, "She needs Her own resourcefulness to live Her life as much as She needs the residents of The Boarding House. She is stronger than you think, and full of Spirit. This is a time for her to learn an important lesson."

"She is half dead with grief," Knower says, comforted, but still full of compassion for Her suffering. "What kind of lesson could this be?"

"The lesson is one of strength," Jesus answers calmly. "Her own."

23
CABIN

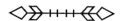

I must have slept. It is past sundown, almost dark. A half-moon is rising, giving a sad, pale blue tint to the air. In the distance I can hear him and yet here he is, his cold body under mine as I lie on his chest. Are you still making your trek to the spirit world, dear Chief? Without me? I try to move but must peel myself off the dried blood that holds Chief and me together. My clothes and his long hair struggle to part, making ripping sounds from the crusted blood, the sound of my ripping heart. After this terrible thing, I weep some more, falling back on him. Then after a long, long time, when the forest is as still and dark as my soul, I know I need to let him go.

I get to my knees, weak and feeling faint. My light head is playing tricks on me, because as I squint, heavy-lidded, toward the dark outline of the cabin above me, I hear Chief bark. Or maybe it my heart playing tricks on me, because I want to hear him so badly. His bark seems to come from the cabin, like a memory.

"Our cabin, Chief," I croak.

I crawl out of the ravine, feeling pain as if I've had an accident. I keep moving on all fours, remembering this place as if it is a friend, pulling myself up each step to collapse on the porch. Finding shelter with this cabin is both a comfort and makes me miss Chief desperately. I wonder if he was killed by the mountain lion we've seen up here at the cabin, and shiver. It's a scary guess, and as I imagine what that would have been like for my poor Chief, I shiver some more. I lean back against the cabin door but it is already unlatched. It swings wide without me twisting the handle. Seeing in the darkened room is difficult with eyelids so heavy and I don't know why they are. I drag myself in rolling onto my back.

I hear a strange sound deeper in the cabin, a high whimpering that I don't recognize, and I startle. What's in here?! I hear the scurrying of paws on the wood floor, racing toward me, and I cringe away in time to feel a rough, wet scraping on my arm. Something is licking me! Is it the cougar? I clobber the mouth of an animal knocking its many teeth together, making it yelp and I yelp too. I scramble away in the pitch-black cabin, away from teeth that may want to eat me.

That awful high-pitched noise I heard before—it sounds like it's by the stove—is being made by more than one thing, maybe terrible things, like big rats behind the walls or a thousand bats in the ceiling. Or the sound might be under me. Perhaps under the floor is a den of snakes, writhing and hissing together. I would run out the door, but whatever was licking me is in my way, a great shaggy thing, and coming toward me again! "Help!" I cry out. *No! No! No! Please God, don't let it get me.*

The huge shape I can barely make out comes for me again, trying to lick at the blood. I gather all my courage and shove it hard. It yelps and barks. Bark? It barked? My brain tries to recall if wolves bark, or coyotes? I wish I could see it, but it's too dark, and my eyes are swollen to mere slits. A swish of a tail sweeps across my face, a long tail, plenty of hair, then a happy-bark. Bark, bark, bark! I recognize that bark.

"Chief?"

Bark.

"Chief?"

"Woof, woof," another happy bark.

My heart lifts at the sound, foolishly, hopefully, even though I know Chief is dead in the ravine outside the cabin—I saw him.

The animal leaves my side and goes toward the feeble crying sound. I move in that direction, but think better of it and shrink back.

"Chief. Come," I say, hopeful again.

He pushes into my side and I reach for him. He feels real! Very real. He licks my face.

"Chief! Chief! Is it you?" I throw my arms around his neck. He feels right and doesn't shrink away! He pushes against me, and tries to lick again. I reach to feel his velvety earflaps. Yep. I feel the long muzzle my hands have memorized...yep. I run my hands down the thick chest fur, then his back, then squeeze a hand down his tail feeling for the slight knob that's near the tip. It's there. This is my dog. This is Chief! It has to be!

I get to my feet, jumping and hooting. "Chief! Chief!" He paws me first, then dances his rear into my legs, almost knocking me over, and goes back over by the stove. I fall to my knees and look to the heavens with praying hands, just like in the movies only this is real life, "Thank you, Jesus! Thank you! You did answer my prayers!"

I'm not eager to follow Chief, even though I know whatever's making noise over there can't be too bad if Chief's not afraid of it. It doesn't sound as loud or ominous as it did when I was hearing it with my fear as well as with my ears, but I sure wish I could see what it is.

Chief pushes a muzzle against my arm and leaves me again, going in the direction of the strange sound. I head over cautiously until I'm by Chief's side on the other side of the stove. My eyes, still so heavy, are slowly adjusting to the faint light and I see a square shape in front of me. I kneel down, trying to remember what's here, and when my hands reach out tentatively and I feel the smooth surface, I remember: an old box. Whatever's making the noise is inside the box!

Chief barks again. My heart soars at the sound of it and him being right here next to me, all while being nervous about whatever's in the box. Let me tell you, that's a whole lot for a girl's heart to hold all at once. But, not being a stranger to a heart having too much to hold, or a stranger to dangerous things, I lift my hand toward the open top of the box. I reach inside and feel wet, soft moving things.

"Ick, ick, ick!" I yell and yank my hand out of there shaking the grossness off. "Chief!"

Then he does what he would never do, even when I baited him. He whines over the box, just like Lassie! He whines so much and so well I wonder if this could be Chief. I take a deep breath and put my hands over the box again. I freeze, so Chief has to nudge me. I hold my breath to gear up and become as brave as I have ever been. I hate slimy things. I'm not a chicken about most things but I'm a chicken about this! I reach down, feel around, and pick something up, carefully feeling its parts and finally figuring it to be an itty newborn pup, blind and helplessly crying.

Puppies!

My relief at figuring out the mysterious sound, and my relief at having my dog back at last, balloon up and fill the whole cabin. Chief nuzzles me, then whines with the best of them, whines just as good as Lassie.

"OK, Chief!" I laugh. "Okay! We'll take care of the puppies!"

He barks happy and prances his front feet back and forth in front of the box.

"I hear you. I know you—great dog of mine!" I hug him and hold onto him as long as he lets me, which is awhile. I keep saying his name over, Chief, Chief, Chief, getting back to myself. I feel like I left part of me outside, and that piece is coming back to me now.

I'm still shaky but my body feels electric, sparking. I'm thinking clearer, so I remember it's dried blood pushing my eyelids closed. I understand the dead dog outside was never my dog Chief, but it's a collie for sure, maybe the mother of these pups. Maybe she's the stray who had to rub up against the log cabin since there was no one around to pet her. This is my best guess. How and why she died I will probably never know, but I grieved mightily for her and I'm glad for that. I lost my heart to her, as if she was my Chief, and she deserves at least that.

What I know for sure is that Chief bolted from the car at the farm and the breeder called my dad about it. And that I found Chief right here with puppies and he's already a caring daddy, even though they can't be his, because he's had plenty of practice with a girl like me. He adopted me first! And now that we found each other again I need to figure out what to do about my other adoption. Am I going home? I better be. This thought scares me. I haven't fit with them before. How will I ever fit again knowing I was stolen from my family and then adopted to them? Do they know I was stolen? The thought makes me sick, so I try to stop thinking it.

Besides, first things first. I leave Chief with the puppies and go outside and down into the ravine to locate my knapsack, knowing Chief and I need food and some way to save the nine puppies I counted. I stop near the dead collie to kneel and whisper, "I'm sorry" with a promise to do all I can for her pups. I wish she could tell me how she died. Did she die while birthing the litter? I know nothing about such things. Somehow I will bury her, but for now I take my best cowgirl shirt from out of the knapsack and lay it over her, tucking it gently under her even though she is dead.

Thankfully, the red-handled water pump is nearby to wash off the blood I had painted all over myself like a Sioux warrior. I won this battle. What a lucky, lucky girl. The water is freezing, and since I am sticky with blood and dirt over much of my arms, neck, and head, washing up gives me a chill. But Chief will warm me. Chief will warm me! I shout loudly toward the cabin, "I'm coming, Chief. I'm coming!" This time it's true! Chief happy-barks from inside. I yell, "Thank yo—u!" into the heavens, loud and clear.

On my way up the cabin steps, I say one more prayer—for Tim-Daddy—feeling bad for how I treated him. I was awful. I pray that he returns to who he once was and becomes who he is meant to be. Amen.

I need to gear up for walking into our house tomorrow. I don't think we can make it back in the dark after such a long day. I'll think about trying. I fill my lungs with the cool night air. The lifeless dog lying under my shirt reminds me of being hit by that semi-truck and lying under the chassis. I hope I didn't leave any parts of me under that truck. I'm gonna need everything I got to see my family after running away.

Maybe it'll be okay to go home for Chief and me. We're armed. Armed with puppies! Isn't this why Chief left in the first place and what started my running away?

Once I'm back inside the cabin, Chief eats what I give him of the venison jerky I take from my knapsack, gulping it down without tearing it apart with his teeth. I think of it sitting in his stomach and talking back up to him. I'm chewing and stewing over the puppies. What to feed them? I don't know if they suckled their mama before she died. She didn't feel warm now that I think back to earlier when I lost my mind in her blood. And even now with my mind back, I don't know how to save her babies. Chief has saved them so far, carrying them inside to the box by their tiny scruffs, or maybe holding them softly in his mouth, one by one.

By the time my arms and face have dried from washing up, the temperature drops and it's cold inside the cabin, even with the jacket I pulled out of my knapsack. The puppies aren't moving much, or making much sound either, so I click my fingers for Chief to lie down and push him over to his side. I take my jacket off, lay it on the floor next to Chief's belly, and lay the puppies in one by one. Then I scoot the jacket of babies beside his belly to warm them pulling the jacket over him to seal them in.

Chief lifts his head and I see the whites of his crazy eyes complaining about the weird action on his tummy. He is their mommy and so am I, but we have no milk. I lift one of the helpless babies to my face and ask for wisdom from all powers that have saved me so far, feeling sure that I will get a life-saving idea. I cradle the puppy under my neck and feel my heartstrings go taut, the miracle of babies again. I tuck the pup back in the makeshift womb. I nuzzle Chief with my nose like he does me, and hug his neck saying, "It's okay, Chief, we'll fix this," saying this also for me to pump myself up, to get an idea. Any idea would help.

From my knapsack I take one of my thin leather gloves used for gathering firewood, or for moving through rocks, or to make a

campfire ring. I get my canteen and some of the hard cream candies
Ol' R & R Ernie pressed in my hand as I left the lean-to at the Shooting
Range, his eyes all gooey with caring for me. For being a hobo he sure
is mushy! I smile at the thought of him and start winging it, once
again counting on help from above. My mind flashes to the mustard
seed and all the faith I had when I was so frightened. 'If ye have faith
as a grain of mustard seed… nothing shall be impossible unto you.'
And Chief here with me is the proof. Yes. I have faith. I pour a little
water in one of the fingers on the glove, suck on the candy and spit
the sugary saliva in the water many times. It's not collie milk, but it's
all I can think of.

I forgot to make a hole in the glove so a puppy could suck the
sugar-water out, like a makeshift nipple. Propping the glove so the
sweetness doesn't spill, I dig through the knapsack for something
sharp, knowing that I don't have a needle, but thinking one could
appear. It could! You just never know in the miracle business! One
doesn't appear. I dig around for my pocketknife.

The leather on the glove is thin but very tough. I poke a hole
with the knife, screwing it back and forth in the leather and ending
up spilling some of the hard-to-make sugar-water into the palm of the
glove but I made a hole.

I move to Chief's nipples, dab the sugar water on one and place
a pup, dab and place a pup. Chief lifts his stately head to crazy-look
with the whites of his eyes again, like an animal in danger, but I tell
him to stay, to lie still, that we are mommies for now. I suck another
candy and mix it with water in the glove to keep this 'milking' going.
We haven't killed any of them yet, that's all I know for sure.

With so many pups it's an endless meal so we all need a break. I
let Chief outside. I don't watch. I don't want to know if he visits the
dead collie. As the slow minutes of night tick by it's a balancing act
for Chief and me, us sharing water and food, us warming pups against
our bellies and doing our best to feed them something.

I figure Ernie and Hatch won't still be at the Shooting Range
waiting for me. It's too late. And Tim-Daddy? I don't know where he

went. Hopefully he made it down safely since it was getting dark. It didn't work for me. I tried two different ways of walking down the road tonight towards town, once carrying the big box of pups which turned out to be too cumbersome, and once with them whimpering at the top of the pack. The half moon has risen now, but it only took one stumble in the near dark that ended in a trip and a fall and catching myself on my arms to protect the puppies before I turned around to wait until morning. That's why we are here feeding.

I gather the pups in the jean jacket between Chief and me and sleep a shallow sleep on my hip on the hard floor. I wake to a rumble and voices. A hotrod gets louder. Hotrod? Lights shine in moving shadows around the room, and the car ignition turns off near the cabin. Two car doors shut. I listen to hear low-sounding voices. Men! Could Tim-Daddy help Ernie and Hatch find the road to this remote cabin? I'm struggling to think fast and decide they would. Except more headlights shine across the front yard of the cabin and another car is turned off. Two cars?

Chief listens, his ears twitching. Harshly whispering, "No bark! No bark!" to Chief, I hear several loud male voices scare my brain empty. Hunching over to not be seen out the window I peek outside, panicking at seeing several teen-sized boys by their cars, slugging down beers, a few in lettermen's jackets. They're here to party and have a private time doing it. Quietly as I can, I hustle around trying to open the windows to climb out. None will even budge. We're trapped.

I crack the door to see if I should risk running past the three guys now sitting on the steps. People make fun when a lot of ladies get together and start talking, calling it a hen party. That's nothing compared to the noise of these roosters crowing. The grief they give each other and the hard, friendly slaps and slugs go with their drinking. I think I would surprise them so much that I could make it past them and run for my life. We might make it! Just before I bolt I remember I must shove things into my knapsack along with the puppies! I gather them inside the jean jacket and set them in the top of the sack, cinching it and buckling the flap with my hands shaking. I gently put this on my back and peek through the door, preparing to leap. I bend my legs, rocking-ready like at the start of a running race. Chief puts his face in the crack of the door below me and I hold his muzzle. Just as I'm ready, new guys with wide backs join the others on the steps, blocking my way out. I almost push out imagining I can climb over them and in their shock they would not grab me. Chief could make it, leaping right over the top of them. I'm ready, committing. Then another two huge boys come up to the steps, enclosing the porch opening and sealing us in.

Are these the teens Hazel said are taking girls to the cabin? I don't see a girl, only guys, gulping down beers. Unless that girl is me. Ah— h! Pulling Chief with me, I back toward the far corner in a panic. My body feels like I've taken one of the emergency asthma pills from the bracelet on my wrist—heart racing, trembling, everything in my body screaming run—but how? If I broke a window to jump out I'd have to escape fast to get away before they rushed in. And Chief would have to jump through the window. We'd both be cut up and bleeding as we ran to town, which will seem much farther away being wounded and traveling in the dark. I must think of a way to outsmart them.

The noise of the guys grows louder with the steady crimp-fizz of opening cans. Their voices don't sound right; beer is talking. Could I casually walk out and say hello and use my friendliness and the shock of just appearing to get past them now? I think about it. Maybe.

A shotgun fires! The porch shakes! Close. Out the window I see they've created a shooting gallery, glowing yellow in their car lights. With some of the teens off the porch now, I have a path out, but I'm not too keen on going out there when there's hunting rifles in the hands of boys getting drunk. A couple guys drag the dead collie out of the ravine and prop her over a large rock, laughing. How'd they find the dog? Several of them take turns shooting at her. I pinch my eyes shut tight and turn my head away, puke rising to my mouth.

These aren't the 'boys will be boys' type. These guys with their broad shoulders are going for broke. 'Hell on wheels' my parents would call them, and now I know what that means. Only God knows what they'd do with me. I cringe hoping they'll have no reason to come inside the cabin. Is there any way I can block the door? I move to the woodstove which is the only free- standing heavy thing in the room. With all my fear gathered into strength I push the stove. It doesn't budge even a speck. I think to lift and scoot it grabbing the cast iron lip of the top but it is the same stubborn heavy weight. Now that I think about it, the sound of the stove dragging across the floor would probably draw their attention and bring them in anyway. There's nothing else I could use to block the door. Maybe if they try the door, I could hold the door shut against them and maybe they would give up? Then I think about the muscles in this group and think that if they want in they might enjoy the challenge of shoving a difficult door open. They might be getting drunk enough to shoot at the door, making it a target.

The only thing I can do is hide on the far side of the large cook stove. I keep my pack on and scrunch as best I can but there is no way to keep the puppies quiet. Even though I know it's a bad sign for the puppies that they aren't making as much noise as when I first got here, it's good for me and Chief, and I can't help but be glad they're quieter. Chief is willing to sit right beside me and I pet him endlessly for comfort. His ears move as he listens to their ruckus.

When I hear voices coming back toward the cabin, I shrink back further, hoping they'll just sit on the porch again. There are heavy steps on the porch, closer and closer, and then I hear the door swing wide open. I gasp and stifle a whimper and Chief jumps out and barks like collies can bark, nonstop, deep, and meaning business.

"Sh—it! I almost crapped my pants!" one of them says.

"Shit is right!" says a low voice.

"Pretty nice dog. Come 'ere buddy boy," says a third voice.

There is a lot of shuffling footsteps telling me the room is filling, maybe all eight of them are in here. A scuffling takes place and Chief low-growls.

"Ok. Got him. What should we do with him?"

"Should we shoot him?" asks a slurring voice. Nobody talks while they think about this idea and I don't dare get up to tell them "No!" for fear they'll start thinking about shooting me too. Feet keep moving in the room but so far they don't see me.

"I don't want to."

"Nah, me neither."

"La—ssie! Where's Timmy?" They laugh their drunken laughter.

One of the boys come into view and we both startle when his eyes land on me. "Jesus H. Christ!" he hollers when he sees me, his hand flying to cover his heart as he stumbles backwards. "What the hell are you doing here?"

The whole group comes to take a look, pushing into each other to get a better view.

I cross my arms over my head as if a bomb went off and stay put.

"Get over here kid!" a gruff voice demands. I'm trembling inside and out, my mouth dried like starch pressed into a shirt. I can't think of any way around it so I get up, hunch my shoulders, pull my head down into them, and put a scowl on my face hoping to look tough and boyish with this scraggly hair. I sidle along the wall, keeping to the shadows thrown by the car headlights.

One of them comes over, looming large, and reaches over to scruff up my hair. "What the hell happened here, your head meet up with a lawn mower?" They all laugh. That's exactly the kind of joke my Dad would make. Hell Creek humor is not original. He grabs my arm and pulls me away from the wall, making a circle around me. I take a better look at them now and wonder why they would wear coats with their name on the front and big football emblems on their backs when they are acting like hoodlums. I can read. I even know who a few of these guys are from watching the high school football games. Chief is trying to push through their circle but they're blocking him with their legs.

"This your dog?"

I shrug my shoulders. Maybe I can get by without talking 'cause no matter what, I sound like a girl.

One of them gets Chief by the scruff of the neck and grabs his tail, yanking hard on it. "This your dog, kid?" Chief snarls at him and he kicks Chief in the underbelly. Chief yelps and is knocked into the circle. "Don't hurt him!" I scream and grab Chief around the neck. My cover is blown if I ever had one.

"Do—on't!" the kicker imitates me in a high voice.

A couple of the guys pull me off the dog and several get hold of Chief. Another one heads for the door saying, "I'll get some rope."

"Why?" asks the biggest, beefiest football player with the name of Jan. "Too weak to hold down a scrawny girl?"

A couple guys laugh darkly but my skin is crawling at the thought of them holding me down.

"To handle the dog," the guy answers snidely.

Satisfied with this answer, this big linebacker, Jan, turns his attention back to me and ask, "What are you doing in our cabin?"

But there's no safe answer to this. There's no safety here with these boys at all, and I know if I have any chance at all I have to run. Run now!

I push off between them toward the door grabbing Chief's fur but I'm tackled just like at their twenty-yard line. I crash on my stomach against the hard floor. Ka-BAM! It knocks the wind out of me, and the guy gets off. I hope the pups riding my back aren't dead with all this rough handling.

"Geez, Ray! You didn't have to tackle her!" someone teases.

"I didn't mean to, so go screw yourself!" Ray yells.

"Shut-up, dickhead!"

I scramble toward the door again hoping for a lucky breakaway. And I get it! Getting to my feet, I leap off the porch and dart around the guy with the rope, who is no small pancake. My lucky break doesn't last long. He runs after me, gets a hold of me by both arms, and keeps a firm grip as he drags me back up the porch where the guys are watching. They back up so he can drag me inside.

"Look who I caught running away!" he says cruelly, and they all laugh and nudge each other.

I wonder about my older brother and whether he and his friends will act like this in high school. I decide no. He couldn't. The other really huge guy starts in on me again. "So what are you doing here?

Shouldn't you be home in your little nightie? Isn't it way past your kindergarten curfew?" This gets a big laugh.

I shrug again.

"You know, girls shouldn't be out here all by themselves. You might run into the BOO—gieman!" he says, leaning toward me, his voice deep and horrible, and a look of pure evil in his eyes. The name on his jacket says something like Francis in its red and white longhand script but he's the Boogieman to me now.

"Yah! Bad things can happen to little girls!" says the one who has a firm grip on my arms. Hazel's news about the group of teenage boys hurting girls up in the cabin becomes real enough that my chin starts to quiver and I become scared for my life! I must, must, MUST get away.

And just like that, they form a tighter circle and start shoving me across the circle and into the arms of another, who then faces me forward to push me across again. I worry about the pups riding in the bag just below my shoulders, but I'm more worried about me, because they're joking and arguing about who "gets to go first this time."

"Maybe the newbie," someone says, elbowing the guy next to him, who looks nervous but determined.

"Shut up," he answers and they all laugh.

Chief tries pushing into the circle to rescue me. One of the boys goes for him, and the circle immediately tightens, blocking any hope of escape. Through the thin spaces between the teens' bodies, I see the boy yank Chief's back legs out from under him. Chief is really growling and squirming now.

"Get the rope!" Jan yells. Before I know what's happened, a couple of them have tied all four legs together like it's a rodeo event, and I'm sure it hurts him. I'm too scared of what they'll do to me next to fuss. I hear whimpering, but I couldn't say if it's coming from Chief, or the puppies on my back, or from my own mouth. Chief writhes on the floor to get loose and tries biting at the rope. They grab the tail of the rope and drag him into the small kitchen area. He barks and barks and this gives me confidence.

The teenagers pull in tighter, shoulder-to-shoulder, like a well-practiced marching band. I wonder how many times they've done this before if they don't even need to talk about what to do next. I look to the "newbie" for help, but his eyes are hungry on me and he's following their lead. Someone rips off the knapsack and throws it. High-pitched sounds grow louder and the boys stop messing with me so a couple of them can investigate the noise in the pack. I'm so dangerously angry I could start screaming! But being petrified keeps me from doing it. As they turn toward the puppies I try to break out of the circle to get out the door again, fighting and squirming to get out of the boy's grip, but I am not successful. Once the puppies are rough-handled and left in the corner near Chief, the boys turn their attention back to me and seem even more threatening.

I get tossed back and forth again but their faces are dark. I don't know what they're going to do to me, but I know they don't plan to stop at this. I'm right, too. Someone rips off my shirt in one hard tug and I hear the ripping of fabric. I cover myself as my bottom lip trembles. Tears pour down my cheeks, even with my eyes wide open in fright. Someone behind lifts me under the arms while Boogieman looms forward and pulls off my cowboy boots, throwing them into a corner. No one's talking about what they're doing or what they plan to do next, they're just yelling "Woo hoo!" and watching as the horrible teen in front of me yanks off my jeans, leg by leg. Boogieman rips my panties as he tears them off me and it hurts, leaving red welts along my hips.

My arms are released at last, and I'm left to stand naked with my arms tight around my waist. They yip and holler and check out my stick figure.

"Take your stupid socks off!" the Boogieman orders, and I do. I hop on one foot at a time. He reaches out his open hand. "Set 'em here," he says in a creepy voice. "Nicely."

24
THE BOARDING HOUSE

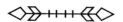

Watcher with Owl has seen enough and so has Knower. They understand the boys intend to rape her. Owl screeches an alarm. Name Schmame will attack first.

Gangster and The Babe stand at the ready.

Lonely has wandered out sensing there may be something coming for her. She hangs back out of the way.

Defender Name Schmame pushes out the revolving door in a blink of an eye, and She comes in through the revolving door to rest in Her Safe Place, where she will stay until the sexual threat has ended.

"Ar——rgh," I growl loud like a madman, tuck my head, and charge into Boogieman's stomach. I won't succeed at this for long because these guys are way bigger than they looked from inside The Boarding House. At least I caught them off guard, for a quick sec. Next!

Name Schmame returns to The Boarding House as The Babe goes out.

My turn. Not to worry. I'm The Babe. I've handled this kind of thing before... I know the smell of desire in a room. I jump into the middle of the circle and put on a very wide wiggle, strutting in front of each of these boys with a hand on hip, head down and eyes looking up with that look, you know, the one that men want. I wiggle around the circle like I mean business, their kind of business, and this catches them off guard, whooping and laughing and congratulating themselves. I stop in front of the boy who looks the most shaken by my presence. You know the one, an innocent, his jaw dropped to the floor? He must be new to their game.

This is such a beefy group of young pups, they have a lot to prove and are looking for all the trouble they can get, so I figure I better give them a little something before I walk away with the virgin. I blow a sexy kiss to each one of them as if it's a promise for later. There won't be a later, but they don't know that.

Nobody will get what they are wanting from me.

I stop once again in front of Virgin and bid him to follow me with the come-hither crook of my finger, way too obvious, but he's too young to know. I turn around, widen my wiggle and walk outside.

A ruckus of "Ooooh's" and "Ahhh's" fuels the Virgin to follow me as everyone pats him hard on the back, like he is the hero, the winner. I take his hand and walk him out through the tall grass, dropping down the slope into the Juniper forest. I can hear him breathing hard behind me as he holds tight to my hand, as if he thinks I'm not real. You are right, sucker. I'm not real.

The Babe makes room for Gangster.

"Good, Sweetheart." Gangster praises The Babe. *"You got him up against the tree and feeling weak."*

I knee him with all the force I can muster right in the balls. Gotcha!

He's down. Just a couple other firm kicks to his face and She will be safe to come out and run.

Gangster and The Babe return inside The Boarding House, and She comes out of Her Safe Place and right out the revolving door. All in the blink of an eye.

Lonely shuffles back to her room mumbling, "No baby for me today."

25
HIDE

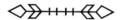

I run naked as fast as I can down the slope of trees. Low branches slap my tender skin; dry pine needles break off and poke into my feet as slivers. They pierce deeper with each stride. Fear pounds extra heartbeats into my ears. *Run fast! Get away! Get away!*

I hear them thundering down the porch steps, coming after me. *They're coming! Get away!*

Oh no! My dog, my Chief, tied up as helpless as the puppies! I can't stop. I can't. Don't think about him! Just go! GO!

The only thing that matters is not getting caught—again. I hear them yelling, cussing, calling me terrible names. I hear them crashing through the trees, breaking tree limbs, moving as bears—fast, angry and maybe able to track my scent. I descend the bluff and escape into the badlands, darting through this familiar landscape like a wild animal on the run. I feel my lungs tighten up. Uh-oh. Asthma! Please don't slow me! I ask for Jesus's help and angels to carry me, for Father Sky to shine the way, and for Mother Earth to hide me. Let me be a mountain lion—leaping rock, pounding up the sandstone pass. Breathe for me! Give me breath! I'm wheezing and injured—fair game—the hunted for the hunters.

I must know these badlands better than they do! I must!

I know where to go. I know where to hide! On the sandstone face carved by rivulets of water eons ago I need to slow down to save my ankles from twisting or jamming a foot down into the slippery grooves. I'm probably slightly visible as I climb out of the gully and wish I could move faster to get onto the saddle of the pass before they come out of the trees and spot my moving white backside in the half-moon, starry night. I'm running well, my asthma settling down, a miracle.

Tall formations with narrow trunks capped by huge rocks standing guard over the sides of the pass are my warrior Indians. I head left to get up into a hiding place, crossing the layer of red scoria. It rips my feet and I come close to hollering in pain from the sharp pebbles but I can't slow down to pick my way across; my silhouette is too easy to spot running on the top of the pass. It's bad enough to be leaving them a glowing, bloody trail in this moonlight.

Their voices scare me, echoing through the night. Someone yells loud and clear into a cloudless sky, "Your other dog will die toni—ght to—o!" and they fire off a few shots.

My heart breaks for my poor helpless Chief but I keep going, like a bat out of hell. I just escaped from hell and will return if these teenagers get another chance with me.

I climb to the backside of a formation I call Two Licks—two spires that bridge together, each with a chunky, half-eaten cone shape on top. I'm headed to a cut-away section up high that forms a natural bench where I can hide and wait the guys out. It's hard to scale, but I've done it before, last summer, getting out of a downpour. It was fun then. I monkey-climb—knees bent out to the sides of my body with feet gripping flat against the pillar so I can push up. I fall from the hold again and again, barely catching myself before my bare butt hits the rocky ground. I'm doing more damage to my feet and starting to panic. I must get off the ground and get myself hidden. I must!

With eight boys to split up and cover ground, I won't stay ahead of them for long. I can hear them searching too, some far from me but some close. Too close! Even if they come right here, the cap rock covering the bench will keep me in shadow, I'm sure of it, if I can only get there. I keep trying. This way of climbing puts naked private areas on my heels and almost against the pillar, but I can't worry about it! I push with all I've got, shaking with effort. My chest and inner arms scrape against the sandstone leaving behind more skin. Sandstone is a close relative to sand paper. Ouch! I stretch for a handhold, a rock shaped like an alien spaceship sticking out the side of the pillar. I throw one knee up onto the ledge—more scrapes—but in one swift move I'll be up onto the ledge. It's a tricky one. I'm holding steady, gearing up. I hear rifle fire, coming from the cabin I think. Four more shots! My sinking heart for Chief hits the ground. I'm slipping… slipping… falling! Those God damn stupid assholes! Dog killers! Massive anger rises in me, enough to power me up onto the ledge. I nearly tumble off, but get my feet under me as I get into a squat.

Just in time! Someone is very close by under me and he fires a gun. Help me, Jesus! The loud echo bounces between Two Licks. From up high I catch sight of something moving up the opposite side of the pass from the cabin. It's the way I normally go with Chief, and the way I came with Tim-Daddy. I think to myself, run mule deer! Hide! Hunters are out tonight and will kill you for no reason at all!'

But how did I escape their clutches in that circle of teens? How did I gain the freedom to run through the trees? The last thing I remember is a sickening metallic taste as I stood naked in the circle of towering, drunk jocks. They went from bad to worse to dangerous so fast. Unless they stole those letterman jackets, these guys are supposed to be people the whole town turns out to cheer for. Small town heroes. I guess it doesn't take much to be one.

I huddle against the wall holding onto the bench and peer around the pillar. From my perch I can see shadows behind me in a gully, sneaking out and around rocks then darting behind again, making their way up the pass, but I don't think these shadows are from the teens, who I've been keeping sharp eyes and ears on. Besides, it's coming from the other direction, not from the cabin. Animals run from rifle fire, so if that's what it is, these shadows should be long gone. Maybe this is a different animal. Maybe a few of the teen boys split off to drive down and around in order to catch me climbing down the gully on this other side of the pass. That would be a smart move on their part.

The child-hunters keep trying hard to flush me out with their rifle fire. They fire here and there, wherever they think I could be hiding. Guns aren't a big deal in our area. Around here most boys grow up hunting young; it's not uncommon for a first grader to tag a doe. Hauling rifles and lots of beer at the same time tells me these boys are pretty cozy with firearms.

I watch down that far gully behind me, blinking hard to focus better in the barely lit night. The shadows continue moving carefully, acting as if they are hiding too. This doesn't add up—these guys aren't crazy enough to shoot each other, are they? I don't want to know that answer. Unless they're trying to sneak up on me without being seen. That has to be it.

I have no plan except staying hidden, stark naked and cold. Summer nights in Montana turn nippy. It was only a few hours ago that I found Chief, and now look at me! I can see my breath coming out in tense puffs. I hug my shins and imagine a campfire. Warmth is all I think about for a while, hoping it will help. It doesn't.

I watch and catch the shadows moving again, ducking behind shapes just like in a Hollywood western. Except, I'm far from a comfy theatre with buttery, hot popcorn. I think I see two shadows making headway. I haven't heard anything from down on the pass lately so maybe the teenagers went back to their makeshift shooting gallery and their cans of beer. And my Chief. But I can't think about that. I can hope they only said they'd shoot him to try to scare me back to them, the way they came up here to fire off shots hoping I'd be too scared to stay hidden. But I think of that evil glint in Boogeyman's eye and I remember the shots fired right after they said they'd kill my dog and I shake and shake, and not from the cold.

The two shadows behind me are moving a little faster, the leader even more so. The other drags behind but still comes. It makes me think of a man and a woman, making me think of Mom and Dad, but they wouldn't be coming up that draw. They don't know how close I am to home. They don't know anything at this point, but soon they will. I may have to go home no matter what now and I might go home empty handed because I might not have Chief or puppies. Or even clothes, nothing. I guess there might be a slim chance Chief and the pups are alive, but I can't risk going back there alone. Not even for Chief. I get angry with those boys all over again. I am beside myself with burning rage, shaking for a whole new reason!

The two moving targets are nearing the top of the pass. As the first shadow rises over the edge I imagine I see long, dark hair swing away from broad shoulders before disappearing out of sight. I lean around the sandstone pillar as far as I can. Hatch? Hatch? I can't see him now. What if the slow one is Tim-Daddy? I watch, ready to spring if there is a chance I can make out light hair on the second shadow. I think I do! Maybe? I wait to get a better look as they come up on the pass since I must be one hundred percent sure before I move a muscle.

But they've disappeared. It's been some time now. I imagine whoever it is would still be scared of gunshot. Somehow I still imagine I saw Hatch and Tim but it could be that wild imagination I'm reported to have.

I lose more skin sliding down Two Licks as if I'm hugging a tree. At least I don't tumble down the slope. My feet hit the ground in terrible pain and my teeth bite down on my lips to keep from screaming. I lay flat against the pillar for a while before getting brave enough to call out, "Ceta—n!" It pierces into the night sounding high but not very bird-like. I'm scared by this boldness but it's too late now!

Creeping to a vantage point, I stop to peek spread-eagle with my naked body pasted against the rock. I'm still not sure if the idiot with the rifle sits around the other side waiting. If they were smart, they would've split up and stayed posted until one of them finds me. They have enough guys to pull this off. They'd know I'd eventually have to move out from hiding but this would take smarts and planning and these guys act stupid and drunk. But they're not too stupid to circle around a little girl without talking. At this thought, my heart pounds a warning to climb back to safety.

A strong hand covers my mouth!

I am so worked up I scream into the palm for a long time, unable to hear "Cetan, cetan…" and then I realize who it is and the fight drains clear out of me and I'm spent and slumping. A shirt goes around me before I am wrapped in Hatch's arms, safe.

"Help me, help me," I whisper over and over, weeping a wide river now.

"Coca Joe, Coca Joe," he whispers, holding me until I start to settle enough to feel the wounds all over my body from my escape. He sets me down and turns his head away while I pull the shirt over me, then he tells me Tim is waiting in the group of formations on the other side of the pass. We start down the slope but I'm clean out of fight. The pain of my feet and body has turned me stiff and stumbling. Hatch scoops me up, which also hurts, and carries me down the pass and into the arms of Tim-Daddy. He weeps freely, looking to the heavens with his head hanging back. I'm jostled as his chest heaves with sobs, tears pouring over his cheeks and onto me. I say *I'm sorry, I'm sorry* but he can only cry.

"When I heard those shots I thought you were… were dead with your Chief," he finally chokes out amidst his sobbing, "… gone forever. I couldn't bear it." He sets me down and I groan from my injuries and hunch over. Hatch and Tim share concerned looks and Hatch picks me up again. I'm not used to needing all this cradling, but I do.

"Chief is alive," I say, "unless those drunk boys shot him like they swore they would. We need to get to him now because I need Chief! I need him! I need him!"

"How many boys are there?" Hatch asks.

When I tell them, they both hiss, *eight?* Hatch squeezes tight saying, "Oh, Coca Joe, Coca Joe, how did they hurt you?" I wince from pain, which makes them both angrier. I can't be cradled like this as I start to describe what happened and I struggle out of Hatch's arms. He says, whoa, whoa, let me put you down gently, and when he does I hide my face, finishing the story of what I thought they wanted to do to me once I was naked. I tell them about Hazel telling my Mom about the teenage boys that are bragging about taking a girl to the cabin and doing things to her, and I say that maybe these are the same guys because they argued about who got to go first this time. I describe that I got away and how I ran but that I don't know how I escaped. Both Hatch and Tim are dangerously angry.

Hatch says I must be cared for right away, but I say. I don't want to go anywhere without seeing if Chief and the puppies are okay. They ask together, puppies? I explain about the nine puppies. They forcefully disagree, worrying and fussing and wanting me heading to town. I argue, no way can I walk on these feet, I need my boots. I need my clothes. They are frustrated, but I keep on, "Please, please, Chief and the pups! Pleeease."

The only way they agree to go looking for the dogs is if Hatch goes alone first to see if the boys are still at the cabin. It's no argument. He goes off alone and I am relieved.

While we wait, Tim pulls himself together to tell me in a strong voice that the reason he left me was to go get Hatch, and that if Hatch and Ernie hadn't been there, he would have gotten help in some other way. He reports that Ernie has not budged from the car and will be waiting there for us until noon. Then Tim apologizes over and over for leaving me, saying that at the time he didn't think I trusted him enough to be of help, but that he should have stayed with me no matter what anyway. He says he is sorry, and we squeeze each other's hands and I apologize to him, too.

Tim tells me he made rock cairns along the way so that he had a way to get back to me and that nearer the bottom he followed the road to the Shooting Range. He earns grace points with me. He said he didn't know whether I would still be here, but that he couldn't live with himself if he didn't try. He said they talked about trying to find the cabin in the car by road, but since it is so remote he didn't think he could figure it out, and he was sure he could backtrack the way we had come. Then when gunshots were first heard, he and Hatch were still a long way from the cabin. They didn't know where the shots were coming from, because it echoes all around the badlands, but they just kept coming, being more careful once they got closer and it was clear the shots were, in fact, coming from the area of the cabin. Tim says Hatch agreed that if they hadn't found me at the cabin they would have figured out some way to find out if I made it home safely.

I tell him he made the right decision to not come by car, because the main road curves far off and around on a circling bluff, and the one-lane road leading off it to the cabin barely looks like a road. He hugs me.

Tim says Hatch was cussing himself out the whole way up into the badlands for not going along with me in the first place. Tim confesses that he and Hatch, and even Ol' R & R Ernie, weren't thinking as clearly as they should have been. They were all so excited to have their child back they wanted to be sure and get legal papers to the courts so they never, ever lost track of me again. Tim says it's not an excuse; it's just a fact that everybody regrets. He looks sick and sorry and worried and says he hates himself for leaving me.

This is what happens when I act so tough. I make it way too hard for people to help me.

We watch Hatch's silhouette climb the upper part of the pass and come back to us. I reach for a hug and Hatch holds me tight then reports that the teens must have been very drunk because they left four guns outside that he gathered and hid in the trees. He asks if I knew how many they had but I don't. Hatch said he could hear sleeping sounds in the cabin but could barely see inside. These teens must not have a curfew, or else aren't the type to keep it. Hatch thinks he saw Chief but can't be sure. Both cars are there and no one was in them. Our plan is that I will hide in the trees as Hatch and Tim take the guns, rouse the guys and get them loaded into their cars. Once they are out of the way I can come and get my clothes on and see about Chief and the pups. Hatch assures me that if Chief is alive he'll bark over the commotion he and Tim create. I don't want to hang back, but for my safety I have to agree.

Tim-Daddy and Hatch discuss what to do with the boys once they are in the cars. They want to take them to the rez to charge them with attempted rape and attempted murder because they must pay for what they have done or they'll keep doing it again. I tell them that these boys seem to have this routine down, like a marching band, everyone in their place and everyone knowing who is in charge. Both Tim and Hatch turn angry and Hatch cusses under his breath. They fuss and worry about hauling them to the rez, but say it would be the two of them, both Hatch and Tim, who would go to jail instead of these local boys if we turn them in at the police station in Hell Creek. Tim-Daddy adds, "This is the way it is. Even though I am a white man, because I am with an Indian, I am considered a white traitor and I will be treated as rough as Hatch." They explain they can't take the risk, even though I am from Hell Creek because justice never favors the Indian.

We move out. Hatch carries me piggyback down the slippery, hardened sand of the face of the pass. He moves like he has no passenger, but his passenger is in great pain. We go steady until we are up on the slope and midway through the forest. All my lost skin causes bleeding through Hatch's shirt that I am wearing, and it soaks onto his naked back. He notices the moisture saying, "Do not worry Coca Joe. We will get you fixed up soon. Your Auntie Sue is a great nurse and will know just what to do. I promise. Then we will get you home to your parents."

"No!" I say, tightening my arms around his neck. I have managed not to think of this much, but I remember how frightened I was when Hatch wanted me to give myself up and get in the car with Mom, and a portion of that fear floods into me now. I still don't know why I'm so afraid, but I've always known something was wrong at home. I just didn't know how big it was until I met Hatch and Unci and Tim-Daddy. Even this dad, who didn't get to raise me, already shows me more care than my dad in Hell Creek. I suddenly know I can't go back. Not without Chief and not without Hatch either. "Can't I go home with you Uncle Hatch? Please? I don't want to go back."

Hatch stops and pulls me off his back, which is a feat because I'm still clinging to him. I'm afraid he won't want me, or that he'll say it takes more love to give me away than to keep me and that I need to get on home. But I can't go back. Hatch feels more like home than the house with my folks ever did.

He looks me carefully in the eye. "You don't want to go home?"

I shake my head.

He exchanges a sad glance with Tim-Daddy and now I'm even more afraid he's going to tell me no. "Do they hurt you there, Coca Joe?"

I shake my head no, I don't know why. I just know I don't want to leave Hatch again. He looks like maybe he doesn't believe me, but I don't want him to ask that question again. "I just want to go home with you? Please? Is that all right?"

Hatch sighs and his face softens. He pulls me into a hug. "Better than all right, Coca Joe," he says softly, and I melt into his answer. "It is what everybody wants, you home, back where you came from."

I want to cry from this feeling of belonging. "Chief too?" I ask, holding on to hope that Jesus has seen fit to save my dog from death again.

"Chief, too," Hatch says, pulling me back and looking me firmly in the eye. "But I need you to be strong right now. Okay?"

I nod because I know he's right. If we're going to save Chief and the puppies, we all have to be strong.

Hatch makes me solemnly swear on "all my good ancestors" that I will stay hidden in the trees.

"No matter what, Coca Joe, you must stay!" Tim-Daddy asserts his authority. I'm proud of him for doing so on this wicked night.

"No matter what," I agree so they will get moving. I want my dog!

Hatch doesn't trust me. He's smart, he shouldn't. "Listen. We cannot worry about you right now. You know that. We are outnumbered and are lucky they have not found us out already. You will hear us call you when it is safe, but only when it is safe. Even if we sound like we are in trouble you must not come! Go down into town and get help first, barefoot and all. Will you agree to this, Coca Joe? Promise me!"

I don't trust my voice. It's choking on a lump of fear, so I nod my head yes.

"You are not to break your promise to me again."

I shake my head. "I won't." I mean it as much as I can. I intend to try really hard to keep this promise.

Before Tim and Hatch step out of the protection of the forest and head to the cabin, they whisper for a long time. Their scheming makes me bold and mad. Good, make a plan to get even with these bad boys! If those teens were smart they'd be gone by now. Maybe they already left and I didn't see their headlights.

Hatch and Tim's shadows in the night are now out of my sight, so all I have to rely on is my hearing. So much time passes I get impatient, then imaginative. Did the boys see them coming, sneak up on them and slit their throats? Stop it! Stop it! I've watched too many westerns. Besides, I'm close enough I think I'd hear if there was any scuffling going on. Wouldn't I?

I shouldn't have worried. When their plan starts, it explodes! Hatch's orders are so loud and forceful, *I* almost do what he says. "On your face! On your face! All of you! Get on your face! Hands behind your back!"

Barking! Chief, my Chief! You're alive! You DID it, Jesus!

"No funny business or your guns go off and we shoot you all!"

A gun fires, followed by more barking. The shot echoes through this forest, telling me it was shot into the sky.

"Do as you're told! Face down! Hands behind your backs and stay that way! Do as I say!" I don't know this Hatch, and don't ever want to. His voice is so big and great it rumbles in my chest.

I only break my promise a wee, tiny bit. I stay hidden in the trees, but get close enough that I can see through the branches. Even in the dark, barely-lit night, I think I see bodies file off the steps and disappear around the side of the cabin. I might have seen Hatch, his black hair swinging past with rifles in his hands.

Then I hear nothing, for too long a time. It gets me nervous. I hear my one and only, my Chief, bark somewhere near the cabin. I want to run to Chief and not obey instructions. I'm just a kid so why shouldn't I? Or maybe I'm not anymore. Did I stop being a kid when I lost my mind over the dead dog, or when the boys had those looks in their eyes after they ripped off my clothes?

"Coca Joe!" The call finally comes.

The splintered, scrapped, bleeding feet do not want me to run on them. I run anyway. New pine needles poke into the bare bottoms of my feet but I don't slow down. Hatch and Tim are near the steps of the cabin, both still holding guns in each hand. I yell Chief's name and he comes around the corner of the cabin, running toward me! I kneel to hug him. Like a good dog he tries to lick me but I won't let go of his neck, I can't, my joy and relief are too strong. When I get my fill for now, I notice Hatch and Tim are out of sight again. Chief and I go into the cabin to first look for the puppies, and I find them curled in the jean jacket on the side of the stove where I was hiding. Chief sticks his nose into the jacket and pushes some of the pups around, then sits and looks up at me. "What?" I ask him, nose to nose. He holds me in view. "I'll do my best to save them Chief." I think I see his ears pull back. "I promise you Chief!" This must satisfy him, because he lies down with his nose near the jacket.

My clothes are near the pups, folded in a pile, but I doubt the teens did that. I start to get dressed, but there's a problem. Boogieman ripped my underwear off so they can't be worn. I hide them in my jeans pocket feeling hot-faced shame. My shirt was ripped down the front by one of the brutes so I put it on backwards, tie it behind at the waist, and put Hatch's bloody shirt over it. I have little to hide, front or back, but this makes the most sense. I lift the jeans, knowing I'll hate pulling them over these missing layers of skin, so I grab a big breath and bite my lips to keep quiet. I pull slivers out of my feet but there are way too many, so socks and boots must go on. I'm wounded and there's nothing I can do about it besides buck up.

When I'm dressed I get my knapsack on and gather the jacket holding the puppies in my arms, speaking softly to them and begging

God to save them. Chief runs off the porch when he hears a clear whistle from around the cabin in the direction of the teenager's cars. I see movement in the ravine, and getting closer, see the top of Tim-Daddy's head in the ravine rising and falling as he does his best to bury the collie. He kicks dirt loose with his boot and scoops it over her with his hands. He wipes the back of his hands under his eyes and sniffles his nose and I love him crying. He is honoring the dead and maybe crying for his buried wife as well, my mother Josephine. I allow myself to cry with him so he's not alone.

I've lost this cabin home-away-from-home, the happiest place I ever felt playing house, pretending to be a wife and a mommy when I was sure nobody was watching besides Chief. Now it will never be safe or happy again, and this mommy-me is not pretending. There are precious babies to save from death. These little pups seem barely alive.

Tim-Daddy washes his hands and sticks his head under the water at the red pump. I say thank you for burying the dog once he climbs out of the ravine. He nods and says in a gentle voice, "That dog was a stray, Coca Joe. She was so thin and matted. Down in the ravine where we first found her, I found a few dried bits that could have been afterbirth. I'm guessing she whelped her puppies there and perhaps died giving birth. Maybe she had trouble." Tim's eyes are still red and I bet mine look the same. As we walk toward the cabin, I think again about the tufts of collie fur up on the cabin porch, and wonder if this is where she lived sometimes. I wish I had found her sooner, before she died. I would have tried to take her home.

Tim breaks through my thoughts with a warning. "When we get to the cars, don't look too closely at those teenagers in the back seats. Trust me, you'll get an eyeful. We took their pants for the ride to the rez. And their hands are tied behind their backs real tight—so are their feet—so they can't hurt you anymore."

He leads me to a GTO with lots of chrome and a Chevy with mag wheels.

Hatch stands between the cars, pointing a gun back and forth between them. Chief is on guard in the front seat of the Chevy. Each car has four guys stuffed into the back seat, causing the cars to rock up in front. The guys look terrible as dawn breaks. Their shoulders are forward showing their hands are tied behind their backs. Hatch looks serious. He wears one of the letterman jackets and Tim-Daddy puts on one too. They both put on ball caps. Hatch hands a gun over to Tim. They each walk to the driver's door of a car.

"What do you think Coca Joe, where do you want me to put these attempted rapists?"

"Prison!" I yell, feeling bold now.

Hatch tucks his hair up into the cap, borrows a pair of sunglasses and tries like heck to not look like himself. I climb in the front with Hatch, a rifle between us. I've shot skeet lots of times and gone bird hunting with Dad, so I've been around guns plenty, but I'm still uncomfortable around them, especially since my older brother has a dead friend from a hunting accident.

We drive off in the loud cars, and there's mumbling from the back. Tim-Daddy drives the other car right on our dusty tail, with Chief sitting tall in the front seat; I can see them every now and then from the side mirror. I keep my back off the seat to keep even more space between me and these bad guys.

I give Hatch directions, going north first on the back road out of the badlands. Up high on this badlands bluff, the full sunrise really shows off. The road drops into farmland below and makes its way west to the old highway. Hatch knows his own way from here. The dirt road is high-centered in places and the car scrapes on the worst parts. I think it's Boogieman groaning the most, so it might be his car, but I'm not going to look back there to check. The rest of the road is washboard, and Hatch drives carefully.

The puppies in my lap are mostly quiet and still. Their feeble cries make me want to pet their tiny forms. In studying them one at a time in my hands, I find they're not pure Collie but some sort of mix. Like me. I'm a mixed breed, too. Three of the pups are black and one of them has a white blaze down his nose and white paws and belly. Two are brown with splotches, and there's a grey and black. Three are dark tan with irregular white rings around the neck, all white bellies and paws. Their tiny tales are tan then black then white tipped, and their noses are a little long. That's probably from their Collie mom. I don't know what kind of dog the dad would've been, or if we'll ever be able to tell. We'll see how they grow. I wonder if the dad was someone's pet on the loose, or if he was a stray too. Maybe he'll show up at the cabin, but for as long as I was there with his pups, I think he would've come around if he were nearby.

The pups start crying louder and it makes me hate the teens even more. What's wrong with these guys? How could they ignore this brand new life that needs care? Do all these teens have a screw loose upstairs and a cold stake in their hearts?

Boogieman is the only one brave enough to speak so far, and he asks where we're going.

Hatch answers, "Well, not Hell Creek, but it will seem like hell for each of you."

"Not to threaten you mister, but my dad is the Chief of Police and he won't like someone like you messing with me."

"Then you needed to keep him in mind when you ripped the clothes off this young girl, intending to have your way with her. Policemen do not like criminals who hurt children."

"It was a mistake. I was stinking drunk. We all were. We didn't know what we were doing. Honest," Boogieman says. He might be a big jock at home but he's a whiner here.

"Mistake? The way my niece tells it, you guys have a real tight routine you use. That means you've done this before and there are other girls around town who you have abused this way. And do you know what that means?" Hatch asks, looking back in the rearview mirror. "It means you need to be stopped."

"Well, my dad is a city councilman and he'll protect us," says another boy.

"And two of our dads are lawyers!" says the voice I recognize of a boy named Jan.

"Which is why those people will have nothing to do with your punishment!" Hatch says in his dangerous angry voice. "Look down at yourselves. Go ahead, each of you, look down at your laps. See how powerful you are now? Look around you. I do not see any of your fathers in this car, do you? That is a lucky thing for you. I would not want to bring this kind of shame on my family."

Hatch is boiling mad and the boys keep quiet.

Hatch doesn't seem to be heading to the old highway that runs along the river. He zigzags off and on dirt roads along sections of farmland seeming like he is lost or going in circles. But after running across this land with him and knowing he posed as a migrant worker, I realize he must know where he is and where he's headed. He checks the mirror regularly for Tim and notices me holding onto the dash and staring at him. I don't want to question him out loud, but once he crosses over the highway that leads into Canada and I see a sign announcing the Port is thirty-two miles, I point a look at him. He whispers that he's entering the reservation from the middle of the northern border, a longer trip, but safest with our cargo.

The teens are behaving. As we've gone through the few tiny towns, Hatch told them to duck down and to stay that way. They did. He has them scared. I'd be scared too if Hatch looked and talked that way in my direction. Tim has been riding our tail, but at the one stoplight in the biggest town, he pulls up beside us and looks like a teen, cranking the radio and bopping to music, pretending to chew gum. He's fitting the car.

"I need to piss," Boogieman cries out.

"Go right ahead," Hatch laughs. Boogieman grumbles.

"I hope you know what you're doing, mister," Jan can't help defending himself, "because we didn't do anything to hurt that girl. Nothin'."

"Yes, you did. You mean you just did not get a chance to hurt her like you wanted to," Hatch says in a hard voice that shuts everybody up.

It's more than an hour later before we're on the rez and pulling up to a cinderblock building with bars on the windows. Hatch asks me to go in and ask two policemen to come out armed and ready, and to tell them that Walks With Knees Quaking is out here with eight prisoners. He steps out of the car with the rifle and points it at the boys. As angry as he is I think he would shoot them. Tim-Daddy gets out and does the same. Hatch shoos me inside, so I leave the puppies on the warm spot of the seat.

No doubt I look weird wearing Hatch's bloody shirt over mine, and walking gingerly on my feet. I look at Hatch before turning the corner to the front of the building and catch his sad expression watching me.

It looks sleepy in here when I first open the door, but as I say my peace to the guy behind the desk, two Indians dressed in light brown uniforms with badges come out from a hallway joining in to listen, their hands over their holsters. The older one looks at me with his eyebrows raised in question and I catch the clue and point them to the left side of the building. They go out the door to investigate but I stay planted because I feel really scared, like a cold wind has blown me over. This is terrible timing, but I can't help it: I go weak from so many hard days and nights. I feel like I'm going to fall over right in front of this stranger.

The Indian policeman comes from behind his desk to help settle me on a folding chair. I wince at every movement and he reads me loud and clear. He seems collapsed in the middle by slenderness—sunken at his beltline—like he was slugged in the gut so many times for being wimpy he had to curve around it to protect himself. I wish he would eat more. I wish that I could eat something. My lips are cracked and dry. He asks, "Can I get you something? A glass of water?"

I give him a blank stare like he didn't speak English. Everything is too much. Finally I come back to myself, answering, "I need a way to feed newborn puppies." It's his turn to stare. Those weren't the choices he gave.

He brings a glass of water and a Butterfinger candy bar, something I imagine my buddy Jesus would bring in my time of need. I smile at this man like he's lit me up in glory light, that's how much I love a Butterfinger. He gives me a crooked smile, awkward-like. I'm so hungry I rip the paper with my teeth and spit the wrapper onto the floor like a trucker, like one of the hicks that work for Dad who sign their checks with an X because they can't read or write. I gulp back the water at a rate that should bring up a non-ladylike burp, and fill my cheeks to poking with the candy.

As I chew the shredded, crispy candy bar, I bend over to pick up the trash I'd spit on the floor, and I'm still hunched over when the door opens and the shuffling of many, many teen feet disrupt the calm of the room. I don't want to draw attention to myself by moving, so I stay low to the ground. A parade of teenage butts file past my face, and I'm closer to their behinds than I should ever have been. I have the smarts to keep quiet, but not to close my eyes. Curious is as curious does.

I sit up to see the pantsless prisoners have caused the nice policeman's mouth to drop open, but he recovers in time to dig a large ring of keys from his pocket and set out down the hall. I should have warned him who was being brought in; that would have been polite! So far, I'm batting a hundred on bad manners with this cop, and the thing about kids is, if we start out buried in poor behavior, we don't usually grab a shovel to dig our way out. We dig deeper until there's not a ray of hope we'll grow up to be decent.

Hatch carries in a load of blue jeans, and Tim-Daddy brings their rifles. I smile as Chief walks in behind them with the bill of a ball cap clenched in his teeth.

"Don't we get a phone call?" yells one of the teens after I hear the heavy clunk of iron bars shutting them in down at the end of a hallway. The policeman shuts the hall door, seeming to want to double protect me from those boys, and I take my first normal breath since they walked into the room.

"I know this looks like very big trouble, Richard, and it is," Hatch says. He gestures to Tim-Daddy, who's hanging back a bit. "You remember Tim Stratmore, my sister Jo's husband, don't you?"

Richard nods once. He reaches his hand out to Tim as an afterthought like he might not want to touch him. Tim shakes his hand but keeps his eyes on the floor. If they met before, it wasn't pretty.

"And Richard, this is Tim and Jo's daughter, Coca Joe Stratmore," Hatch says.

Richard turns his attention to me. He swallows hard, his large Adam's apple bouncing. "Nice to meet you Coca Joe," he says kindly before looking back to Hatch. "So what's the story with all these white boys in my jail?"

Hatch glances at me and takes Richard by the arm, pulling him to the far side of the room. He lowers his voice and I can tell he's telling Richard the story of what happened to me, because even though they're trying not to let me hear, I get snippets of it and they keep glancing at me with sad eyes.

Then Richard straightens hard, looking at Hatch, and says in a loud voice, "Hell Creek? These boys are from Hell Creek?"

Hatch looks like he just took a blow to his cheek. He squints his eyes at Richard nodding yes.

Richard grabs Hatch's elbow and leads him outside. I can just barely hear what he says through the glass door. "Hatch! You crossed a county line to drag these kids here! Do you have any clue how big this trouble is going to get? Last time we messed with anything in that town we got our asses chewed." I scoot to the window so I can peek out. Richard takes the jail keys out of his pocket again. "This is nothing I want the tribe getting into. I'm sorry Hatch. We can't help you."

This gets my heart pumping! He's going to let those boys free? What will they do to me then? I sense Tim-Daddy coming up next to me, as if to reassure me of something, but he doesn't say anything. I'm too busy watching to care anyway.

Hatch jumps in front of Richard to stop him but Richard shoves him out of the way of the door. Hatch grabs Richard's scrawny arms, but he breaks free of his hold.

"You are way out of line here!" Richard barks into Hatch's face. "I should lock you up!" I wish I hadn't eaten that candy bar he touched if he's going to treat Hatch like this.

"Please Richard, they attempted to rape my flesh and blood. Just listen to me!"

"No! Our locked bars are for our own native people. Nothing good can come from this."

"Richard, please. Give me a little time. I will get them out of here, I will, as soon as I get another holding area set up!"

"Where do you think you're going to take them?"

"I'm going to call an emergency Tribal council. Yellow Bird—"

"Yellow Bird will not approve."

"You don't know that."

"Well I do not approve. Get these white boys out of here now!"

"Richard! They've broken the law and no justice would prevail if I took them to the authorities in Hell Creek. You know that! If I'd taken them there, you would be driving to Hell Creek trying to get me and Tim out of jail, and good luck with it too. We would be charged for the crimes of these teenage boys, not them, because that's how it has always been and you know it."

I see Richard is starting to soften, but I still cannot relax until I know he's not going to let those rotten boys out to do who knows what to me.

"We must hold these boys accountable," Hatch continues, "not just because they hurt my relative, but because it is the right thing to do. And as I said before, this is probably not their first offense! That's reason enough, but I will say to you that I am tired of our Indian people being afraid of the white man," Hatch says powerfully. He pulls himself up to his full height as he speaks, shoulders back and proud. "These Hell Creek teenagers have scoffed at their behavior, claiming their brutality was due to drunkenness and that they should be excused. But I will not excuse them and I say it is time for our Indian people to rise against their wrongdoing and leave a permanent impression that we are no longer afraid of Hell Creek and we will no longer be treated like Indians are barely human."

As I hear Hatch speak, I see him standing thigh deep in prairie grass, a washed-out Montana sky behind him, wearing a warbonnet with feathers lifting like wings in the wind. Richard says, "Talks With Knees Quaking, you talk like the chief of our tribe and yet so far you have chosen not to lead your people."

Hatch presses his lips together, seeming to know the truth of what he just heard. "You speak truth and I respect you for it," Hatch says softer now, the heat going out of both of these men. "I have been hearing the ancestors call, and I recognize the time for me to lead is near. I am praying and awaiting Wakan Tanka to guide me into my future as chief of our nation."

Richard nods in understanding. "That is good. Your words have been spoken with power, and I respect them, but you do not spend your day like me, straddling the ways of our people and the laws of the United States government. You put the tribal police in a dangerous situation and there is no other way to view this."

"My niece will be in danger if you let those teens out, and you know it."

Richard takes a breath and looks toward the door, then his eyes find me looking out the window at him. His face softens.

"Twenty-four hours," Hatch says. "That's all I ask."

Richard looks at Hatch, then gives a slight nod in agreement. Hatch lets out a big breath and I do too.

The two men come back inside, quiet and sober. Richard walks over to his desk and plunks down in his chair looking exhausted, flipping the ring of jail keys around in his hands before putting them on the desk and looking at Hatch.

"If you're going to press charges, we'll need official statements." He looks at me and I straighten. I don't want to give a statement. "She looks like she needs medical treatment first, though."

Hatch nods. "Tim can give you his statement, but I'd like to take

Coca Joe to Sue first for care. Since Sue is the nurse medic for the tribal police, can Coca Joe give her statement there? It might be more comfortable."

Richard nods once in agreement. "I will call Sue and inform her you will be coming over and I will fill her in on what has happened. But remember what I said," he says, looking at Hatch. "I will not keep them for longer than twenty-four hours."

"I understand. Let's go, Coca Joe." He gestures me toward the door, but hangs back as Richard gets up to whisper in his ear. Though I'm heading for the door, I'm not out of earshot. "Were you saying she is the baby that was abducted from the car?"

I keep walking and wait for Hatch in the car. When Hatch comes out, I search his face but he watches his feet the whole way to the car and doesn't glance my way once inside it.

Abducted is a bad way to be adopted.

26
CARE

<⟩⟩⟩┼┼┼⟨⟨⟨⟩

The puppies might be done for in this world. Their tiny lumps are mostly still in the jacket and they make no noise. Chief jumps into the backseat and puts his head over the front to look at the babies. He looks at me out of the corner of his eye. He's counting on me.

As Hatch pulls away, he says, "We'll get you home and taken care of, Coca Joe."

"But what about the puppies?"

"We'll take care of them after."

"No! Hatch I can wait, but they can't! Please. Look, these two aren't even moving."

Hatch looks over at the puppies, then up at my pleading face.

"I can wait, Hatch," I say, determined to ignore the hurting wounds all over my body. "The puppies need help."

Hatch sighs and nods. "Alright, Coca Joe. We'll go to Janet Red Feather first. If anyone can take care of the puppies, it's her."

There is not a face we pass on the street that doesn't turn to look at the loud muscle car motoring by. Hatch is quiet-quiet, like the power he used on Richard took him off somewhere, off away from the seat behind the steering wheel, off nowhere near this car. I try to get his attention, asking if he's planning to wear that Hell Creek team cap all day. He takes it off and shakes his hair down making me want to touch it, making me miss my own long braid. I don't touch. He's not ignoring me, Hatch isn't like that—the wind got knocked out of him and is left blowing in the war bonnet feathers. I leave him alone, turning back into dog-mommy to whisper to the pups, egging them on to live. Live!

We turn off the paved road at a wide, rocky creek and follow it for several miles. The shocks on the tricked-out car hate the rutted road, so it feels like I'm riding an elephant while balancing the pups so they won't be bashed around.

Janet Red Feather does not fit her wispy name; she's tall as a house and seems instantly mad when she sees me, but I don't know what I've done wrong. Thick black braids shine like her dark reddened skin. Her low forehead ends where beautiful eyes take over, but these eyes cut me with a look that says back off. What did I do? The words "And she'll huff and she'll puff and she'll blow my house down" cross my mind. Between the road, the ride, and this woman, I am queasy.

Hatch hugs Janet long and hard and she giggles like a schoolgirl, even covering her face. Uh-huh, I think, I know why she's giggling... crush, crush, crushy-wush-wush. Who could blame her?

When she puts the puppies on her table, she chases a chill down her spine with a few body shivers. Chief settles so close to her chair that Janet bumps her arm against him as she moves, but doesn't seem to mind. He settles his muzzle on the table and watches her work on the litter. I'm not used to playing second fiddle to Chief and wish he was watching my every move like he is watching Janet, but then I feel stupid for feeling jealous over a dog.

Janet lights a match to a clump of dried sage lying in a large seashell on the table. I watch her take her time lighting all around it, slowly and carefully, and have to fight off the urge to scream, *Get those puppies fed right now!* She doesn't know how long they have been without milk, or that I did my best and fed them the sugary water hours and hours ago. But no, now she uses a large feather to fan smoke from the burning sage, using her other hand to draw the smoke over the pups, seeming to scoop it on top of them. Then she starts to sing loud in her native language, as if the animals are deaf! Her voice sounds like there is gravel in her throat. I clear my throat, to give her an obvious hint, and Hatch gives me a hint right back, widening his eyes first and then squinting them at me, his mouth in a straight line. I shrug one shoulder but stand corrected.

Janet turns on a heat lamp and gently takes each pup from the jean jacket and places them under it. She gets Hatch and me to work, filling syringes with some special looking milk she mixed in a bowl. Finally! After she removes and cleans a puppy's umbilical cord and gives the pup a check, she hands it to one of us to feed. Meanwhile she keeps rubbing the litter. She makes noises I don't recognize, like she is disgusted. Next she sings a Sioux lullaby so sweetly it sounds like someone else came in to sing instead of the gruff woman I've known so far. While she sings, she rubs the pup gently with the tips of her forefingers, pulling the sage smoke over to it again and again.

By the end of her medicine, she is able to save seven of the nine puppies. I cry for the loss of the two, and Janet Red Feather looks at me with a blank face, no sympathy. It takes us a long time to feed the living newborns. In the meantime Janet gives Chief water and food then stops to look at me like I'm making one big mistake after another. Hatch sees this and pats me on the back but gives me a warning face, shaking his head no only once. I appeal to him, tight-lipped and eyes wide and begging, but he shakes his head once more.

As we head off, Janet shoves a bag of supplies at me and is rough putting the dead puppies in my arm. But she is gentle placing the living puppy box in Hatch's arms, squeezing his forearm and smiling and flashing her pretty eyes up at him. I bow my head to her, Oh-Princess-With-A-Crush-on-Talks-With-Knees-Quaking. Chief licks her hand, and walks close beside her so that now both my guys have turned on me over this giantess! I'm fuming, and Hatch better deal with me before I huff and puff and blow her house down.

"What's wrong with her?" I ask before he revs the car.

"Nothing."

"What'd she have against me? I didn't do anything."

"She does not know that."

"Well why didn't you tell her? Why'd you keep the reins on me like that?"

"You will need to get used to it, Coca Joe, Indians do not act like white people. We walked into her house uninvited, which is okay, but we needed help with animals that were nearly dead, which for Janet Red Feather is like bringing a carload of nearly dead relatives to her door and asking her to save them. Remember our beliefs that we are related to all? We believe that we are related to the pups, and to all four-legged, mitakuye oyasin, we are all one. I wanted to show respect for Janet as a healer and as a friend. And you had to also. You wanted to take care of the puppies first and we did. While we were busy looking after those little lives, your feelings were not what was most important, but that does not mean that you are not important to me at all times."

I'm mad and sad and tears make hot tracks down my cheeks and drop on the two dead pups in my lap that I wish weren't there. "But Hatch, it wasn't my fault these puppies died, and I'm very sad they did."

"Dear daughter, sometimes native way will not fit with white way, with what you understand. I would have let you explain to Janet but it did not matter. What matters is that she gave good medicine to the pups, and to Chief. You know, he has been through a lot, just like you," his voice softens, "and Coca Joe, you need someone to care for you now while I go handle the mess with the white teenagers. You are hungry and hurt and very tired."

I sniffle, "You called me Daughter, and now you are leaving me?" My heart beats, *please... please... don't turn me away.*

He lightens up. "I called you daughter because you are my sister's daughter and because of that you are also mine. This is what I would have called you even if Jo was still alive and raising you here. It is our way. I am not leaving you, my daughter. I will take you home Coca Joe, to your home and mine, at Tanka Unci's. You disappeared from your great grandmother before she had a chance to love you as much as she desires. She has said she has vivid dreams of you living with us.

I will ask your Auntie Sue to nurse you at great-grandmothers house, and since Sue has earth medicine, you will heal quickly. Plus, Sue will want to put some meat on your bones, and your cousin Teenci wants to be your friend."

I want to put my head on his shoulder as a thank you, but instead I look down at the sad, little bodies in my hurting arms. "What do I do with these puppies that died?"

"I will bury them, Coca Joe."

"Can you bury them close by so that I can cry over them when I need to?"

"I will put them in the earth behind Unci's house, and it will be easy for you to find them because I will place rocks over the dirt so other animals do not dig them up."

Just knowing they will be there is already a comfort. When Hatch parks the car, he tells me he will go get Auntie Sue to come and nurse me first, and then will bury the two pups. I hug each teeny dead pup and gently place them in his hands, as if they can feel it. I am so hurt and tired, it seems a long way to the door to carry the box of newborn pups, my knapsack and myself, even though it isn't.

Tanka Unci heard the car park outside and is on the porch with her hand over her mouth, and old eyes wide. I carefully set the box down beside her, and when I get into her arms, I notice how bloody and dirty I am but she doesn't seem to mind, squeezing me forever. She has strong arms for such a small old lady and she goes on long speaking in my ear, the Lakota language melting me. But she slows down when she notices Chief, and runs her hands over him, holding his muzzle to peer in his eyes, pets his long nose with her gnarled fingers. I tell her his name and she joyfully repeats it from deep in her throat. Once we are inside, I set the pups on the coffee table and slip onto the couch, having lost all steam. She pets my head and Chief's, and keeps praying.

Auntie Sue and Teenci arrive some minutes later, and Sue makes a fuss at seeing me and Chief, then peeks in the box and fusses some more, overjoyed! Teenci pets Chief, admires the newborns, and then leans against the armrest shaking her head while pinching her nostrils. She smiles, saying with a plugged nose, "Pew—ie! You stink worse this time!" Tanka Unci still pets my head so I look at Teenci with the dreamy slit-eyes of a sleepy cat, rolling a purr off my tongue until she laughs. Even Tanka Unci stops her praying to giggle.

Aunt Sue ruffles a hand through my hair and puffs of dust fly up. She laughs and says whew! as she shuffles into the kitchen with a bag of groceries.

"Fry bread with honey," I croak like a parched cowpoke, my goofiness rewarded by their laughter. What a relief to be here, to be myself, to be free from the worry of finding Chief or having to figure out how to save my life or the life of newborns. I look for Chief and see him stretched out on his side, taking up as much floor as he can to sleep. I let him be even though my heart says to go to him.

"I'll get the fry bread going Coca Joe, but first you'll eat a sandwich and then you need some medical attention. Richard called me from the police station so this is both an official and a medical visit. Understand? Hatch came by and told me I would find you here so I brought my nursing bag and the medicinal herbs to treat you. I'll need to get those stickers out of your feet."

Hatch comes in the door, walks right past us, and is already running the bathwater, same routine as my last visit only this time I am family. When he sees I haven't left the couch he warns, "Don't look in the mirror until after your bath Coca Joe, trust me! It might take two baths for you this time!" Then, after he teases me, he fills me in on some news. "I thought you might want to know that while I was at Sue's I got a hold of someone at the Vagabond Hotel in Hell Creek who is going to go find Ol' R & R and let him know we found Chief and that we are back on the rez. Knowing Ernie, he is probably still waiting in his car at the Shooting Gallery." Hatch and I smile at each other.

Hatch asks Teenci for another outfit of clothes to borrow, then whispers something in her ear so her face lights up. She skips out the door. Must be good!

"Sue, where is Nathan?" Hatch heads into the kitchen. It doesn't take him long to spread peanut butter and honey on bread and put it in my hand, then another for him. It doesn't take us long to devour them, either.

"Under some car I think, helping Roger Leaping Bull," says Sue.

He pours a glass of water for me and shoves another sandwich in his mouth. "Good. I am going to need him and most of the leaders. I also need your help, Sue. Can you ask your friends to get makeshift bedding ready tonight, I need eight, and have them brought to the lodge before bed time?"

"Yes, Hatch. I spoke to Richard about … those boys. The tribal women will gather all the supplies we can."

He goes to turn off the bath, and when he returns, he motions Sue over to the kitchen. I stay put listening. My Tanka Unci goes to her chair and closes her eyes as if to nap but her lips still move slightly, maybe in prayer. Hatch says, "So you know that the jail will not keep the teenagers much past today. I am planning to put them in the lodge if the elders will allow. I do not know where else to put them… maybe the school gym. We will have a tribal council meeting in a couple hours if all goes as planned. And Sue?" Hatch takes a breath. "More than anything else, the most important thing we want to do is take care of Coca Joe. Her safety comes first. She is my daughter now, this is what my sister would expect, and my daughter has been through the worst."

Hatch drops his voice to a whisper, but my big ears hear. "I suspect that even her home life may be unsafe."

Hatch stops whispering and is speaking with power again. "You were there earlier this spring, Sue. You heard the message of the American Indian Movement leaders. Perhaps it is their truth-telling about the injustices we are forced to endure on and off this reservation, combined with the terrible treatment of Coca Joe, that makes me want to act against Hell Creek on her behalf. She is an Indian too! So will you spread the word in your calm way that a change is beginning to take place, a change bigger than our family and our tribe, a change meant to benefit all the native bands represented on this reservation?"

Sue doesn't answer. She waits and then asks in a respectful way, "Is there more you want me to know?"

"You can know that people living in Hell Creek, and even those on this reservation that work their crimes against us are not going to keep getting away with it. And let people know I will probably need the help of everyone who knows me," Hatch answers.

"Everyone knows you, Talks With Knees Quaking."

"That is who I need, then."

Hatch walks over to me on the couch, places his hands on my shoulders and long-kisses the hair above my forehead, then he kneels to one knee and looks into my eyes. "You are safe and you are going to be well cared for, and I could not be more glad to have you back here with us at home."

Tears jump to my eyes surprising me.

He squeezes my shoulders and smiles. I can hardly stand this amount of attention from him. His eyes stay on mine, while at the same time I seem to see them go off to the prairie again where a war bonnet catches a firm wind.

"It is time." Hatch says in a strong voice, rising off his knee and removing his hands, "Time to let Wakan Tanka make me ready to lead!"

Sue sucks in a surprised breath and I look over at her. She is looking at Tanka Unci who sees something in the room that I can't see. They both seem to watch whatever it is move toward Hatch.

"Grandfathers, Grandmothers, it is good to see you again," Sue says, bowing her head, crossing her hands over her chest, and releasing a slight shiver.

I go still, watching my uncle with eyes wide. He raises his hands to the sky, cupping them as if something will pour into them, and then he steps back, seeming to fill the room. That is the only way to describe it—he fills the room.

Uncle Nathan and several friends come into the house without a word. They look at Hatch like the same wind went through their spirits and blew them here. Nobody moves. I feel the same holiness I sense in the badlands Sand Circle, feel it move into this shack of a house.

Tanka Unci sings out so loud and shrill I snap like a rubber band back into this room instead of thinking of my badlands. The house fills with a choir of Lakota singers. The only thing missing is the drum, but I somehow imagine its beat anyway. Teenci weaves through the men and comes to reach out a hand to hold. Who knows what look my face wore, but she saw something and must have guessed I need a tether. Words being sung that I do not know lift me anyway. The song is pitched high for men but they sing beautifully on a melody as tricky as the meadowlark. Slowly they draw into a circle in the tiny living room. I can't imagine my dad and his cronies doing anything like this in our living room at home.

After the song dies down Hatch says, "Time to cleanse and listen to Spirit. Time to sweat with Yellow Bird. Let me get my pipe." He goes down the hallway and after a minute returns carrying a deerskin bag out in front of him in both hands as if it is an offering. The men go out the front door behind him as if this is what they came for.

All this didn't take much time but something happened during that one song, something holy.

After a few minutes Aunt Sue asks me to meet her in the bathroom and once there she asks me to describe my wounds to see how she can help. As I do, we notice that I am wheezing and she says we need to take care of my asthma first before anything gets out of hand. She offers to get my medicine and so brings me my knapsack and some water for me to swallow my pills. Sue praises me for being responsible about caring for my asthma. I tell her I've had it since I was six so that I'm used to it. She tells me I probably had it from birth but that I didn't have noticeable symptoms until I was six. I frown, not knowing anything like this before.

"Now, you. I will get you something for your pain," she says going off to the kitchen. I'm glad, because I'm ready to not be hurting so much. She comes back with a small armload of dried plant life and a stone bowl with a fist-sized smooth rock resting inside.

I blink at it all. "Why can't I just have some Bayer?"

"Bear? Who eats grizzly for pain?"

"No, Bayer aspirin."

She giggles showing that she is teasing and proving she's one of the nicest ladies I know. "I'll give you aspirin if you still need it. Promise."

Then Aunt Sue chooses different plants and grinds them, saying she will make a poultice to lay over my abrasions. I ask her if she's got something against Mercurochrome and regular ol' bandages.

"Seems like it. Other than mercury solution hurting you worse than these awful scrapes, I don't have anything against it." She chuckles.

I smile. "Where did you get these weeds?"

"These herbs come from different places. There is a badlands area on the eastern side of the rez that has a special kind of taopi pejuta, wound medicine. I find this only there around the prehistoric bones."

"Really? Are you kidding me?"

"Not kidding. This one here is a type of milkweed, itopta sapa tapejuta. I found this at the prairie dog town and it's going to help with your swelling."

"Sure seems like you are teasing me."

"You will see how well it works. The old ones knew how to heal us by using what is on this land. Are you ready to let me have a look now?" I'm not. I use cheerfulness to ward off what's ahead. It doesn't stop it from coming.

I pull off my cowboy boots and my white socks are covered in blood. She helps peel them off and I'm biting my bottom lip from pain. She examines the bottoms of my feet with a sad, sorry face, shaking her head and blinking her eyes slower than normal. "You've got more than the slivers here... looks like they've been chewed up." She gently rubs a special oil on the slivered bottoms. I wince and tears pop out the corners of my eyes. She very carefully sets my feet back on the ground—a sweet gesture—as if I haven't been walking on them for hours.

She keeps her eyes off mine and asks me to show her more.

I take off Hatch's shirt and untie and drop my shirt to show the bloody scrapes, cuts, and large bruises all over my upper body. I try to pull down my jeans, but they stick to me in places from blood and pus, and it takes both of us to slowly rip them away from the flesh. She gasps and says with pity, "Oh dear girl." I look down at my body and try to stay here in the bathroom, try not to go back to last night in my memory.

"Where are your underwear?" she asks innocently.

I watch her face awhile, twisting my mouth to the side to chew on my cheek, thinking it's best to keep this secret. She reads my mind. "There is no reason to hide anything Coca Joe. You are safe with me, don't you think?"

I know it's weird but I seem to be hearing *'Never tell the nice face! Never tell! Never tell!'* I scowl at the voices. It takes me some time, but I say, "I think I'm not supposed to tell you."

"Did someone tell you not to?" she asks in a near whisper.

"It's strange, but I hear voices in my head telling me not to tell." I hang my head as far as it will go.

"It sounds like those voices are trying to help you, trying to keep you safe, don't you think?"

"I don't know."

"Well, Coca Joe, you don't have to tell me anything you don't want to."

"I don't?"

"No, you don't. I mean it. What happened to you last night isn't your fault. Do you hear me?" She tucks her hand gently under my chin so I will look at her. "You did nothing wrong. Someday later you will have to tell the whole story, but tonight you only need to tell me what you want to. I am here to listen, but also to assess and help you with all your injuries." I like the sound of this in her lilting, warm voice.

"Well, I must have done something wrong or those boys wouldn't have tried to ... tried ... I don't know what, maybe they were going to try to do 'you know what' with me," I say, echoing Hazel's words I heard so long ago. "I'm pretty sure they would have hurt me if I didn't get away."

"Look right here." Aunt Sue points to the deep red marks along my hips. She pokes into them, asking if it hurts. I shrug. I don't want to say.

"They *did* hurt you. I can tell these marks hurt because I'm a nurse and I know about these things. And I know it's not possible for you to use enough force to do this to yourself, right?" I nod my head yes. "And do you know what else I know?"

I stare at my fingernails. Fingernails are very interesting at times of trouble.

"I know that what those boys wanted is something you didn't want to give to them."

Through moist eyes I ask, "How do you know?"

"Richard called because sometimes I help with police stuff just like this. I'm a tribal nurse. Plus you are my relation. I already love and care about you because you are Jo's daughter, and because I knew you before." I stare at her solid Indian looks where in every way she is native. It's hard to imagine she can see me as anything but a fake relative. She continues, "We didn't want you to have to go to our hospital and be examined by people you don't know. I am with you in an official capacity and also as a nurse and your auntie, but mostly as a friend."

She waits while I think about all this. Finally I pull the panties from the jean pocket and set them in her hand. She straightens them out, noticing they are barely held together, and then she holds them against me. She pretends to yank them away as she imagined the boys did and then looks at me with a questioning face. I nod yes.

"I need to do some nursing now, okay? Have you ever been to a nurse?"

I frown deeply. "Lots."

"Good then, you're a pro. I'll make it as quick as I can and then you can get in that bath."

She gets nurse-like, starting at the top of my head and working her way down. When she gets to the place in-between my legs she sees the missing skin along the insides of my upper thighs. "Tell me how this happened." I explain how I climbed the vertical formation like a monkey, and how it hurts if you don't have clothes on. Then I show how I came down from the ledge in a hurry.

"Which of these wounds was made by you running, climbing, and hiding?" I point them out.

"What parts of your body did the boys touch?" Aunt Sue keeps her eyes below my neck. I point around to different parts of my body.

"Did you point to every one of them?" She asks.

"I think so."

"Did any of the boys kiss you?"

"No, I don't remember that. I don't remember everything maybe because I was so scared?" I really don't.

"That's okay. You're doing a real good job, Coca Joe. You'll get to climb in that bath soon. Do you remember how your clothes came off?"

"They tore some off and yanked off others. First my shirt, then my pants, then my underwear. That hurt when Boogieman ripped that off."

"Boogieman?"

"That's what I named the biggest guy. He seemed like the ringleader."

"He sounds scary with that name," Aunt Sue says.

"He is very scary. I don't ever want to see him again."

"If you have to, you won't be alone. You will be kept safe," Sue says forcefully. I shiver because he is scary and also because I am naked.

Sue notices, drapes me gently with a towel and asks me to tell the rest of the story. I don't want to but I do. At one point in my story, Aunt Sue closes her eyes and purses her lips as if trying to control her upset. "I am so sorry for you. This is the last part, I might need to examine you like a nurse because it seems like you don't remember some of this, which is normal. For some people it's normal not to remember when something really scary happens to them. Did you know that?"

"Oh."

"Last night must have been very frightening. Can you tell me what you do remember, because that would really help me?"

I walk to the wall and put my back to her. It doesn't help much. I tell the rest of my story from there as muffled as I can. "But I don't know how I got out of their circle," I finally finish. "The next thing I remember is running through the forest. But... right before I ran I saw one of the boys on the ground, hurt. He was curled over and moaning like he was hurt in between his legs. I don't know how he got there and don't remember how I got there either. Somehow I figured out how to get away."

"I am so glad you got away. Do you think you hurt him between his legs?"

"I don't know. What I remember is that I saw him moaning on the ground and I started running as fast as I could and didn't stop until I was hidden."

"But you don't remember anyone touching you in your genitals or trying to have sex with you?"

"No."

"Do you think that might be what you can't remember?"

"No."

Sue waits for a long moment. "You seem pretty sure about that. Why do you think that is?"

"It's the only place on my body that doesn't hurt. And it hasn't hurt. But everything else does."

"Makes sense to me. You have a lot of wounds that need treated, and I'll bet you hurt like heck all over. You are a warrior, Coca Joe, full of such courage!" I give her a tentative smile. "I need you to be brave for one last exam then you can go ahead into the bath. I'll run some water right now to warm it up. If you will let me see between your legs, I'll see what I can see." I am frightened by this, but she says gently, "I am not doing this to humiliate you. I believe you when you say your genitals don't hurt, and I am just going to look for signs of rape on the outside as I clean the area nearby. I want to prepare you though, Coca Joe, if I suspect more was done by those teens than what you remember, I'll need to take you to the tribal clinic for a more thorough exam. Sadly I've seen all this before and I can't just guess that you are okay by what you tell me. Okay?" I nod. Her gentle explaining is helping. "I'll make this as quick as possible, then you can get in the bath"

I hold my breath as she finishes her examination. Sue reports that she believes that somehow I did fight those boys off and she does not see that they got away with raping me.

"I'll work on the cuts and abrasions later, but being able to see them now helps me know what plants to use in the poultice to make you feel better. The slivers will take time, but we'll get them. Let's see what everything looks like after the bath. I know you are dirty but I'm going to put some drops of healing oil in the tub. It'll help."

I'm barely listening to Sue. I stare at the pure turquoise light trapped in the running bathwater and disappear into its powerful sound. The grit and blood itch beyond belief, like I won't be able to stand it on my skin for even a second longer. I want to leap into the bath, but wait for Aunt Sue to bow out. With all these scrapes, getting into the bath burns so that I cry out and hold my body taut. The water turns ugly fast—red and brown mixing—hiding my body beneath the surface. At first it's a relief to lose myself. Then I poke a knobby knee through the liquid coffin, claiming life.

I hear Aunt Sue humming the Lakota song all the men sang earlier and this reminds me of my Hell Creek Mom's whistling that meant all is well, you can come out now, our trouble is over. I know this isn't true anymore. This time trouble is churning up thick like water mixing with dirt to make dangerous gumbo. I dunk to the bottom of the tub being as still as I can, holding my breath, floating to the surface, lighter from knowing what is wrong at home is one mess that I don't have to figure out. This time.

The scrubbing of such a filthy body makes dirt soap bubbles glom onto the side of the tub like the scum in ponds us kids call Indian soap. I think about this, staring, wondering if calling it that meant something rude, wondering if I've made Indian soap because my blood in here is part-Lakota. I let the water out of the tub, but stay in it. The water runs out around me, and the dirt grooves the bottom like sand in the coulee blown by the wind. I see I'm still sprinkled with dirt, cinnamon-like, so I rinse under the spigot. Its flow takes me back to the red-handled water pump behind the cabin. I fight these thoughts, trying to stay right here in the bathroom.

As I brush my hair, I notice that chopping it off took away any sun-kissed parts, and the roots seem a bit darker. Nothing like Hatch's deep black hair, but not the ashy blonde that didn't seem to want a color. Even my nose has decided it might have a bit of an Indian look, or else I never took much notice of it before. If I hang out on the reservation any longer, what else will turn?

Aunt Sue had asked me to tell her when I was out of the bath, so now she comes to rub in the poultices. I complain of the stink, telling her I'm not a garden, my skin is not soil to be tilled. Like all good nurses she knows when to ignore the troublemaker.

Once I am covered in plant-life Sue carefully wraps me in a buffalo robe, the hide side in, and the soft curly hair out. It is as heavy and big as a large quilt. She leads me to rest on Great Grandmother's bed and asks me to stay wrapped in the robe because there is power in the great buffalo. She layers deer hides on me saying that warm resting in a quiet place will help me heal. Before she leaves she reapplies the oil mixture on my feet while praying in Lakota. I yank my foot out of her hand, away from the sharp sting, but give it back. She removes what slivers she can, saying they are already looking better. I started young with painful pokes at Dr. Mattenstadt's in Minneapolis, so this is nothing. I tell myself to toughen up as Aunt Sue works.

I don't know how long I was in the darkened room. There were times my feet were worked on and times when warm rags gently removed the poultices and they were reapplied. I slept through the care, so tired, and safely snuggled in the hides.

When Aunt Sue wakes me I feel heavy and far away. I must shake my head to clear it. Sue pulls off the deer hides protecting the poultices and invites me to go stand in a warm shower.

"Are you still hurting?" she asks as the water rinses me and she gently rubs gross, stinky plants off my back. My eyes are closed and

I'm plugging my nose and she giggles. My wounds are better, even my feet, and I tell her so. It doesn't seem possible.

Sue leaves and I find one of Teenci's simple cotton dresses and a pair of beaded moccasins in the bathroom. I hold the moccasins to the light to admire their beautiful geometric patterns. The best I can do is clutch them over my heart since they're way too beautiful to put on these hurt feet.

When I go out to the living room, Teenci smiles, holding something in her fist, and gathers some of my hair and puts it into a barrette. I touch it, feeling a miniature ear of corn. I click a thumbnail across it liking the sound of rows of seed beads and I know it is pretty since Indian designs always are to my eyes. Teenci tugs the moccasins from under my crossed arms and puts them on my feet so that I cry from her kindness. I can't stop, I keep on crying, hiding my face in my hands unable to stop until fry bread tacos hit the table. Eating tear-stained is what I seem to do at great grandmother's table.

I am home. Tanka Unci sleeps in her chair, a picture of peace, even with a thinning string of drool reaching from her mouth to her sagging breast. If she wasn't so ancient and dear I might poke fun at her spit.

27
THE BOARDING HOUSE

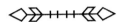

Knower is in the sitting room resting with Katrina. He doesn't have any record books nearby, which is surprising. He has never left them all on his desk before. Even Katrina's hands are still. All her chores are done, even the mending.

"This is why there are no record books of Her as a little baby when She lived here with Her family on the reservation. She didn't need The Boarding House," Knower says.

"Creates quite a lull," Katrina says.

"Watcher with Owl are paying attention and we will be alerted if our rescue is needed," says Knower.

"It's nice as it is, knowing She's fine," Katrina sighs.

"The residents of The Boarding House will be doing our jobs soon I think. I can imagine They are searching everywhere to find Her. They are serious about getting Her back. And when They do, all residents will be busy doing jobs to keep Her safe."

Katrina says, "This is nice for now. We have never had much of a rest before."

"Yes," Knower agrees.

Watcher with Owl, Katrina, and Knower have never closed their eyes before, and they aren't going to start now.

28
SAFE

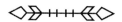

I am so happy to see Hatch again after all the deep trouble that I can't stop smiling at him. He squeezes my hands saying, "I have good news. I contacted help from outside of the United States, somebody I told you about that I knew in college. I would trust her with my life."

I am feeling chipper so I tease, "Is it the beautiful Karen Carter in the photograph with you?"

"Yes," Hatch smiles sweetly then gets serious. "The tribal council has approved this action of seeking outside help. America has a long habit of turning its back on its Indian people, but some Europeans are interested and willing to help us. A tribal legal team, along with other professionals, some of them from off the rez, as well as Karen Carter will begin negotiations with Hell Creek. Because you are a Hell Creek citizen, not just a native girl from the rez, it will help, since you grew up there and your adoptive family is there.

"You will be kept safely hidden from the Hell Creek teenagers while they are still on this reservation, so I do not want you to be afraid of them being here. Your Hell Creek parents will know you are on the rez soon, but we believe it unwise to have you make contact with them just yet. Is that what you want?"

"Yes." I say firmly, trying to not get worked up. I'm still tired. "And at least I called them." I talked to them long enough for them to know

I am safe and that I found Chief so they could stop worrying. I did have to hang up on Mom's yelling though.

"Right, at least they know you and Chief are safe." Uncle Hatch softens his voice. "But sweet Sister of the Wind, this is all my business to figure out. Your business is to rest and take good care of yourself and all your dogs. You can go out in the yard, but please do not go any farther. Everybody is busy today, even Tanka Unci. I have many responsibilities so make yourself a sandwich and I will come back soon."

As I eat alone I notice a door across the small hallway from Tanka Unci's room. I'm curious. If this is another room, why do Hatch and I sleep in the living room? The door is locked with a hook from the inside. Strange. "Is somebody in there?" I ask in fear. What if someone else lives here and I don't even know it? Creepy!

I push the door open the length of the hook. It's too dark to see through the crack so I squeeze a hand inside to find a light switch. Got it. Only one eyeball can look through the crack, seeing feathers and smelling lots of old stuff. I turn my face on its side so both eyes can see and I didn't push hard but the door flies open and I fall flat on my back inside the room.

I scream at seeing an old Indian standing in front of me dressed in beaded hides and wearing a warbonnet with feathers that go to the floor! I stare with my eyes popping out then scream again and yell, "I'm sorry, I'm sorry! I didn't mean to fall in here!" I cover my face with my hands, squeezing my eyes shut and hoping he will walk away since he's blocking the doorway and I want out!

I make myself open my eyes. The clothing I saw on the Indian is now hanging on the wall. No real Indian. A warbonnet hangs there too, looking like the one he wore. I hold still, afraid he will return if I move. I dare myself to look around the room but don't have the guts. I run out fast shutting the door and shaking. How was the door locked from inside an empty room and how did it open?

I catch my breath, picturing the Indian. Even though all I saw later was clothes, he was there when I first went in the room. I'm sure of it.

He didn't look mad at me for bursting in, either. He looked kind, like he knew me, recognized me. I back away from the door remembering his face, and now I see him in the badlands Sand Circle, the light bouncing off the sandstone walls casting a warm glow to his face. I look around and see I'm standing there with him. We face each other in my beloved badlands, the circling breezes lifting his feathers as Big Elephant stands guard over us.

He wants to say something. I wait, watching his mouth. His eyes fill with tears. Mine do, too. The vision of him is blurry so I brush away my tears hoping he doesn't disappear. He's still there. I'm still there. He speaks in a language that sounds like Lakota but I somehow understand the words, hearing it in my own language at the same time. His words light the air, white sparks crackling between us as he says, "Daughter, follow me to the baby. Follow me home."

Somehow I understand all that this means. I search his face of coulees and pitted sand, seeing rivers in his worn-out eyes. A few moments pass where I hold all the knowledge and understanding of his words, we hold them together, 'Daughter, follow me to the baby. Follow me home.'

Then he's gone and so is the understanding of what he spoke to me. I can still hear the words but they make little sense to me now.

As quickly as he is gone I find myself instantly back in the hallway by the door. "Come back! Come back!" I beg. "Great Chief! Please, please, come back!" I want to understand everything!

"Who is with you Coca Joe?" Hatch yells, running in from the front door and eventually through the kitchen and into the hall.

I startle, chest heaving.

"Coca Joe! You are as white as this door!"

"Hatch! Hatch!" I hold one hand over my throat and one arm straight out in front, blocking him. I'm afraid he'll be angry. "I went in the locked room. I met the old chief. I'm sorry for making more and more trouble!"

But Hatch doesn't look angry. He comes closer, his expression encouraging me to say more.

I straddle two worlds, one here in this tiny hallway and one there in the badlands. I picture the old chief. I say in a whisper, "He spoke to me."

"Yes?" Hatch coaxes.

"He called me Daughter."

"Yes," he whispers, gently taking me into a safe hug.

"And he said, 'Daughter, follow me to the baby. Follow me home.'"

Hatch doesn't answer, he just breathes into my rats-nest hair.

I pull away needing to speak to Hatch's dark eyes, knowing what happened to me was important. "We were in the Sand Circle in my badlands! He spoke in what I thought was Lakota and I heard it in English at the same time."

"You were not afraid?"

I shake my head. "He cried, Uncle Hatch. He cried real tears, like he was real! And I cried with him."

"Waste´. Good. You joined through water. Water is our first medicine. When each of us comes to Grandmother Earth it is in water that we grow in the womb. You joined through the water of your tears, so when he spoke you understood him."

"I did understand him, Hatch!" I say, happy he doesn't doubt the miracle. I feel an urgency I don't know what to do with. "I could see far past today and also a long, long time ago, like time wasn't anything. The words he spoke made sense, like they had something to do with me, except... now I don't understand anymore. Do you, Uncle? What baby? How do I follow this chief? Where is his home?"

"He will show you the way when it is time. He will join with you again."

I don't know how he can be so sure, but there is such certainty in his voice, it starts to settle my fear that I've lost an important message forever. But that doesn't stop me wondering how all this works and how the chief will join me again. "But Hatch... he isn't 'real' real! Except his clothes. They're the ones hanging on the wall in there."

"How do you know they are his?"

When I explain how I got inside the locked room and first saw the chief, Hatch says, "I would have screamed, too." We grin at each other. "Coca Joe, his message came to you through the cante´ ista´, a Lakota phrase meaning the eye of the heart."

"Chahn-te´ ish-tah´," I try it on my tongue. I know this is important. I feel it running wild through my body like the powerful Missouri River, but the meaning of the message is slipping farther and farther away.

"The chief brought this specific word to you, maybe for your future. First the two of you joined through water, and then you received the whole meaning of his message through the eye of your heart. Seeing fully through the cante´ ista´ is a true gift, an honor!" Hatch's eyes shine with an excitement I've never seen in him before. "Could you tell me more about him?"

"His face is as old as Tanka Unci's. Older. And his eyes are old but bright, like the sun wears them and the rivers run through them."

"I am curious," Hatch says, his face seeming to be lit by that same sun, "if he is the ancestor spirit of Chief Matohota, Chief Gray Bear, our forefather long ago who wore this hide clothing from the deer he hunted and killed with his arrows. Gray Bear's warbonnet is made only of sacred feathers, and each feather tells a different story of his tremendous bravery. He earned each eagle feather through the path of his life." I think about how many feathers were on his warbonnet!

"Uncle Hatch have you met him? I mean, like me?"

"I have not had the honor, Tate Tanksi." Hatch's eyes shine for me. I'm proud but shy. I didn't do anything to deserve a visit from such a courageous chief. I shouldn't be rewarded for being so nosey. But I hold it all close to my heart anyway, wondering what it all means.

Hatch is off again taking care of business. I'm on my chair-bed with my mouth hanging open, exhausted. My eyes are at half-mast, but my foot searches for Chief, who is having a dream right at my feet. It seems like a running dream because he whimpers, sounding almost like a horse neighing, and his legs shake. If I was a dog I'd be doing this same thing, to try and shake off everything I've just been through. I reach down to comfort Chief, and I tell him everything is okay, we've made it home. Home.

I slump down even more in the chair, pondering.

It wasn't long ago that I used to be different than who I seem to be now. I didn't receive mysterious messages from a dead Lakota chief, then watch my movie-star-handsome uncle get excited about it. I didn't call myself Sister of the Wind or have a family call me Tate Tanksi or Cetan. I like being called Cetan after my mother. I like imagining her and me circling on the wind, high above the badlands. I can almost feel it.

I didn't have any idea I would find my real family, and that they would circle around to protect me, just like that herd of bison do with their young.

I have a sweet new friend in my cousin Teenci. I see giggly things for us in the future. I used to have only one favorite grandmother, Grandma Naomi in Minneapolis. I imagine her finding out I am an Indian. I think she'd say, "Oh, yo—u!" with the most love of all. I hope she gets to meet my other grandma, this great one, Tanka Unci. As strange as anything could sound, I think they are cut from the same cloth, and that cloth is settled comfortably around my shoulders.

I've lost my mother, but think I've been pretty lucky with Tim-Daddy. He's been by to check on me, Ol' R & R Ernie too, which makes me hope drinking and the hobo life didn't ruin him after all.

I yawn so big I'm sure my face cracked. I rub my jaws to put it back together. I glance at Chief for comfort, feeling tired but on the edge of something that sets my heart to racing sometimes. It's like a build-up of floor wax, this feeling. Slippery.

I used to whisper simple questions like, "What's wrong with this family?" into the velvety ear of Chief before we'd run down the coulee into our badlands home. I spent time looking in the window of our house in Hell Creek, Montana watching my folks and wondering who are these people and what are they doing with me? I have an answer to that now, but still a lot more questions. Since I've been away from them, I don't carry my shoulders so high around my ears. I'm not sure why yet. I don't know how I'm going to manage to stay here for good when I know my parents will want me back, but I trust Hatch to help me.

And I'm safe. Chief is safe, and the puppies are safe. I've found my family and they're far better than the adoption story I made up as a child, about my real mom and dad being dumb enough to leave me on the orphanage steps. That sad story got me purple suckers and special sad smiles aimed right at my heart. There's not a person alive who doesn't have sad stories, you'd be a paper-doll cutout if you didn't, but one of the saddest parts of my story is that I finally found my family and my mother is dead. Knowing she died from asthma makes me hate my asthma like never before. But I will ride the wind in my mind with her, and take comfort in the truth that my Lakota family seems to love me.

So my Mom in Hell Creek is wrong. It didn't take more love to give me away than to keep me. It took more love to find me and never want to give me back.

I live on the rez for now, waiting to see what becomes of me and the boys who hurt me. This broken-down chair is my whole purple room, but I don't mind. The knapsack beside it is my ticket out of here, if for some reason I need it. And a flirty Lakota boy sometimes comes to mind, with the name of Tommy Cetan Ska. Tommy White Hawk!

And Chief? He's busy with adoption. It isn't easy, even with puppies. Chief and me? We're going nowhere fast, just like Montana promises.

Keep your eyes peeled for:

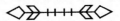

I CALL MYSELF SISTER
OF THE WIND

The next installment of Coca Joe Stratmore's story.

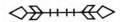

Visit

www.ArrowKeane.com

for the latest updates and to join Team Coca Joe News!

ACKNOWLEDGEMENTS

Firstly, and rightly so, with all my heart I thank my incredible editor, Donna Cook, for your gifts of passion, intelligence, precision, time, and dedication to give Coca Joe's voice a fighting chance at being heard clearly and beautifully.

I humbly and lovingly thank Jolee Goodtrack, for your deep wisdom, encouragement, love, and patience while editing the Lakota in this story and teaching me about life on the reservation. It is out of the utmost respect I have written about Native People.

My big thanks to Elyse Ross, for your thorough and intensive review that got this writer on her toes and most assuredly improved this book.

Authors dream of having fans that savor their words like the most delicious chocolate, so Katherine Cranford, I thank you for your exuberant love of me and Coca Joe, and for your divine editing and proofreading.

Amber Dillon, thank you for formatting this book and for your years of dedicated help. Your wise counsel, your gentle ways, your brilliant mind, and your belief in me becoming all I can be are gifts unmatched.

With real love and true heart, I thank Kristina Wayne for your deep and everlasting friendship, and your loving dedication to all levels of my life and work, as well as for your videos of my ReadSing, and my author photos.

I thank thee, George Washington, the founding father of my earliest proofreading, for your kind and wise help.

I am deeply grateful to the people who came early as discerning readers and encouragers, to: true friend Margaret Melvin, who read first and then many drafts, and told me Coca Joe speaks to you; to Greg Bishop, for loving Coca Joe and supporting me through this long leg of her journey; to Ann Washington and Anna Goodwin, who said this book would win a Nobel Prize, bless you, can't get better encouragement than that; to Sue Hart, whose loving spirit listened and prayed to help bring this book into its truest light; to Julie Glascock, for loving belief in my music and writing; and to John and Cathie Havlina, who saw who I am and where I am from, and encouraged me to keep the Lakota in the story; to Lila Standing Tall Weeks for your blessing that this book will touch many hearts and spirits, and for seeing who I am; to Chief Walks With Prayers, Rudy Escamilla, for your outpouring of wisdom and blessings on both me and the words chosen for this story. Mitakuye Oyasin.

Deep thanks to early readers who sang praises that truly mattered: Dan Rogness, Dakotah Bishop, Cheryl DuPree, Joyce Hickerson, Monic Hackett, Jennifer Wildeson, Sherry Welsh, Lisa Plummer, Trisha Rochford, Linda Short, Nea McCauley, Cindy Riedlinger, Sherry Munroe, Alice Dieter, Judith Hansen, Sandy Sterhan Dickey, Sunny and Bill Murray, Norm and Jean Bishop, Rovonna Caraway, and Jean Larson.

Much gratitude to my fabulous beta readers: Barbara Bainum, Laura Cesare, Ruth Hallows, Greg Likins, Barbara Martin, Audrey McCoy, Lance Morris, Gretchen Mullins, Sara Westbrook, and Jennifer Wheeler.

Overwhelming thanks to these who have lovingly cared and helped me in deeply meaningful ways: Debbie Markley, Dorothy & Steve Larson, Harry & Sue Hart, Thea Loughery, Sherry Munroe, Trina Montgomery, Donna Zaitz, Lisa & Phil Plummer, John & Trisha Rochford, Linda Rochford & Paul Sandholm, Toni Scharff & Tim Cashin, Beverly Hoy, Alice & Bruce Preston, Sandy & Tim Schwartz, Cynthia Schember, Tracy Rockholt, Lorna Milne & Jon Motl, Carole Yapuncich, Doug Rogness & Liz Hayden, Patrice Lynn, Pamela Graham, Ellen Spencer, Karri Jones, Pat & Roxey Coast, Kelly & Eric Sheffield, and all my relations.

I am super grateful to these who helped with specific information for the story: my kind, long-time friend Jim Thielman, Sandy & Dave Barnick, Tanner Parker, and Marilyn Kutzler.

To my children, Dakotah James and Angelie Grace, thank you for letting Mommy write! You are the most amazing children I could have ever hoped for, and I love you with my whole heart.

If this book shines it is not my light, but is the grace of God to whom I am grateful above all else.

BOOK GROUP DISCUSSION QUESTIONS

1. How does the quote at the beginning by Martin Luther King, Jr. relate to Coca Joe's story? What silent things matter in this book?

2. What do you think Coca Joe means when she says, "Pretending who I am is all I got that's real"?

3. What is the mystery behind Coca Joe losing things or finding things that she didn't put there? Is somebody playing tricks on her?

4. Do you think it's a good idea to tell kids that are adopted that "It took more love to give you away than to keep you"? What would you tell your adopted child?

5. Coca Joe says she can't feel any bruises, saying "never have, never will." What does she mean by that?

6. When Coca Joe first meets the Indians at the train depot in Livingston, Montana why do you think she gives them her made up name, Coca Joe Stratmore, instead of her real name?

7. The bigotry and hatred toward Native People in this story was pervasive in the late 1960s. Nearly a half-century later, has public opinion changed? When you see a multicultural representation of people in the media, is there normally a Native American in the group?

8. Since the 1800s, Native American children being removed or stolen from their family on the reservations hit epidemic proportions and is still happening today. What's behind it?

9. Coca Joe says she can see visions of ancient Indians on the land. Is this only her imagination?

10. Adoption records were permanently sealed during Coca Joe's adoption in the mid-1950s. Even today, in many states you cannot get them opened. What is the big secret and why was

it kept? If you didn't know anything about your birthparents would you try to find out who they were? Would you try to find them?

11. Describe how you think it actually works when a Boarding House resident helps Coca Joe.

12. In regards to Coca Joe having a Boarding House of residents to help her, do you think you could spot someone like Coca Joe when she is living her regular life? Did Coca Joe show any signs that she has a Boarding House when she is living her life? Do you think there would be obvious signs?

13. What do you think the Hell Creek teenagers were experiencing when The Boarding House springs into action to rescue Coca Joe?

14. How far would you be willing to go to save an important pet? Do you relate to the depth of love and devotion that Coca Joe has for Chief?

15. Does Coca Joe know what her adoptive parents are doing to her? Does anyone know?

16. Using your best guess, what do you imagine the ancient ancestor Chief Matohota means when he tells Coca Joe, "Daughter, follow me to the baby. Follow me home?"

ReadSing!

Catch an inspired mix of readings from the Coca Joe story, underscored by original songs at a ReadSing. Crafted for entertainment and intrigue, Arrow Keane's vocals and guitar add the finishing touch to passages read from I Call Myself Coca Joe. In both song and written word Arrow takes skillful aim.

LA Times reports:

"In her songwriting she has a knack for probing the deep psychological barriers, setting these closely observed, nakedly emotional stories to melodies that are pretty and sweet."

Music critic for The Times wrote:

"(Arrow) is capable of a loveliness that can make it hard to hold back tears."

The Orange County Register says:

"Arrow's shimmering vocals could melt steel."

See you at the ReadSing!

ARROW

Pop onto

www.ArrowKeane.com

for the tour calendar, books, music, downloads, audiobooks, videos, and more!